I WILL DIE FREE

NOBLE ALEXANDER
with
KAY D. RIZZO

Pacific Press® Publishing Association
Nampa, Idaho
Oshawa, Ontario, Canada

For current Information on the persecuted Church,
Please Contact:

The Voice of the Martyrs, Inc.
PO Box 443
Bartlesville, OK. 74005
(918)337-8015

Edited by Marvin Moore
Designed by Tim Larson
Cover photo by Betty Blue
Typeset in 10/12 Century Schoolbook

Library of Congress Cataloging-in-Publication Data:
Rizzo, Kay D., 1943-
   I will die free / by Kay D. Rizzo.
      p.   cm.
   ISBN 0-8163-1044-0
   1. Alexander, Noble. 2. Persecution—Cuba—History—20th century.
3. Seventh-day Adventists—Cuba—Clergy—Biography. 4. Adventists—
Cuba—Clergy—Biography.   I. Title.
BX6193.A37R59 1991
272'.9'092—dc20   91-11308
[B]   CIP

99 00 01 02 ● 15 14 13 12 11

Contents

"To all Latin American Christians who, in the midst of lack of understanding and in the blessedness of the thirst for justice, are preparing, in the manner of John the Baptist, for the coming of the Lord in socialism."

Castro Talks on Revolution and Religion With Frei Betto.

Five Minutes From Hell

Even as I gazed out over the darkened auditorium, a strange mixture of exhilaration and sadness pervaded my thoughts—exhilaration following a successful opening meeting of the youth revival in my church and sadness over the chronic fear I sensed in the upturned faces of the young people before me. "Phrases like, 'living in the last days,' 'a time of trouble such as never was,' or 'the evil times in which we live,' no longer apply to the future by and by," I thought. "For these Christian youth, the evil times are here, and the troubled times are now."

They had come to the meeting to be fed, to be reassured of their part in God's eternal plan of salvation. Had I satisfied their hunger? Had I met their needs? Did I reassure them? Did I give them strength to face the threats that pervaded every aspect of their lives? I didn't know. I hoped I had, but I didn't really know.

The chairs stood empty, the hymnals closed. Suddenly, I sensed I was not alone. Placing my Bible in my briefcase, I straightened and turned to face the intruder. Pastor Vásquez, the church's senior minister, strode up the center aisle. "Ah, Pastor Alexander, you are still here. How did the meeting go?"

"Very well, I think." I smiled, trying to shed the strange foreboding that haunted me all evening. "It comforts me to know that the forces of heaven will triumph, that Satan and evil will be defeated in the end."

"Yes," Pastor Vásquez agreed, "I know." The thoughts we didn't utter spoke more loudly than the words we shared. "How many would you say attended the youth meeting this evening?"

"Oh, about 200, give or take a few."

"Then it was worth it?"

Pastor Vásquez and I had debated for some time whether or not, in the face of the increased persecution from Castro and his supporters, to cancel the planned series of meetings.

I glanced at the pastor, his face shrouded in the shadows. "Oh, yes," I assured him, "it was worth it. If you could have seen the despair in some of their faces, the uncertainty, even terror. I can't explain . . ."

"I know, I know. " Pastor Vásquez nodded. "I sensed the same disquieting tension in the adult meeting."

The new Communist regime had been hovering over organized religion in Cuba like an anticipated tropical hurricane. A number of times I'd been detained and questioned by G-2 men, Cuba's newly formed KGB. Pastor Vásquez cautioned me that these interrogations regarding friends and acquaintances who had escaped from the island could lead to my eventual arrest. Two days earlier, the pastor and I had considered canceling our series of meetings rather than risk further persecution from Castro and his men.

"Things aren't good, Noble, they aren't good at all," Pastor Vásquez warned. "I have half a mind to postpone in spite of your protests to the contrary. " As senior pastor, the final decision was ultimately his, but I hated to see our long hours of preparation come to naught.

"I share your worries," I hastened to assure him, "but can we afford to let this opportunity go by? Because of what is happening. . . . How long do we have? Who can tell but that these meetings may be the spark that sets this country on fire for the Lord?"

The Christian church in Communist Cuba was operating on borrowed time. Daily, Castro and his henchmen harassed first one denomination, then another. Catholics, Protestants, Baptists, Seventh-day Adventists, it didn't matter who. Christianity of any kind drew the Cuban people's allegiance away from him to a Higher Power that could create martyrs and dissension and could ultimately threaten Castro's government. After praying together, Pastor Vásquez decided to take the risk. We would faithfully do our part, and God would have to do the rest. Considering the results of the first meeting, the decision had been sound.

In silence, Pastor Vásquez and I walked to the door. I paused and glanced back at the darkened room. My first revival meeting. Yes, I told myself, it had been a success. Together we stepped out into warm night air.

"It is too bad that Yraida and your son could not be here tonight to share in your happiness," the pastor commented as we made our way to the church parking lot.

"I just hope Hubert isn't coming down with a tropical fever of some kind," I said. "When Yraida couldn't get him to stop crying, she thought it best to stay home with him."

"Yes, well," Pastor Vásquez chuckled, "that's the way it is with babies, you know, and new mothers."

Guiltily, I recalled my impatience at Yraida for the late start we'd gotten. Then to have our two-year-old start crying and refuse to stop even before I'd started the car's engine—I was certain I'd never reach the church in time for the sermon, let alone in time for song service. If the truth were known, when Yraida had offered to stay home with him, I leaped at the suggestion. "It was for the best, I'm sure," I demurred.

Pastor Vásquez and I shook hands and said good night. I watched him cross the parking lot to his car. Then I climbed into mine and shut the door.

Maneuvering the automobile into the late-evening traffic, I glanced at my watch. "Hmm, 84 miles—an hour and a half should do it," I thought. Automobiles, trucks, buses, and bicycles jostled for position amid the usual throng of pedestrians in the main street of Matanza. By the time I reached Marianao, where I lived, the streets would be dark and empty.

Out of the corner of my eye, I noticed my son's hand-knitted sweater and baby bottle. "Ah, yes," I thought. "Yraida's purse." I reached under the front seat and removed my wife's beige handbag from where I'd stuffed it. In her haste to get Hubert back to our apartment, she'd forgotten it, along with the sweater and bottle.

"Ah, Yraida, what a good sport," I thought. I knew it wasn't easy trying to balance being a mother of a two-year-old and a pastor's wife at the same time—especially during a series of meetings. "I'll have to be sure to tell her how much I appreciate her when I get home." Glancing into my rearview mirror, I noticed a blue-and-white Oldsmobile tailing me but gave it little thought.

At the edge of Matanza, the traffic thinned, and the moist woolen-blanket atmosphere of the city lifted. I rolled down the window and let the island trade winds blow through the car. Miles rolled beneath my wheels as I relived aloud the evening meeting. Step by step, I reviewed the story I'd told regarding the fall of Lucifer, his desire to be like God, and his rebellion and expulsion from heaven.

"One-third! Think about that number. One-third of heaven's angels believed Lucifer's lies. How the loving Creator must have mourned the loss of His children. He is a God of peace, not war." I paused and smiled. I'd felt the Holy Spirit's presence in the auditorium that evening. The young people had felt His presence too. I knew by their response. A surge of joy and triumph filled me.

"Yes!" I pounded the steering wheel with my fist. "Praise God!" I shouted out of my window, honking the car horn in celebration. "You used me, Father, to touch their lives. Thank You, thank You, thank You." What an incredible honor, I thought—to be used of God.

The quiet drive gave me time to come down off the natural high preachers get after such experiences. By the time I saw the lights of Mariano, I had to fight to keep my eyelids open. The empty streets narrowed and darkened as I passed the downtown section of the city. Again, I glanced through my rearview mirror and recognized the automobile directly behind me—the same one I'd noticed before leaving Matanza.

As I entered an alleyway less than a block from my home, my headlights illuminated a second blue-and-white 1957 Oldsmobile parked in the roadway. Thinking I'd need to back out onto the other street, I slowed to a stop. Immediately, the car tailing me pulled in behind me, blocking my only available exit.

Before I could decide what to do, two men dressed as civilians with guns in hand jumped out of the rear vehicle and approached my side of the car.

"Oh, no," I thought, "not another questioning. Not at this hour of the night. I am so tired."

The taller man bent down and peered into my open window. "Are you Humberto?" he asked.

"Noble," I replied.

"Nevertheless, you will accompany us to G-2 headquarters. We have a few questions to ask. It should take no more than five minutes or so," the man explained. "If you will come with us . . ."

At the sight of his Red Star gun and the set of his jaw, I knew his invitation was not open for discussion. I sighed, climbed out of my car, and walked to the other vehicle as ordered. I could see the outline of a third officer in the driver's seat. Once there, I got into the back seat. I knew the routine well. The back seats of these 1957 Oldsmobiles were outfitted with manacles—handcuffs attached to the floor of the car. From outside the vehicle, it looked to passersby as if the person in the back seat was loose when in reality he was securely cuffed.

The first officer slid in beside me on my left and aimed his gun straight at my heart. The second officer rounded the back of the car and flanked me on the right. The routine didn't bother me. I was used to it by now, though I wished they had picked a more civilized time of day in which to conduct their interrogations.

During the twenty-minute drive to G-2, Castro's KGB headquarters, the policemen remained silent. I tried to recall my every move during the last forty-eight hours, hoping to find a clue for this latest detention. Had one of my friends or parishioners fled the country and I was again being questioned regarding their absence? If so, no one had mentioned it. I had been so busy preparing for the meetings. Nothing came to my mind that could possibly incriminate me in any way. I would later learn that I was but one of hundreds of Cubans arrested as political agitators during the early days of Castro's regime.

At G-2 headquarters, my captors wasted no time. They whisked me through the doors and down a long, dark corridor. In my mind I imagined the gray stone corridor to look much like the proverbial passage leading to the abyss of Revelation. We entered a brightly lighted room, and a policeman placed me in front of a camera. A card with the number 30954 was placed on my chest. At that moment, I never imagined how deeply those numbers would burn into my memory.

"Face left," the lieutenant barked. I obeyed. The camera flashed.

"Face right." Again, I obeyed.

"Officer," I tried to explain, "I have a letter in my wallet from General Samuel Gonzáles Rodríguez—a character refer—"

The officer closest to where I stood slapped the side of my face and shouted, "Shut up! Speak only when you are spoken to."

My hand flew to my stinging cheek. I staggered backward to maintain my balance. Now I knew I was in more serious trouble than in times past. "This will be more than a five-minute detention," I thought, as one of the policemen grabbed my left hand and pressed each of my fingertips into the ink pad, then onto an official arrest sheet.

"Empty the contents of your pockets onto the table," the officer demanded. Dazed, my mind switched into automatic. Somewhere beyond myself, I heard my watch, my wallet, and my car keys hit the metal tabletop. I thought about my car parked illegally in the alleyway and wondered if the traffic cops would tow it away in the morning. If only I could get word to Yraida. She could go pick it up.

The officer sifted meticulously through my wallet, reading every scrap of paper within. He even read the message written on the back of my wife's picture.

"Take off your clothing—everything!" The man inspected each item of clothing, tearing at the seams and hems of each garment, searching for contraband of any kind. Satisfied there was none, he handed everything to a waiting policeman. I watched the second officer scoop up my belongings from the table and carry them to a locked closet. As he stuffed them inside and relocked the door, I thought, "There goes Humberto Noble Alexander. There goes my identity."

"No, no, that is not true," I reasoned. "My name is recorded in the books of heaven." I lifted my chin and squared my shoulders at the thought. "They may strip me of every earthly possession, but my identity as a royal son of the King of the universe is eternally mine!"

The door to the hallway opened, and a barber entered the room. Without a word, he cut off all of my hair, down to the scalp. The photographer shot a second series of pictures. A second barber arrived to shave my face. He held the straight razor to my right cheek and pulled. I cringed from the pain. The blade hadn't been sharpened in years, I was certain. It felt as if the razor was yanking each hair out of my face, one strand at a time. He finished the job in three strokes: one from my right cheek to my chin, the other from my left cheek to my chin, and the third from the base of my throat to my chin. Blood was streaming down my face by the time he finished.

One of the officers shoved a paper towel into my hand. "Here!" he ordered. "Clean yourself up with this. Hurry! We haven't much time."

The camera flashes blinded me as the photographer barked out his instructions a third time, and I moved accordingly. I was still dabbing at the blood oozing down my face when a guard shoved me into a gray metal chair beside a dilapidated oak desk, where one of the arresting officers sat, his hands poised on the keyboard of an old standard Royal typewriter.

"Name?" he asked.

"Humberto Noble Alexander."

"Age?"

"Twenty-eight."

"Occupation?"

"Youth pastor of the Seventh-day Adventist Church," I replied.

The officer mumbled my answers as his fingers clicked in a hunt-and-peck fashion across the keyboard, recording my answers.

"Address?"

"146 Street East 49."

"Married?"

"Yes."

"Wife's name?"

"Yraida Seull Alexander."

"Children?"

"Humberto D. Alexander."

When he'd recorded every detail of my life since birth, the lieutenant turned me over to a helmeted policeman.

"Follow me," the man ordered. His right hand caressed the butt of his gun as if daring me to refuse.

We crossed the room, then walked down a dimly lighted hallway. At the end of the hallway, he opened a heavy metal door. The pungent odor of stale excrement accosted my nose. I followed him down a long flight of narrow stone steps. The atmospheric temperatures dropped as we descended. At the bottom of the stairs, my eyes adjusted to the dim lighting enough that I could make out an empty corridor. The sound of our footsteps echoed off the metal doors lining the cement block walls.

The hall was broken into short segments, and each segment was barred by a steel door and a set of guards. No one spoke as we approached the first door. Without losing a step, my guard whistled a coded message. A whistled reply came from beyond the barricade. The door slid open, then clanged shut behind us. Not another human could be seen.

Wordlessly, we continued on to the next door and the next, until my guard halted before cell number six. I had seen no other prisoners and no prisoners had seen me until the guard shoved me into my new quarters. The heavy metal door clanged shut behind me.

A sudden wave of nausea swept across me as I struggled to regain my bearings. The stench was unbearable. I swallowed hard and gasped. I felt as if every pore of my body was being invaded by the choking odor of human excrement.

The cell was nothing but a concrete cage. High on the back wall, a vent made of concrete was angled in such a way as to prevent a prisoner from seeing outside his cell, yet it allowed for a change of atmosphere from outside the cell. Lower on the same wall, a rusty pipe with a broken faucet dripped stagnant water. There was no toilet and no washbowl. A hole in the opposite corner was designed to act as a toilet, but it had long since clogged. Piles of excrement lay about, barnyard like. Some piles were hard and old; others were fresh and putrid.

In despair, I glanced about my temporary quarters. My eyes struggled to adjust to the darkness, and I sensed I was being scrutinized. A moment later I saw them: twenty-four eyes staring at me from nine metal bunks chained to two of the concrete walls. My mouth dropped open in disbelief as I studied the disheveled and desperate faces about me.

A sudden rattling at the door broke the silence. "Ilegó carne fresca" (fresh meat has arrived), the prisoner nearest the door shouted as a large tray slid through a slot at the base of the door. My cellmates dived for the food. One whiff of the putrefied meat, and I knew I couldn't put any of it in my mouth. It stank worse than the human waste strewn about the floor.

The arrival of the food loosened my companions' tongues. They craved information from the outside more than their empty stomachs cramped from hunger.

"What is happening outside?"

"Did you overhear the guards discussing our release?"

"Castro. Will there be a coup?"

"Have you heard anything about an invasion?"

"Will we be freed?"

The inmates bombarded me with questions. I told them what little I might have picked up from street gossip and from the state-controlled newspapers. Mostly, I knew nothing about any coups or invasions or political threats to the Castro regime. I was a pastor of young people, not a man of the revolution. I didn't then appreciate my cellmates' insatiable appetite for fresh information. I would come to, in time.

After a while, we lapsed into a haunting silence. While no one spoke, our thoughts were of the same things—family, home, and freedom. Hours dragged by. "If only I could fall asleep for a few hours," I thought. "If only I could escape into the oblivion of a dreamless sleep." But in spite of the darkness, sleep eluded me. The earthy grunts and groans of my fellow prisoners constantly reminded me that I was not alone. I heard someone to my left mumble. A man on my right whispered the words to a familiar Catholic novena. And every few minutes, or so it seemed to me, one of the prisoners shuffled over to one corner of the cell to relieve himself.

Since sleep seemed out of the question, I thought about the evening meeting and the young people who had, for the first time, dedicated their lives to the Lord. I praised God again for their faith, then prayed for each one individually. When I'd completed my list of names of people who'd come forward at the first meeting of the revival, I leaned my head back against the stone wall and closed my eyes. "Who will Pastor Vásquez get to deliver the second youth sermon of the series?" I wondered. I hated to have the meetings close because of my detainment, yet I knew that when I finally got released from this hole, all I'd want was a bath and a place to sleep for twenty-four hours.

My thoughts grew hazy, and my head rolled to one side. Suddenly, a shout startled me. One of the men had cried out in his sleep. I could only imagine the nightmare that triggered the outburst. I was again alert to my surroundings.

Perhaps, I reasoned, if I played a few mind games, I could blot out this freakish melodrama I'd somehow landed in. Imagining myself in our apartment with Yraida and my son, I walked through each room, examining each piece of used furniture. Mentally I ran my hand over each nick and scratch. The faces of the relatives who had so generously donated each piece to us when we were married surfaced in my mind. How proud my wife was of our first home. "Our little love nest," she called it.

The vibrant colors in the afghan on the back of the small brown rocker warmed me. I could see it wrapped around

Yraida's shoulders as she sat nursing our son. My eyes misted over at the treasured moment. I leaned my head back against the cement block wall and sighed.

"Has Yraida heard about my arrest?" I wondered. "If not, she must be worried sick by now. If she knows, has she contacted Mama?" Yraida's purse! I'd left Yraida's purse on the car seat! "Oh, no. It will be long gone by morning. Oh, well, not much I can do about it now." I found out later that Yraida didn't learn of my arrest for three days. "Pastor Vásquez—has he heard yet that I'm being detained? Probably not. Not until morning at least." An emptiness filled my innermost soul. Realizing that these thoughts only intensified my misery, I forced them from my mind.

I rolled my head from side to side, trying to dislodge a kink in the back of my neck—a minor irritation compared to my surroundings. Some five minutes! Obviously the officials made a mistake. "Just how long will they keep me here?" I wondered. Questions drifted through my semiconscious mind. Questions that had no answers. After a while, I stopped thinking and just stared into the impenetrable darkness of the crowded, filthy cell until a bone-weary tiredness overtook my body, numbing my mind.

This was February 20, 1962. Fortunately, I did not know that I would remain a captive in Castro's awful prison system for twenty-two years.

Storm Clouds Over Cuba

Cuba, my homeland, is often called "the pearl of the Antilles." When Christopher Columbus landed on Cuban shores, he wrote in his journal that he had found the most beautiful land that human eyes had ever seen. It was a land where the sparkling blue waters of the Caribbean Sea lapped softly against white sandy beaches and coral reefs, where the warm, tropical trade winds gently whispered through tall, willowy palm trees. It was a land abundant in lush green grass, fruit trees, brilliantly colored flowers, and exotic birds—a tropical paradise.

The Greater Antilles—Cuba, Haiti, the Dominican Republic, Jamaica, and Puerto Rico—are a part of the island chain Columbus erroneously named the "West Indies." The main island of Cuba is almost the size of all the other islands combined. There are more than 1,600 smaller islands, most with only a few people inhabiting them. One exception is the Isle of Pines, about ninety miles south and east of Havana. As a boy studying the geography of my country, I never imagined how well I would one day become acquainted with the deadly, yet beautiful Isle of Pines.

Many have compared Cuba's elongated shape to a hungry alligator, with the capital city of Havana in the north resting on its tail, and Santiago de Cuba in the south in its open jaws.

During my growing-up years, Fulgencio Batista had ruled Cuba, first through a series of puppet presidents from 1934 to 1944, then from 1952 to 1958 as the head of government himself. Cuba was regarded by many as the tropical playground of the United States. United States businesses invested heavily in the development of the country. In later years, Batista was rumored to have amassed a large fortune ($300-$400 million) for himself at the expense of his countrymen's needs, along with rumors of extreme brutality against those who opposed him. His avarice

15

and cruelty paved the way for the young, charismatic revolutionary, Fidel Castro, and the subsequent rise of Communism. This is what history books will tell you. Native Cubans have a slightly different tale to tell.

As a small child living in the small inland community of San Germán on the southern end of the main island, I was unaware of politics and government strife. My parents, both of pure African descent, emigrated to Cuba in their youth—my father from Trinidad-Tobago and my mother from Jamaica. There, in the southern province of Cuba, they had met and married.

My father, an auto mechanic, trained to become the best lathe man in the community of San Germán. He owned his own shop, and because of his reputation for exceptional work, he contracted regularly for jobs at the American naval base in Guantánamo. This involved many miles of travel to and from the base. Neither he nor my mother appreciated having him away from the home and his family so often. Certain that his work at the naval base would continue indefinitely, he called a family counsel and decided that he would sell our home in San Germán and move south. Once there, he established a new shop in the seaport town of Caimanera. Two years after our move, my father was working on his lathe when one of the grips broke. The high-speed machine swung free and hit him in the chest. His injuries hospitalized him for two weeks. During his hospital stay he decided it was time for him to teach me the business. After a short recuperation, my father announced his intentions.

"Noble," he said, "I won't always be with you. You must learn to run and repair the machines."

"After your brush with death," my mother protested, "you want to endanger our son's life?" She argued with my father and lost. I began by learning how to clean and service the machinery. I disliked the work from the start, but in our home, one never defied my father.

On Friday, March 19, 1950, only two months after his accident, my father came home after completing some work at the military base. The family spent the evening talking, retiring for the night a little after ten. The next morning when my mother called my father for breakfast, she found him dead of a heart attack. Since our move, I'd spent more time with him. We'd become friends, and suddenly he was torn from my life. Shocked and isolated by his death, I mourned my loss. My mother promptly sold the family business.

My friends and I attended the local grade school run by the Catholic Church until we reached high-school age. That is when I left my friends to attend the *Instituto Guantánamo*, a school near the American base. I attended the institute for five years. During that time, my mother and my sister Paulina, both tired of the constant political upheaval, emigrated to the United States. I chose to stay in my homeland. I felt that, as a black man, Cuba offered me a better future than did our neighbors to the north. It was during my years at the institute that I accepted God's call to the ministry. My future seemed set, secure, predictable. And then came Castro and the revolution.

Cuban leaders throughout history have known that revolutions and insurrections always begin in the hilly province of Oriente. Fidel Castro, seven years my senior, grew up on his father's sugar plantation in the province of Oriente. Coming from a fairly wealthy family, he attended the best Catholic schools in the area. He was a good student and an excellent athlete. Though I did not know him personally, it was rumored that he had had a number of problems by the time he reached the university. In a struggle for power at the university, he supposedly killed his own cousin. During law school, he became deeply involved in radical political groups. He was active in student riots and demonstrations that repeatedly got him into trouble with the police.

In 1952 he completed his degree in law and ran for congress. This was the same year Batista feared he might not win the elections, so rather than risk humiliation and defeat, he staged a revolt and suspended all elections. But this political unrest had little to do with me and my preparation for becoming a minister of the gospel of Jesus Christ.

Rumors regarding the growing revolution crisscrossed the island faster than a spring hurricane. In 1953, during a carnival parade, Castro and his men disguised themselves as Batista's soldiers, entered the Moncada Headquarters Hospital, and killed eighteen hospitalized soldiers. Batista was blamed for the deplorable act. Eighteen months later, after a series of such attacks, the government deported Castro to Mexico, where he built up a mercenary army. In 1957, outfitted by monies collected from people in the United States and South America, and with the help of former president Carlos Prio Socaras, Castro and his men slipped back into Cuba and again committed despicable acts against the people of Cuba, all the while disguised as Batista's men. The people logically turned against the Batista regime.

Many Seventh-day Adventist leaders, while not politically active, believed that Castro would have the power to build a more stable condition for the country. In the Sierra Maestra, sympathetic church leaders became more directly involved, not with the fighting, but with feeding and guiding the revolutionary soldiers. More and more Cubans joined the movement.

In the final days of 1958 it became evident that Batista's days as leader of Cuba were numbered. Rather than face defeat, Batista slipped out of Havana on December 31 and headed for the Dominican Republic. Two days later, on January 2, 1959, rebel troops took over Santiago de Cuba and began a week-long triumphal march northwest to the capital city of Havana.

Castro and his men arrived in Havana sporting their rosary beads—a ploy to convince the fervent Catholics that the revolutionaries were indeed loyal to the church. A closer look revealed a different picture.

His cornerstone men, men like Ernesto (Che) Guevara from Argentina; Camilo Cienfuego, a member of the Cuban Communist Party; and Raúl Castro, Fidel's brother, who at age fifteen had visited the USSR, were staunch Communists.

After placing these men and others like them in key positions in the Cuban government, Castro began to use plainclothed military men to harass the churches. The Catholics and the Jehovah's Witnesses were the first to feel his iron fist.

In Cuba, the Catholic Church commemorated "La Virgen de la Caridad" (The Virgin of Charity) on September 8 each year. The tradition had begun with the first settlers of our country. But because it was connected with religion and God, Castro refused to allow the people to conduct the accompanying parade. He claimed it would be dangerous, since factions of Batista's men were still at large in the capital city.

The priest decided that the people would hold their parade anyway. They would march around the block where the church was located. Castro's plainclothed militia armed themselves with metal pipes, chains, and bats, all innocently wrapped in newspapers. When the people emerged from the church to begin their parade, the fighting broke loose. Hundreds of worshipers were injured or killed. Batista's men were blamed, but the people of Havana knew better. From this event on, Castro removed his mask of innocence. He openly deported priests to Spain and incarcerated his countrymen en masse.

The Jehovah's Witnesses' conflict with Castro centered around their refusal to serve in the military and salute the flag. Furious at their defiance, Castro arrested them by the score and confiscated their properties and belongings, then had them thrown into prisons, mainly the Isle of Pines and Combinado del Este. They were stripped, beaten, and thrown into cells filled with homosexuals.

By this time, I had finished my education at the institute and was working with Pastor Vásquez in the city of Marianao as a youth pastor. I also sold Christian books to supplement my income from the church. We knew from the start that it was only a matter of time till Castro would begin harassing other Christian organizations, including us, the Seventh-day Adventists.

Castro's Marxist regime viewed the church as a threat. During the revolution, Castro's people had nicknamed him "el caballo" (the horse). So when our pastors preached on the beast of Revelation, they were accused and convicted of fomenting political rebellion.

Within months of Castro's coup, the governmental leanings toward Communism became evident even to the nonpolitical population of the country. The new leader had promised that his revolution would bring sweeping changes to Cuba—its economy, government, and way of life for its people. And it did! In 1959 and 1960, Castro still had not declared himself to be a Communist, yet the flowery speeches he delivered at public rallies fell crushed beneath the boot of flagrant injustice. Once certain of his power, Castro rounded up his enemies, charged them with committing crimes against the revolution, and conducted speedy mock trials. Some were sentenced to prison; others were publicly executed. Journalists declared that his treatment of his enemies was similar to the way Russia disposed of its dissenters.

Like Hitler's Youth Movement in Nazi Germany and Mao's Red Guard in Communist China, Castro organized a children's group called the "Pioneers." The members possessed unlimited authority. They broke into homes, ate whatever food they desired, ordered citizens to turn out their lights for the evening, and took personal possessions—all confiscated as "people's property." Anyone with a shortwave radio would be accused and found guilty of listening to the enemy's voice. The least infraction, real or imagined, was considered a crime against the state. And crimes against the state never went unpunished.

Relations with the United States worsened after Castro nationalized all American-owned oil refineries. The United States placed an embargo on all trade with Cuba, and Castro retaliated by confiscating all U.S. businesses in Cuba. On January 2, 1960, Castro charged that all the employees of the U.S. Embassy in Havana were spies. Within forty-eight hours, all embassy staff members were removed from the country, and the angry U.S. government broke all diplomatic relations with my country.

When Castro first came to power, many Cubans escaped from their homeland, including a large number of doctors, lawyers, writers, professors, and engineers. They left rather than have to work for the new government. During that time, I helped many of my personal friends and church members join the exodus.

My mother and sister, now living in Massachusetts, urged me to leave Cuba for the United States while I could still escape. I would have, except for one complication. By now, I had met and married Yraida. She and I had discussed applying for a visa for some time. However, before we could leave the country, my young bride became pregnant. Unfortunately for us, the new government passed a law that did not allow any pregnant woman to leave Cuba. Too late we realized that we would not be going anywhere, at least not until after the new baby arrived. Maybe later, we consoled ourselves. Maybe six or seven months after the birth of our first child.

When Castro saw how many professional and educated people had applied for visas to leave the country, he closed the borders. Yet, in spite of his best efforts, people continued to slip past border guards and secret police. And I admit, I assisted my brothers and sisters when and wherever I could. It is difficult to understand how precious were the liberties we Cubans lost! Perhaps no one knows until they are gone.

Then came the planned Bay of Pigs—April 15 to 17, 1961. Cuban counterrevolutionaries, along with the American CIA, planned to invade the island along a remote area of beach called the Bay of Pigs. With the help of air cover promised by the United States military, they would retake the island from Fidel Castro's revolutionary army. In Cuba itself, former Batista supporters and others who opposed the Communist takeover of their country prepared for the invasion.

Castro and his soldiers, having learned of the planned invasion days before the event, rounded up hundreds of people in the major cities of Havana and Marianao. He locked up 70 percent of the inhabitants, male and female, in schools, hospitals, stadiums, warehouses, even the zoo—any place they could convert into a prison. At the same time, the regime commandeered the home of Marquez Sterling, one of the earlier presidential candidates killed during the revolution, turned it into the Cuban equivalent of the Russian KGB Headquarters, and called it G-2.

The security leak that allowed Castro to prepare for the invasion and the United States government's failure to carry through with the promised air support caused the attempt to fail. After the Bay of Pigs fiasco, Fidel Castro's paranoia intensified. He had his agents searching for American CIA agents around every street corner and behind every sugar cane plant on the island. The most innocent action on the part of a private citizen came under immediate suspicion. Many of my friends faced his firing squads—friends like Armando Rodriguez, Perez Lopez, Jesus Cueva, and Enrique Hernandez. Others were taken into custody and simply disappeared, never to be heard of again. Protestant ministers and Catholic priests were particularly suspected to be CIA agents because of the international connections their positions afforded.

Like other Christians throughout Cuba, my wife and I lived in fear. Each time I left home, Yraida and I kissed one another goodbye, knowing we might never see each other again this side of heaven. The first time I held my newborn son in my arms, I wondered if I would live to see him grow into manhood. Yet, in spite of the hassles, in spite of the raids, and in spite of the killings occurring around us, I believed that I had a job to do. More than ever before, the terrified people of Cuba hungered for the assurances found only in the Word of God. More than ever, they needed the hope for a better tomorrow.

Company in Cell Number 2

The once-a-day arrival of food broke the monotony of prison life. After the first meal of less-than-fresh meat, our daily diet consisted of a four-ounce serving of a pale yellow gruel made with cornmeal and water alongside a slice of rock-hard bread. Fat white worms floating on the surface of the gruel supplied us with protein. But no matter how hard I tried, I couldn't make myself ingest either the gruel or the bread. The other prisoners didn't mind benefiting from my delicate stomach. I sensed they were wondering how long I would hold out before I began eating the putrefied food.

As I watched the other prisoners eat, I wondered how long each man had been incarcerated in this hole of death. From the little I could see, some of them had been here for quite some time. What had each one done to deserve such inhumane treatment? Murder? Theft? Blackmarketing? Member of the underground? I could only imagine the extent of their crimes against their country. I thanked God that once my captors realized my arrest was an error, I would be released and allowed to return to my family.

I had no idea how much time had passed when the face of a guard appeared in the little window on the cell door and he called, "Is Alexander there?"

When I answered Yes, a bare ceiling light bulb blinked on. I shaded my eyes from the bright light. The food slot in the door opened, and a clump of clothing plopped to the floor at my feet. "Dress and get ready," the guard commanded. "The interrogation officer is calling for you."

I picked up a blue-and-white striped T-shirt and slipped it over my head and stepped into a pair of red overalls. As I adjusted the straps on my shoulders, I glanced down at my garb and chuckled in dismay. Humberto Noble Alexander, a minister of the gospel of Jesus Christ, wearing such a strange and flamboyant get-up—I could only imagine what I looked like. My cellmates laughed in spite of their seminaked condition.

"Don't worry, you'll get used to the zebra look," one of my fellow prisoners said, his voice tinged with sympathy. "We all do."

I grimaced and shrugged off his remark. Inside I thought, "There's no way I'll be here long enough to get used to any of this." Yet my reason wrestled with a nagging disquiet within me. What if the worst happened? What if I were not released? No! I shook myself in disgust. I would not think such negative thoughts. I had to believe that any mistake the military police might have made would be cleared up quickly and efficiently. I just needed the opportunity to talk with someone in charge, and I'd be on my way home.

Steel scraped against steel as the massive door swung open. I stepped out of the cell into the faintly lighted hallway. A wave of fresh air greeted me. My fatigue fell away as I inhaled the refreshing aroma. I could handle anything, I thought, except the foul atmosphere I'd just left behind.

My military guard with his grizzled beard and rumpled army fatigues resembled any one of the hundreds of imitation Fidels roaming the streets of the capital city since Castro's successful coup. The guard slammed the cell door shut behind me and nudged me forward with the barrel of his sidearm. Our footsteps echoed down the long, empty corridor.

Along the way, he decided to harass me. "When we get through with you, you won't continue distributing your opium to the people," he said.

I thought for a moment, then asked, "Opium? But I—"

I winced as he ground the gun's barrel into my spine. "The opium of the masses," he snickered. "Christianity!"

As I walked with the gun pressing against my backbone, I smiled in spite of my pain. "Of course, the gospel of Jesus Christ"—'opium of the masses,' according to the Castro regime. Is that the reason I have been arrested, for preaching the gospel?"

One of his hands grasped my left arm, and his other hand leveled the gun at me as we proceeded through the labyrinth of gray, tomblike hallways, barred doors, and uneven stone stairwells. As we trudged the length of the corridor, I saw no one; I heard no one. Suddenly he ordered me to stop, then turned me to face a large metal doorway.

In code, my guard escort rapped on the door. The door opened, and the guard shoved me inside a small interrogation room. A wave of cool, refrigerated air hit me, as if I were stepping into a cold-storage locker. I would learn later that the room's temperatures could range anywhere from scalding hot to a deep-freeze cold, according to the designs of the interrogator and the degree of discomfort to be inflicted upon the prisoner.

A man I immediately identified as the officer in charge in spite of his civilian attire paced back and forth behind a small metal desk. His scraggly beard imitated the mustache and beard worn by his commander-in-chief, Fidel Castro. With his hands folded behind his back and his chin jutting forward, he strutted like a lightweight bantam rooster anticipating a championship cockfight in the center of Havana. For a moment he stopped pacing and leveled his gaze at me. The cold glint in his eyes contradicted the friendly tilt of his head and slight smile on his lips. An empty metal chair stood in front of the desk.

Without a word, my guard escort and a second soldier who had been standing in the shadows grabbed me and stripped off my clothing. For some time, I stood naked, waiting for further instructions, while the three men, each dressed in heavy, warm clothing, laughed and talked among themselves.

"The revolution will last forever!" my interrogator declared as he seated himself in the chair behind the desk.

"Yes," the second soldier agreed, gesturing with his arms. "It is great and invincible."

"It will surely last for more than a thousand years," my guard escort replied. "I do not know if there is an eternity, but if there is, the revolution will outlast it."

I trembled from the cold as the three men extolled the virtues and the longevity of Castro's revolution. After a few minutes, as if to purposely allow the cold air time to seep into my body, the interrogator ordered me to sit on the empty metal chair. I obeyed.

When I sat down, the second officer turned on the light fixture above my head. An 800-watt light bulb directed straight into my face blinded me. I blinked but could not escape the light's intense glare. I closed my eyes, but the intense light penetrated my eyelids, causing intense pain in my eyes. "Father," I prayed silently, "You have promised to always be with me. Be with me now. Give me the strength to endure." I took a deep breath and waited. From experience, I knew there are three things you never do when being questioned by government agents: speak before spoken to, ask questions, or volunteer information of any kind.

After a few uncomfortable moments, the officer in charge fired his first question at me. "Why were you going to Guantánamo?"

"Guantánamo?" I asked. Surprised at his question, I needed time to think. What was he leading up to? Nothing made sense. Whenever I'd been questioned earlier, it was about other people's activities, not mine.

"Yes, Guantánamo!"

Then I remembered a trip Yraida and I had made a few weeks earlier. We'd driven down to the Oriente province to see members of my family. I decided he must be referring to that trip. "To visit my relatives."

My interrogator snorted his disbelief. Though I could see nothing beyond my circle of blinding light, I could hear the sound of a pencil tapping impatiently against the metal desktop. "We know that you went to see McDonald."

"McDonald?" My voice betrayed my surprise. "Sir, I don't know any McDonald." I sifted through the bits of street gossip and underground hearsay I had picked up at various times. Oh, yes, I thought. I had heard rumors about an American doctor at the United States naval base in Guantánamo and of his alleged attempts on Castro's life, but I had never met the man.

"Dr. McDonald," the man leaned across the desktop into the light. "You know him!" The officer's patronizing tone matched the sarcastic smirk on his face. "He is a doctor at the hospital on the base. You know that because you went to see him." Apparently pleased with the grenade of information he'd tossed my way, my interrogator folded his arms and leaned back in his chair.

"These guys are just looking for something to hang me on," I thought. "Well, they'll just have to look harder." I straightened my shoulders, elevated my chin, and stared straight ahead into the darkness that engulfed my interrogator's face. In a clear, measured tone, I answered, "I repeat, sir. I do not know any doctor by the name of McDonald."

The scrape of metal against rough concrete reverberated off the bare cement block walls as my tormentor jumped to his feet. I could hear him pace out his anger. Without a word, he rounded the desk. A pair of neatly pressed trousers and highly shined boots came into view, then his left arm and upper torso, while his face remained outside the circle of light. He leaned against the edge of the desk in an attitude of relaxed composure for a few seconds. Then his body tensed.

"Humberto." His voice escalated threateningly; then he pointed a finger into my face, within an inch of the tip of my nose. "I am being very patient with you, but my patience is growing thin. We know for a fact that Dr. McDonald was to give you a bomb to plant in Castro's private plane."

"A bomb?" Incredulous, I stared up to where his face would be if I could see it. Where in the world had they come up with that fantastic tale?

"Don't try to act ignorant with me, Alexander." The man leaped off the edge of the desk as if he'd leaned against a hot kitchen stove. Tension crackled throughout the room as he struggled to regain his composure.

"Yes, a bomb!" His voice cracked, revealing his disbelief and frustration. Taking a few seconds to re-establish his arrogant demeanor, he snapped about and strolled back to where I sat.

"We know—" he said, dragging out the "ow" meaningfully. "You know him!"

I shook my head and shrugged my shoulders. "Well, you all know more than I."

Righteously indignant, he gathered himself up to his full height of five feet five inches and sniffed, "Hmmph! Of course we do. Get dressed. Sergeant, take him to 'the room.'"

As I slipped into my clothing, my brain switched into an uneasy neutral, much like an automobile whose engine needs a tuneup. My fingers refused to work, and my teeth chattered, partly from the frigid temperature in the room and partly from the horrid realization that there would be no easy way out for me this time.

Dazed, I allowed myself to be led from the room. My guard escort taunted me as we retraced our steps through the serpentine tunnel system. "You'll talk. You wait and see, you'll talk."

He took me down one corridor, then another. I glanced at the heavy metal doors, which broke the monotony of the gray cement block walls, and shuddered. Now I realized that imprisoned behind each door were people living in conditions unsuitable for animals, let alone humans. At one corner, when I automatically turned toward the left, my captor redirected me to the right.

"This way," he barked, prodding me in the spine with the barrel of his gun. "To cell number 2, your new home."

I brightened for a moment. Perhaps conditions would be a little better in cell number 2. My first cell must have just been a holding pen, I decided. That would explain why there were twelve prisoners in a cell designed for nine.

My guard stopped in front of the door marked number two. He flicked on a light switch beside the door and removed a wad of keys from his hip pocket. After unlocking it with one of his keys, he slid the door open.

"We'll see if you know McDonald or not after spending a few days in here," he said, shoving me into the barren cell. I glanced about for a bed, but there was none—only a barren concrete floor, crumbling in the dampness of the room. The door clanged shut behind me and the light switched off.

Thinking I was alone, I shrugged and sat down on the cold, damp floor. Exhausted, I lay down and closed my eyes, hoping to block out the last seventy-two hours of my life. "Maybe if I sleep for a while," I thought. I curled up into a fetal position, but my hip bone and elbow soon protested.

I rolled from side to side, trying to find a comfortable position. I wondered how long they would keep me here, isolated from other prisoners. How long would I be able to stand the isolation?

Before five minutes had passed, I learned that my first supposition had been inaccurate. I was not alone in the cell. To the contrary, I could feel tiny feet scurrying across my scalp. I reached up to brush the intruder away, only to discover that my uninvited cellmate hadn't come alone. Out of the nooks and crannies in the walls and broken chinks of concrete swarmed hundreds of bedbugs, cockroaches, and gopher rats. Everywhere I touched, some creature darted out of my reach. I shrank back against the wall and curled my body into as tight a ball as possible, only to hear the deadly hum of mosquitoes circling my newly shaven head.

I flailed my arms and legs in a wild frenzy, occasionally connecting with one creature or another. When I felt the warm body of a jungle snake slithering down the side of my neck and onto my chest, I leaped to my feet and threw it across the cell. I glanced about frantically. How many other snakes hung ready to drop from the ceiling onto my shoulder? Within minutes, I seriously wondered how long it would take before I went insane or got bitten by a rat or poisonous snake and died.

It seemed like a lifetime, but in less than five minutes the ceiling light switched on, and my scurrilous cellmates scattered or slithered back into their hiding places. I stood and brushed the remaining vermin from my underpants.

The door to the cell slid open. My grinning guard chuckled at the look of horror that must have been on my face. He waved me into the hall and escorted me back to the interrogation room. This time the room was warm, and I was seated on a cushion in front of a different interrogator. The officer in charge clicked his fingers. My guard snapped to attention, adjusted the air-conditioning dial, then aimed the 800-watt spotlight into my eyes.

"Alexander," the new interrogator snarled, "you must understand. I mean business. When was Dr. McDonald going to give you the bomb?"

I whispered a short prayer for strength and took a deep breath. "I know nothing about such a bomb."

"Do you admit to visiting Guantánamo?"

"Yes."

"For what purpose?"

"One of my sisters lives on the Cuban side of town. I visited her."

The man beyond the circle of light leaned forward. His voice lost the edge of anger he had originally exhibited. "Now look, Alexander, we only want to know one thing. How did you plan to sneak the bomb on board the plane?"

I remained silent, since I knew nothing of the assassination plot he described. His chair scraped against the concrete floor, and for a few minutes I could hear him pace back and forth behind the desk.

"You do not want to answer because of your contract with the American CIA. We know that you are one of their principal agents here on the island." The voice moved closer until I knew my interrogator stood within inches of me.

"You did not notice the pillow on which you are seated?" he asked. The tone of his voice curled around me like a snake waiting to strike. "It is the cushion in which you planned to hide the bomb in order to place it on board the airplane."

I looked down at the royal blue cushion beneath me. Blinded by the light, I could not make out any details.

The interrogator banged his fist on the table and shouted, "Sergeant, take him out of my presence before I kill him!" The guard grabbed my arm and hauled me to my feet.

"Maybe a while longer in 'the room' will loosen your tongue," the officer in charge growled. "Braver men than you have entered that room strong and stalwart and left broken, when they survived at all."

The metal door slid open, and my guard dragged me into the hallway. I stumbled. He swore and jabbed his gun into my side. I struggled to catch my balance. I felt lightheaded as waves of exhaustion and hunger swirled through my brain.

The walk back to cell number 2 seemed endless. Once back inside the cell, and with the overhead light blinked off, I stood frozen in the center of the cell waiting for my cellmates to return. And they did, with a vengeance.

Since I had no idea how long I would be incarcerated in "the room," I realized I couldn't remain standing. Sooner or later I would have to sit down. Again, I drew my legs up into a tight ball and leaned against a wall. I swatted at my tormentors, hoping to frighten them enough to snatch a short catnap. It worked for a few minutes. I awakened to gopher rats gnawing at my toes. An army of cockroaches marched across my stomach, leaving behind an abominable odor.

Minutes later, the overhead light came on, and the creatures of darkness retreated. When the cell door slid open, I couldn't decide whether to be grateful for the reprieve or fearful for my immediate future.

I was taken back to the interrogation room and ordered to sit on the same cushion. A different officer, one I'd never seen before, stood in front of me. I could sense the presence of a second officer standing behind me.

"Alexander," the new interrogator began, "what were you preaching about in your so-called revival meeting?"

"My sermon was about the origin of sin and its consequences," I replied.

The interrogating officer pounded the table top and snarled, "You said that Fidel was a devil, didn't you?"

"You said that, not I. Moreover, I never once mentioned the word *devil* in my sermon. Nor did I mention the word *Fidel*." I paused. "In fact, if your agent taped my sermon, as I suspect he did, we can go over it together to prove that what I say is true."

The first officer straightened and paused for a moment. "Noble, if you cooperate with us we can make life much more bearable for you. You will be rewarded with fruit, rice, beef . . . if you cooperate." He waited for me to speak. I didn't.

"Fine, if you don't want to talk, we'll give you a sheet of paper and a pencil. You can write out what you were doing. I mean your counterrevolutionary activities."

He handed me a piece of notebook paper and a pencil. Having nothing else to do, I began drawing Christian crosses. The officer in charge glanced down at my sketches. Furious, he ripped the paper from my hand and crumpled it in his fist.

"Give him a phone call!" he shouted.

For an instant, I thought, "Good, now I can call Yraida to let her know." Then I discovered that my captor was speaking of an entirely different kind of "phone call." Simultaneously, two large hands slapped both of my ears with such force that the slap lifted me off the cushion and into the air. Intense pain shot through my ears. Tears sprang into my eyes. I was certain my eardrums had burst. I felt dizzy from the pain. "I will be deaf for the rest of my life," I thought. I didn't realize then how accurate my thoughts were. Twenty-three years later, I still suffer the consequences of their "phone call."

Above the ringing in my head, I heard my captor shout, "Compañero, take him back!"

The second officer held a revolver to my head as I struggled to my feet. My guard returned me to cell number 2. For the next fifteen days and nights, the pattern continued—first interrogation, then time in cell number 2, and back again for more questioning. Even though I'd been denied sleep and food and was weakened by their repeated beatings, I could never admit to their lies. The longer they questioned me, and the longer they kept me in that filthy cell, the more determined I became that they would not wear me down. I would leave the cell unbroken and unbowed.

Baptism of Death

I staggered down the corridor of gray once again, with my guard at my side. My ears rang and my head swam from the "phone call" I'd received earlier. Exhaustion and pain played handball with my consciousness. It had been hours since I'd slept or eaten. "Lord," I thought, "how long does it take before a person breaks under such conditions?"

After the guard frisked me for hidden weapons—where he thought I'd get such a weapon I don't know—he thrust me back inside the interrogation room. There I met a fourth interrogator, a stout, swarthy officer. It was evident by the way he twirled his drooping mustache and stroked his full beard that they symbolized proof of his machismo.

"Have a seat." The officer in charge gestured toward an empty chair. On the seat was the royal blue cushion. I obeyed. "We are losing too much time." The man rounded the desk and leaned against the edge, his left leg dangling.

"You are shaking. Are you nervous?"

"No, I'm cold," I replied.

Arching one eyebrow, he shook his head ever so slightly and curled what little could be seen of his upper lip. "Do you recognize the cushion you are sitting on?"

I shook my head.

"You are sitting on top of the bomb you intended to place in Castro's plane, you know."

He waited a few minutes for a reaction of some kind. "You are not going to tell us about your CIA activities, are you?"

I shook my head. "Not any, that I know of."

"You are not going to tell us how you entered 'Gitmo' [the Guantánamo base] to pick up bombs in order to sabotage Castro's plane?"

The officer's face exploded with fury. He leaped to his feet, jerked his revolver from its holster, and pointed the barrel at my

31

forehead. Purple with rage, he shouted a volley of profanity in my face.

I waited for him to fire. Would I hear the gunshot, then feel the bullet penetrate my skull? Or would I feel or hear nothing at such a close range? For the first time since my arrest, I was truly frightened—frightened to the core of my very being.

I closed my eyes and willed my mind to blot out my situation. The Lord must have heard my plea. Suddenly, I was back in San Germán, in Mr. Harris's classroom at the little Catholic school in our community. I could hear his voice as he pointed at Europe and Asia on the pull-down map on the wall. In my imagination, I glanced about the classroom at my childhood friends, their eyes sparkling with innocence and mischief. I could smell my mother's cooking in our home. I could see my father working over his machines. I remembered the evening walks my parents and I took together during my childhood. In those few moments, I traveled through my twenty-eight years of life, recalling the most incidental experiences, experiences I'd long since relegated to the depths of the mind.

"Alexander, I could shoot you dead right this minute!" The cold steel of the revolver and the officer's insistent tone snapped me back to reality. "After all, what else could I do? You were trying to escape, right?"

I decided that since he hadn't shot me immediately, he probably had no intention of doing so. My fear that he might deliberately shoot was replaced with a new terror. In his fury, the man's trembling fingers might unintentionally pull the trigger. Why that made a difference to me at that moment, I don't know. Frozen in eternity, I prayed.

When the man had spent his rage, he waved the revolver under my nose. "There is no man too brave not to betray or too strong to resist. You'll either do or die!" Then, swaggering across the room, he turned, shook his head, and grunted in disgust. Little did I realize that I'd just been tried, convicted, and sentenced with no room for an appeal.

My moment of terror passed. Silently, I wondered what else my captor could possibly do to me. I soon found out. I was ordered to strip out of the few clothes I was wearing. The guard placed a thick black canvas bag over my head. With my hands tied behind my back, they marched me between two soldiers to a waiting automobile and tossed me onto the floor in the back seat. One soldier lashed my ankles together. Two men climbed into the back seat and slammed their doors. I could tell how many there were by the number of feet resting on my back and the muzzles of their two rifles pressing into one of my sides.

Another door slammed shut, and the automobile's engine roared to life. While I tried to adjust to my cramped condition, I could hear the static of the car's two-way radio. As we rode, the driver responded in monosyllables to the calls from headquarters. My guards scarcely spoke as we rode. I felt every bump in the road as the car bounced across potholes, weaving first one way, then another. While it was a three-hour drive, our destination was actually quite close to the G-2 Headquarters.

As my guards had planned, I had no idea which direction we were heading, when we would arrive at our destination, or what would happen to me when we arrived. All I could think about was my increasingly painful situation.

The car finally slowed to a stop. My four traveling companions dragged me out of the car and down a grassy slope. My feet were still tied together. When they removed the hood from my head, I discovered I was at the edge of a large inland lake, partially frozen by unseasonably cold temperatures. A short wooden dock protruded out over the water.

"Turn around," one of the men ordered. "Put your hands behind your back!" He bound my hands behind my back with a rope while a second man fastened a leather strap about my waist. A heavy sisal rope was attached to the strap. Without a word, one man grabbed my shoulders and the other my feet, then walked toward the dock.

"What . . . what are you going to do to me?" I cried.

"Simple!" One of my tormentors replied as he stepped onto the floating platform. "We are going to toss you into the lake. If you are truly innocent of all crimes against the state, swim out, and we will believe you."

As the two men heaved my body over the side of the dock, the words of Matthew 27:40-42 passed through my mind. "If thou be the Son of God, come down from the cross. Likewise also the chief priests mocking him, with the scribes and elders, said, He saved others; himself he cannot save. If he be the King of Israel, let him now come down from the cross, and we will believe him."

Dark, frigid waters swirled above my head as my body plunged deep into the lake. I gyrated like a marlin on a line, struggling to break free of my bonds. My lungs felt as if they'd burst, my ears rang, and my vision dimmed. I realized I was drowning and could do nothing to save myself. There was nothing left to do but relax and let it happen.

As soon as I stopped struggling, my captors yanked me out of the water by the rope attached to my waist. Suspended between the water's surface and the dock, I gulped and sputtered, gasping for air. I could see the faces of my four tormentors as they laughed at their sadistic joke.

The officer in charge, the one who'd earlier held the revolver to my forehead, leaned toward me. "Are you ready to speak now? Swim out and we will believe you."

I shook my head in protest. "I have nothing—" My protests were cut short by a second dousing beneath the icy waters. Again, I was submerged until I was certain I would drown, then raised and questioned. The lake's cold temperatures soon became more of a death threat to me than drowning. Over and over, the ceremony was repeated until I lost count of the times I was submerged and left to almost drown.

When I could no longer control my chattering teeth enough to answer the questions, the main interrogator again asked, "Are you ready to speak, or shall we try another little game?" His voice shook with anger.

My baptism by freezing ended when I lost consciousness. I came to on the floor of the speeding car. Back at G-2 Headquarters, my guards took me to another interrogation room, where Commandante Nauguera, a higher-ranking officer than any I'd met previously, was waiting.

Nauguera looked at me and sneered, "You believe you have guts? We are going to demonstrate that we are the ones with guts!" Turning to the two guards, he ordered, "Take him to cell 21."

My captors vented their frustrations at not being able to break my will by half yanking and half dragging me through the corridors to my new cell. We arrived at a small cubicle, similar to a shower stall, barely large enough for one person. On the floor was a grillwork that tilted toward the back of the stall. Along the back of the stall, several rows of nails pierced the floor from below, the points sharpened and waiting for the intended victim.

"Get in." One of the guards shoved me into the stall and closed the door. I heard a bolt slide into place. I soon learned that to avoid my heels being pierced by the protruding nails, I would have to stand on my tiptoes. I tried other positions, but there were none.

Then the real torture began. A tiny droplet of water fell from the ceiling and onto my head, followed by another, then another. One by one the droplets hit my head in exactly the same spot. I tried to shift, but the droplets continued to fall in a slow, perfectly timed cadence. Five minutes passed, ten minutes, twenty. By the end of the first hour, the water droplets felt like giant hammers pounding unceasingly on my head. I felt as if I'd go insane.

Over and over I prayed the words Jesus prayed while hanging on the cross: "My God, my God, why hast thou forsaken me?" A battle between my faith and my circumstances raged within me. I prayed that my agony would be cut short. I lost track of time. Whether I spent an hour in there or five, I did not know. When my tormentors came to remove me from cell 21, they were surprised to find that I was still sane. Back in the interrogation room, the officer in charge tried to force a confession from me once again.

"You think you have the best of us, don't you? Well, you're wrong." He stroked his beard and nodded his head for a moment. "I think I will just shoot you and claim you were trying to escape. How about that?"

Since there was little I could do about it, I just shrugged.

In utter disgust, he shouted, "We're not going to kill you. That's what you want us to do, but by the time we finish with you, you're going to prefer dying, because the dead are better off than you will be. I'm going to see that you get a twenty-year sentence!"

"Lord," I prayed silently, "give me strength." I stared straight ahead, refusing to give my tormentor the benefit of knowing how miserable I actually felt.

The guard yanked me roughly to my feet and dragged me down the hall to another cell—a cell crawling with snakes of every kind. During the colder weather, the island snakes, poisonous and nonpoisonous alike, slithered into this particular cell in order to curl up next to whatever warm body was imprisoned there—in this instance, mine. While I'm not certain just how much my cellmates agreed, the snakes and I hammered out an uneasy truce.

A month later, my guards returned for me. I had no idea where they were taking me. They bound my hands behind my back and forced me at bayonet point to proceed through the dank corridors to the rear entrance of the G-2 building. The tropical sunlight blinded me as I stepped out into the prison courtyard. Again the bayonet point edged me forward into the back of an eighteen-wheel enclosed truck, where a number of prisoners already sat waiting for transfer.

As the soldiers jammed the last prisoner aboard, the truck's sheet-metal doors slammed shut, completely sealing off any access to oxygen or light. In the darkness, I listened as the driver started the engine and ground the truck's gears. My bones grated painfully against the hard metal walls and the wooden bed as the truck bounced in and out of a thousand potholes at what seemed to be a breakneck speed. Before many miles, the air supply dwindled. Groans and wails filled our mobile prison cell as we struggled for each breath. Entombed in my own discomfort and the total darkness of my surroundings, I failed to realize until we reached our destination and the doors swung open that many had fainted during the journey. One prisoner, Byron Miguel, died.

La Cabaña Fortress. Built in the sixteenth century, the old Spanish fort was known throughout my country as "the death house." The complex, about the size of four square city blocks, was built with underground galleries interlaced with cavelike tunnels. The number of prisoners relegated to one cell in the long rows ranged between fifty and 243! More Cuban prisoners died in this prison than in any other.

Bullet holes pockmarked the massive gray stone walls from the firing squad executions carried out by the military. In this prison, Batista's former military men and other enemies of Castro's revolution waited for their numbers to be called, waited to face the six-man firing squad.

During the long, tropical nights that followed, I would lie awake listening to the grisly sound of gunfire as soldiers annihilated hundreds of prisoners. I also learned to listen for the occasional prisoner who died shouting, "Long live Christ the King," or "Down with Communism."

But the worst sound I remember was the yelling and laughter of little children running about during the daytime executions. The La Cabaña guards brought their wives and children to the executions as though they were a family outing to the circus. Yet they were not just entertainment. They were also a warning of what happens to counterrevolutionaries.

One by one our captors called our names, assigned us numbers, and allowed us to hop down from the truck, whereupon we were thoroughly searched. Whatever property a prisoner might have brought with him was confiscated for the guards' use.

I was taken to Gallery 12 along with 125 other prisoners. We had to pass the military prison yard in order to reach the civilian prison yard where I would be held until my trial. Hardly more than a cave dug out of rock, our funnel-shaped cell had a bar door at the widest end and a small bar window at the narrow end. The small hole in the floor, also barred, accommodated our lavatory needs.

As is the custom in each of these prisons, the veteran prisoners greeted me at the cell door. I knew the prison routine fairly well by this time and was ready for their barrage of questions. "How is the counterrevolution going?" "Is the United States planning another invasion?" "Is it true Castro has cancer?" "Has the OEA [Organization of American States] censured Castro's regime?" "Is there any sign of weakening in Castro's government?"

I answered their questions as best I could, knowing that they were questions posed by desperate men grasping for any shred of hope I might be able to give them. How I wished I could tell them what they wanted to hear—that Castro and his henchmen were on the brink of defeat, that the United States had launched a successful sea attack, and that in a few short weeks they would be free, but I couldn't. I had to slash their fantasies of freedom with the cold steel razor of truth. Angry and bitter, they turned away— some to hide their tears of disappointment, others to build new dreams with which to replace the ones I'd destroyed. I sighed again, frustrated that I could do nothing to relieve this strange, haunting sickness—people hungering for information, for truth.

As the crowd about me dwindled, a fifty-year-old man stepped up to me and smiled. "Do you remember me?" he asked.

Five feet eight inches of hard muscle and determination faced me. Bright, intelligent eyes stared at me from beneath a smooth, broad forehead. I shook my head. "I'm afraid . . . I'm not too certain . . ." I studied his strong black features for some time.

"Did you ever sell books?"

Was this a trick, I wondered. Has this man been planted here by the military to trip me up somehow? I will have to tell him the truth, I decided. "Yes," I admitted.

"Did you work in the Oriente Province?"

"Yes . . ."

I could sense his excitement growing. "Have you ever been to Puerto Padre?"

A nervous lump swelled in my throat. "Yes, I have."

A huge grin filled his face. His eyes filled with tears. "I am Antonio Diaz—the sergeant who signed the permit to allow you to sell your books in my area."

I scowled as he continued. "You gave me a little booklet entitled *Steps to Christ,* remember?"

I nodded slowly, though I could remember nothing about the incident he described. My stomach felt uneasy. This had to be some kind of trick. I decided that I couldn't afford to antagonize this man, whoever he was. "Perhaps if I just go along with him," I thought.

Antonio threw back his head and laughed. He had read my thoughts. "It's a marvelous book, my friend. It has a transforming power. It is through the testimony of that book I accepted Christ as my personal Saviour."

Suddenly, a veil was lifted from my eyes, and I remembered every detail of our meeting. We embraced, though the term *embrace* doesn't adequately describe the emotions transmitted between us at that moment. Only a Christian in a similar circumstance could possibly understand the joy, the overwhelming joy we experienced. Like a drowning man clinging to a lifeguard or a man who has fallen off a cliff grasping his rescuer, we hugged one another.

Dazed, I struggled with myself to believe it. To find a Christian brother in that house of the living dead seemed too good to possibly be true—then for the brother to be someone I had actually influenced for Christ. Incredible!

"What are you doing here?" I gasped, my voice breaking from uncontrolled emotion.

"Well, as you know, I was a member of the Cuban Constitutional Marines that were overthrown by the revolution. While many of my fellow officers either fled the country or joined Castro's forces, I stayed, and well . . . here I am."

"How long have you been confined?"

"Since '61," he explained. "I was released once, then taken prisoner again. I've been here at La Cabaña since February."

As he told me about his conversion and subsequent arrest, I studied the man's face. Again I shook my head in wonder. When I first met Antonio, his uniform sported medals for the rescue of seven Americans during World War II, when their PT boat sank. It hardly seemed possible that this could be the same man I'd met while canvassing the seaport town of Puerto Padre. The transforming power of the gospel! While the process had happened gradually after his acceptance of Jesus as his Saviour, this man had changed from a harsh and violent military man to a man of God.

After his conversion, Antonio became more of a counselor than an officer to be feared and hated by his men. Through day-by-day encounters, he shared his love for Christ. Soldiers and prisoners alike learned to love and respect him.

"My men began calling me Brother Rivero instead of Sergeant Rivero. Isn't that something?" Antonio's face glowed with gentle pride. "When the revolution broke out in 1955, I could not bring myself to oppress Batista's political enemies. So when a man was arrested, I would help him contact his relatives and a lawyer. It was as if God had been preparing me for just such a time." More than 200 men listened as Antonio told his story.

"After Castro came to power in 1959, the army and navy were disbanded. I, along with my fellow officers, was thrown into prison without benefit of trial. Night after night, we waited to be executed.

"One night, I was taken out of my cell where I joined a large band of prisoners. 'This is it,' I thought." He paused. "Under my breath, I began repeating the words to Psalm 91. 'He that dwelleth in the secret place of the Most High shall abide under the shadow of the Almighty.'

"One of the soldiers overheard my prayer and mocked me. 'Rivero, give glory to God,' he said.

"I answered, 'Yes, glory be to God.' I didn't realize it right then, but an officer standing nearby overheard the exchange and recognized my voice. He was one of the men I had helped while he was in prison," Antonio explained. "The captain stopped the lieutenant and told him that he had an important investigation in process and that I knew a lot that could help. He ordered the lieutenant to return me to my cell immediately. 'Captain, that's impossible,' the lieutenant argued, 'the firing squad is waiting for him.'

"The captain insisted. 'Take off those handcuffs and send him back to the dungeon with one of your soldiers,' he ordered. The lieutenant asked who was going to sign that order and the officer replied, 'Me!'" Antonio's eyes brimmed with tears of joy. "I was miraculously released from certain death that night."

"Praise God," I whispered as I looked at Antonio, my new brother in Christ. For some reason, I thought of the story of Jesus and the ten lepers. While only one leper returned to thank the Master, one did return. The same had been true of Antonio. Antonio had eased the suffering of so many after his conversion. He'd helped so many. And while most of the men left, grateful to be free, one officer found a tangible way to say Thank you by saving Antonio's life.

A murmur of satisfaction passed through the cell as Antonio's words reached our fellow prisoners' ears. I could almost read my cellmates' thoughts. "There is some justice in this world."

Yet I knew better. Antonio's rescue hadn't been the result of earthly justice, but heavenly. "God is so good," I mused.

I looked into Antonio's eyes. He'd echoed my thoughts. With tears in our eyes, Antonio and I embraced as brothers no longer separated by war. I would never have imagined that here, in La Cabaña Fortress, Cuba's famous "death house," I would receive a surge of renewed life. That I would find myself surrounded by God's mercy and His love. In spite of my scars, in spite of my exhaustion, in spite of everything, I felt so rich.

New Life in La Cabaña

A veil lifted from my memory as I studied the face of my brother in Christ. I remembered the abrasive officer he'd once been and the bottle of cognac he'd offered me when I visited his office. I compared him to the new Antonio standing before me and marveled at the transforming power of the gospel of Jesus Christ—truly a two-edged sword.

"I have a plan!" Antonio whispered. Generally, when a prisoner used this phrase, it was an escape plan. My brother in Christ had something else in mind. "Dear friend," he explained, "it is my mission to share the gospel here in this prison. Will you help me?"

Amazed, I stared at him. "Here?" I asked, glancing about the cell. "Where?" The tunnel-like gallery resembled the inside of a huge oil tank or perhaps a submarine cut in half. The beds were stacked four high along each of the walls. A narrow corridor the length of the cell separated them.

"Right here!" he gestured. Even as we spoke, we were surrounded by prisoners on every side. Some sat on the beds, some paced back and forth along the aisle, and still others stood nearby listening, since there was no place else to go.

Antonio nodded and grinned.

"How do we begin?" I asked.

"At the cross, at the cross . . ." Antonio's rich baritone voice echoed off the walls. I immediately joined in. Our first underground church service had begun. Somehow, as we sang the familiar words, the burdens of my heart lightened, and, as the song says, they "rolled away." Before we finished the chorus, a third man, Prado Fernandez, joined us.

"Brother Alexander," Antonio began, "will you 'read' the morning text for us?"

41

"Of course," I answered. "I will be 'reading' from the book of John, chapter three, verse sixteen." With a dignity worthy of the most prestigious congregation, I recited the well-known words: "For God so loved the world that he gave his only begotten Son, that whosoever believeth in him should not perish but have everlasting life."

We prayed for our new mission, for our fellow prisoners, and for our captors. We prayed for strength and understanding; we prayed for guidance and for our own spiritual growth. By the end of our prayer, we felt the presence of a fourth Man. Three sinners and the Christ. We would carry out our ministry. We knew before we began that there would be many foes to fight. However, we knew we were being led by a General who had never lost a battle.

One by one, other inmates joined our little circle of fellowship. Some joined out of boredom. Others joined in defiance of the Communist regime—and by hearing the Word of God were changed. Before long, they nicknamed me "the Pastor."

Some of the nonbelieving prisoners, hearing us pray for our captors, became angry. "How can you do that? These animals don't deserve your prayers, much less an answer from God!"

We tried to explain the love of God, but our explanations fell on deaf ears and hearts hardened by torture and abuse.

We built a makeshift pulpit out of a cardboard box and a sheet. Our church within the dungeon walls was taking shape. A guard called M-2, who, as a child, attended a Christian church with his aunt, smuggled a Bible in to us.

Satan saw the growing interest of many of the inmates and immediately set out to destroy it. First, a few of the more violent prisoners began referring to us as a cult, implying that our worship was questionable. Yet our numbers continued to grow. To accommodate the additional people, we moved our meetings to a larger open area in the center of our gallery. Enrico Vásquez, a nervous busybody type of man, thrived on deceit and violence. While we were careful to leave adequate space for the other prisoners to move about, he complained that we were in the way. Other malcontents such as Mario Simon and José Torreo joined him.

The last thing we wanted to do was to create strife in the cell block, so we discussed our problem and decided to move two of our beds about, and we would worship in the empty floor space.

However, Satan wasn't about to surrender yet. At the beginning of our next meeting, we began to sing a hymn. We hadn't finished the first line when Enrico strode over to where we met.

"Hey!" he said. "I don't like all the noise your cult is making here."

What a ridiculous claim. Night and day, the cell was constantly filled with the natural noise of so many people crammed in such a small living space. It was the hymn to which he objected.

Like a banty rooster, Enrico strutted back to his cot. The worshipers gathered into a huddle. I could see that the old Antonio ached to get his hands on Enrico's neck, but instead, the new Antonio pounded his fist into his hand. "We've got to find a way to continue. We can't stop worshiping together."

"I know," Jesus Arango, one of the newer converts, said. "I could never go back to the emptiness and isolation I felt before I joined the fellowship."

"We can change the hour of our service—meet at different times during the day instead of always at the same time," one of worshipers suggested. We tried his suggestion, and it seemed to work for a time.

Then, around three o'clock one morning, the cell's overhead lights flashed on. The blinding lights and shouts of "*Requisa*," which means "search and confiscate," along with the sound of metal striking metal and human flesh, created instant confusion for the startled prisoners. Sixty guards had tiptoed into the gallery and lined the length of the cell and were swinging two-and-a-half-foot lead pipes against the bedrails, the bed frames, and the sleeping prisoners.

The only means of escape from the terrible blows was through the one door that led to the courtyard. We ran from the cell like frightened deer trying to escape an attacking lion. To do that we were forced to run between two guards who stabbed at us with a stick, sharpened to a razor's edge, while shouting, "Get out! Get out!"

"What do you have that pipe for, corporal? Use it!" The sergeant in command egged on the guard unit to inflict as much pain in as short a time as possible. The prisoners' mass exodus barred the exit, allowing the guards to beat us even longer.

Once the last prisoner had broken free into the courtyard, another set of guards, specialists in ransacking, stealing, and sadism, arrived. The search that had begun in the wee hours of the morning continued throughout the day until 6:00 p.m. While the guard team searched the cell, our terror continued, for next to the courtyard was a rock quarry where dynamiting was going on. Shards and fragments of rock fell about us like shrapnel. With no place to run, we stood surrounded by pipe-armed guards, exposed to the hot tropical sun without food, shelter, or water. Our discomfort dulled into numbness as the hours passed.

In agony, we watched the search team throw out into the courtyard what meager possessions the prisoners might have acquired. Scraps of papers, worn-out books, cigarettes in varying degrees of use, and spare clothing lay in a heap. Without glancing toward Antonio or the other brothers in the faith, my spirits sank. This time, our most treasured possession, our only Bible, had been added to the pile. A moment later one of the guards lighted a match and set fire to our things.

The sergeant ordered us to walk the gauntlet, a corridor between two rows of soldiers. The routine was always the same. At the beginning of the line, each prisoner was required to strip off his only garment, his underpants, and walk to the end of the line. The underwear was then inspected by the last guard in the line. When the guard was satisfied that there were no notes hidden in the seams, he tossed the underwear onto the ground and ordered the prisoner to bend over and pick up his clothing. With searchlight in hand, a lieutenant conducted the final search of the prisoner. By now, a large group of military women stood atop the walls around the courtyard, laughing and jeering at our humiliation.

They herded us back into what was left of our cell to find the beds upside down, split open, and in total disarray. Water had spread all over the gallery floor after their check of the faucet. The prisoners looked about at the confusion, then at one another. We had no idea where to begin to restore order to the chaos. I was to learn that seldom a month went by without a "*requisa.*"

I whirled about as a guard ran his iron pipe along the bars of the door and shouted, "Prepare for breakfast." Immediately, the starving prisoners fell into line. Before we could reach the mess hall, a guard ordered us into the supper line.

While we waited to eat, we stood helplessly by, watching the flames devour our only earthly belongings. I longed to break free, dash to the bonfire, and rescue our Bible, but could not. I could only stand and watch and pray. Before long, our precious Bible was nothing but ashes.

A fog of despair hung in the air as we silently made our way into the mess hall.

When we returned to the cell, Antonio called us together. "Come, brothers, it is time for our worship service. We need to realize God's presence more than ever before."

Exhausted and sick of heart, we dropped to our knees. Immediately, we heard Antonio's usually strong baritone voice weakly sing the first few notes of "What a Friend We Have in Jesus." Another voice, barely above the level of a whisper, joined him, then another, until the ransacked cell rang with praises to our King.

Suddenly, the cell's clanging metal doors scraped open. A young soldier stepped inside our cell. A hush fell over the gallery as the entire prisoner population automatically melted back into the dungeon's shadows. They'd learned their lesson well—in order to survive one must remain as inconspicuous as possible.

"Where is the minister who conducts the religious services?" he asked.

I was in trouble, and I would suffer for it. I knew it. Everyone in the dungeon knew it. The entire gallery population stared at the broken concrete floor without speaking. The soldier's gaze slowly roamed about the circle, as if searching for his victim. Again he asked for the minister who had been conducting the religious services.

"I've come so far without denying my Lord," I reasoned. "Now is not the time to start." I took a deep breath and stepped toward the waiting soldier.

The soldier eyed me carefully, then asked, "Are you the minister?"

"Yes," I admitted, expecting at any moment a blow that would send me crashing to the floor.

He withdrew two Bibles from inside his uniform jacket. "I took these from the fire. Do you want them?"

"Yes!" Speechless, I stared in disbelief as he handed me the torn and partially destroyed Bibles. "Thank you," I stammered.

"Remember, you don't know me," he ordered. With an abrupt click of his heels, he turned and left the cell.

The cell door clanged shut. Stunned, I rushed to Antonio and handed him one of the Bibles.

"I don't believe it," I whispered. "God has His people even among the enemy."

"Praise God," Antonio replied, "praise God."

That was when we realized we had been foolish to make our possession of the Bibles public knowledge. We would protect the precious promises more carefully in the future. We learned to be "as wise as serpents and as harmless as doves." Carefully, we divided the Scriptures into a number of sections and hid the individual portions in various places in the gallery. My favorite hiding place for a portion of the Scriptures was among one of the Communist propaganda books we'd been given to read. That way, when the guards conducted their next raid, at least one or two portions of Scripture would remain secure.

Like the early Christian believers facing the persecution of their times, we added to our numbers daily. Baptist, Seventh-day Adventist, Presbyterian, Methodist, Catholic—our fellowship recognized no boundaries. The walls of Galleries 10, 11, and 12 echoed with praises to our faithful God and King. Prisoners formerly disheartened and empty of hope found comfort and joy as we sang. Though chained by hatred and deprivation, our pitiful group of Christian brothers declared themselves free in Christ.

No walls could keep out the joy we found in that truth. Together, we vowed that since we'd been born free, we would die free. Our tormentors might destroy our bodies, but we would not allow them to destroy our souls. For this, those of us who knew the words sang the triumphant songs of praise. It was difficult for the new converts to join in since they didn't know the words to the hymns or to the Bible verses we shared.

Antonio and I discussed the problem.

"If only we had enough Bibles for everyone," I mused.

"And hymnals," Antonio added, "so everyone could sing along."

"What if we copied off each day's Bible texts for them to take with them?" I suggested.

Antonio tipped his head to one side. "On what? We have no paper."

"Maybe . . ." I smiled. An idea was forming. "We do have paper." I picked up a scrap of a propaganda newspaper. "We have the margins on which we could write portions of the Scripture. We could use . . ." I glanced about the cell, ". . . the inside of cigarette packs for writing out the words to the hymns."

News of our praise services spread beyond the prisoner population and our guards, straight to headquarters. A satanic hatred filled the hearts of these brutal officials. Guards were ordered to break up the services by any means possible. But we could no more have stopped meeting together than we could have stopped eating our daily rations of wormy mush. Praise in the face of persecution provided a link with reality, with hope for a life beyond our daily existence. This link strengthened our determination to survive.

One evening, as we sang the second verse of *"Demos Gracias al Señor"* ("We Give Thanks to the Lord"), a sniper from the opening in the gallery roof opened fire on us with his R-2 Russian rifle. The prisoners who were not worshiping with us scattered for whatever cover they could find. A contingent of guards wielding billy clubs, chains, baseball bats, machetes, and rifles surrounded the worshipers.

"Stop singing!" their leader ordered. "Stop this instant!"

We continued singing. They opened fire, shooting indiscriminately into our circle. Instead of scattering as the guards thought we would, we remained together, singing and praying, as rifle bullet fragments and shrapnel embedded themselves in our flesh. The gunfire ceased, only to be followed by a beating massacre.

A guard's machete blade pierced Luis Rodriguez's cheek. His teeth could be seen through the wound. A second guard pounded Magimby, another brother, with a rifle butt, destroying his eye. We struggled to escape the brutal blows of our captors.

When the guards left the area, I noticed that the ring finger on my left hand was partly torn off. The excruciating pain didn't set in until at least an hour after the attack. Our guards offered no medical care.

At the sight of such wanton brutality, I seethed with anger. My jaw tightened in steely silence. "If only! Like Peter at Gethsemane's gate," I thought for a moment—"if I could only cut off their ears! Just let those Russian rifles fall into our hands." I didn't have long to plot vengeance, however. The injured brethren needed me—not just my physical support, but also my spiritual.

I snapped back to the reality of our plight. Obviously, the prison officials had no intention of supplying any medical attention for the wounded. My anger evaporated almost as quickly as it had arrived.

Whispering promises for strength to one another from God's Word, we bandaged and treated each other's "trophies of honor" as best we could. In spite of our injuries, we praised God for being allowed to suffer for our Saviour.

By the time we'd examined and treated the last prisoner's injury, my heart could once again sing.

Two soldiers arrived at the cell and called Antonio's number. "Headquarters wants to see you."

Antonio stepped forward immediately. "Me? What for?" he asked.

"Who knows? I just follow orders," the officer in charge replied. "You will come with us."

Antonio obeyed.

Since Antonio was a former military man and a very outgoing person, the authorities looked upon him as the leader of our little "insurrection," so they took him first.

Through the prison underground, word drifted back that he'd been taken to the prison director's office. And, like Paul before Agrippa, Antonio spent the entire interview witnessing to the man. His words appeared to fall on deaf ears, for we also learned that Antonio had been sentenced to the dungeon for twenty-one days. At the end of the three weeks, he was returned to the cell. When they returned him to the cell, the same guards called my number. I hastened to obey.

With a guard marching on each side of me, their bayonets poised and ready for trouble, we crossed the courtyard and entered the main door leading to the prison offices. The nameplate on the director's office door read "Captain Lemus." When the door opened, one guard flung me inside, followed, and closed the door behind us.

A large, broad-shouldered army officer in rumpled fatigues glanced up at me from behind the desk. Even before Captain Lemus rose to his feet, I could tell he stood way over six feet tall.

"Are you Alexander?" he demanded.

"Yes," I replied.

"What are you all getting on with in there?"

I scowled for a moment. "I don't understand your question."

"You will!" he barked, reaching for his walking cane. Holding the base of the cane, he extended the cane and tried to wrap the hook about the back of my neck. I backed up to evade the hook, only to have the guard standing behind me push me forward. The commanding officer successfully hooked the cane about my neck and yanked my body forward like an ox or horse's yoke would do.

Making a quick move to the right, I ducked free of the hook. Captain Lemus slammed the cane down on the top of my head. I staggered from the stunning blow and felt something hot running down my forehead. I reached up and touched it. Dazed, I stared at the blood on my hand for an instant. That was my last conscious thought until the next day, when I opened my eyes and found myself in the tiger's cage.

Under our gallery and part of yard number 2 was a large basement, waist deep with rotting garbage and rats, insects, and various other unidentifiable creatures. Above the garbage hung a number of iron-bar dungeons, or "tiger cages," as they were called. Each cage was made of three-quarter-inch steel bars. The cages were about five feet square.

The darkness and the stench haunted my senses as I fought off the rats and lizards. My head ached from the concussion I had received the day before, and my body appeared to be one massive bruise from the iron bars on which I'd lain. I moved about, vainly trying to find a comfortable position in which to sit or sleep and even momentarily relieve the pressure created by the iron bars pressing into the thin layer of skin stretched over my sharp, angular bones. Any cushion of fat I might have had before my arrest had long since melted away.

To take my mind off my discomfort, I thought of Yraida and my little son. I wondered what she'd told him about me. Would he even remember me when I returned home? If I returned home? I struggled to recall every detail of my earlier life. I despaired when some of my memories refused to surface, and I grew frightened when I couldn't recall the faces of various friends and relatives.

Life in the tiger cage took on a bizarre routine. I learned how to tell when the guard was near. A dim light filtered down from the prison yard above me through the hole where the garbage was dumped. While I couldn't make out the man's features, I could occasionally see his silhouette during the daytime.

At night, from the depth of our putrefied tomb, the prisoners in the other cages tapped out messages in a code they had worked out. Using anything at hand, a spoon, a stone, a brick, we scraped out the dashes and tapped out the dots on the iron bars of our cages. This nightly communication kept me alive, supplying me with the will to live.

Every few days, when he remembered, the guard would toss me a bowl of mush. On his day off, the guard would purposely forget to inform his replacement of my presence, and I would go without both food and water until he returned the following morning.

At the end of my twenty-one-day sentence, the guards lifted me out of my smelly hole and returned me to the gallery. Shocked, I entered my cell to a hero's welcome. My incarceration in the dungeon had proved to be a blessing straight from the throne of God. Because Antonio and I had defied the authorities and survived, the other prisoners considered us to be heroes.

Every prison contains prisoners who don't really fit into any definite category, such as political or criminal. Our Christian group referred to this loosely constructed group of men as Moses' mixed multitude. Due to our hero status, many of these men joined our ranks. While earlier they had often violently disagreed with us and our ministry, we now united against a common enemy, the Communists. Side by side, we proclaimed the gospel of Jesus Christ to anyone who would listen. The Holy Spirit blessed our words, and interest in Christ and His love spread throughout the prison at a record rate. God had confounded our captors!

In the face of such a victory, my wounds didn't seem so severe or my bruises as painful. Surrounded by such devastating madness, such wanton cruelty, I could finally see a purpose to my continued existence. God didn't want me to give up and die. He had chosen to use Antonio and me the same way He used the witness of His people throughout all time. By remaining faithful, our spilled blood would become the living seed of truth to men who had long since lost all belief in life or truth.

The Kangaroo Court

Cool tropical breezes wafted through the gallery when the guard released me from the tiger's cage. I inhaled deeply, then stretched my weak and stiff muscles to a symphony of pain. When I arrived back at my cellblock, my brothers in Christ engulfed me with embraces and tears.

Antonio hugged and patted me on the back again and again, repeating, "My brother, my brother."

"I told you I'd be back," I reminded. "Remember, we have agreed that we will all die free!" Glancing about the circle, I noticed some changes—a new face added to the group and a few of the old faces missing. After catching up on the news of the last twenty-one days, Antonio and I discussed the progress of our infant church.

"God has been so good to us, Noble," Antonio said. "Through it all—He has been so good."

"I know. Even during my worst hours in the cage, He reminded me that I suffered in His name and for His sake." My voice grew husky with emotion. "To share in our Saviour's suffering . . ." Humbled by the realization of my experience, I couldn't continue speaking. "Strange," I thought, "that the very persecution inflicted upon us to weaken and debilitate our resolve to serve the Lord should lace our determination with threads of steel." A new sense of peace filled me. I felt as if I'd been touched by grace directly from the throne of God.

I sat on my bunk and reveled in its comfort. Even a canvas sheet could comfort bruised flesh more than iron bars. Later, I lay awake for some time, listening to the familiar night sounds of the prison cell and praising God for the opportunity to witness to my fellow prisoners. One way or another, they would be influenced by my life and by the lives of my brothers in Christ.

Before drifting off to sleep, I prayed, "Heavenly Father, please make my influence as pure as sunlight to these men."

Long before the bruises on my body disappeared, I drifted back into the routine of existing through intolerable days when it seemed as if I'd been in La Cabaña forever and unending nights of loneliness when I remembered every detail of my life before my arrest.

I was arrested in February of 1962. My captors kept me isolated from all visitors and any news from the outside world while they investigated my alleged crimes. I lived the long, lonely hours, one minute to the next. I repeated Bible texts and sang hymns in order to maintain a link with reality beyond the prison walls.

Three months later, they finally allowed Yraida to visit me for the first time. On that long-awaited day, the guards marched us prisoners into a large open room where wives, mothers, children, and other friends waited. A prison lieutenant watched the proceedings from his glassed-in office.

The minute Yraida and I spotted one another, we ran into each other's arms. Tears flowed unashamedly, but no one noticed since each person was caught up in his own tragic melodrama. The cacophony of babble, wails, and moans filling the room made it difficult to hear one another, and I had so much I wanted to say to Yraida. A flood of emotions blocked out every carefully planned question. All I could think of was how beautiful she looked. I tried to speak, but no sound came out of my mouth.

"Noble." Yraida caressed my cheek. "You've lost weight. How are they treating you?"

I shrugged, knowing that every word we shared could be overheard by the guards stationed about the room. "I am surviving. By the grace of God, I am surviving."

She dabbed at her eyes with her handkerchief. "I contacted your mother. She is so worried about you. And little Humberto asks for you all the time."

At the mention of my young son, a pain unlike any I had experienced so far ripped through my chest. How much he must have grown during the last few months! "How much I have missed," I thought. I could think of nothing to say. "I am sorry, Yraida, so sorry."

"I don't understand," she said, searching my face for an unspoken message of some kind. "Whatever did you say or do to end up like this?" She glanced about the room and shivered uncontrollably. In her eyes, I could see that the stark reality of my plight had registered for the first time.

"I honestly don't know." I sighed and looked away. The pain and frustration in her eyes hit my stomach as though I'd left myself wide open for a boxer's solid right-hand punch. What could I possibly tell her? How could she understand what was happening? I didn't understand myself.

"Pastor Vásquez has been to see me," she went on to explain. "Of course, there is nothing he or the conference officials can do for you but pray." I sensed a touch of bitterness in her voice at the mention of prayer. "He says that if they were to even try to intercede with the government for you, the entire Adventist work in Cuba would probably be shut down." Her voice drifted off with a lack of conviction.

I nodded my head. "Yraida, my love, prayer can move heaven and earth, you know."

"Speaking of moving heaven and earth, your sister Paulina in Massachusetts has asked the U.S. government to demand your release. She's determined."

I smiled. "Good old Paulina," I thought. "If anyone could make it happen, she could. She'll wear them down with her persistence." "And the rest of the family?" I asked.

"Raudel says that if you behave yourself and tell them what they want, the government will release you." Yraida's eyes shone with expectation.

"Yraida," I sighed, "don't believe your brother Raudel. He's part of the system."

"No," she insisted. "He really cares."

I took her gently by the shoulders and shook my head slowly. "They are using him as a patsy to break my testimony." How could I make her see that by admitting to one lie regarding the supposed assassination plot I would pound the very nails in my coffin? "All I know is, you and I must be strong, of good courage. The Lord got Peter out of a worse dungeon than this—and on the night before his scheduled execution."

"Then you won't cooperate with them?"

I shook my head and watched as her glistening eyes grew round with emptiness and despair.

I changed the subject. We each had so many questions that

our two-hour limit passed much too quickly. Reluctantly, we parted when the guards announced that visiting time was over. Yraida threw kisses to me as the guards hurried the visitors from the room and pushed us prisoners through the other doorway. Silently, I mouthed, "I love you," as she disappeared from sight. It would be a very long month, I decided, as I plodded back to my cell.

Months passed. Yraida and I communicated as best we could. Others also came to visit—church members who risked imprisonment themselves by smuggling themselves into the prison on visitor's day. So many times during those visits I recalled the words of the Master, "I was in prison and you visited Me," and truly appreciated the sacrifices these brothers and sisters in Christ made, coming to see me as they did. Their reward is sure.

During my first year in prison, the officials did all they could to convince those of us jailed due to our religion that we had no hope, that the churches, our families, and the world at large had long since forgotten about us.

On the thirtieth of August, the guards assembled all of the inmates of our cellblock in the prison yard to bathe. While we waited for the order to proceed with our baths, soldiers burst into the yard and opened fire on us. At the sound of the first rifle shot, I fell to the ground and covered my head. Some of the other prisoners didn't react quite so quickly. Four hundred and sixty prisoners died for no apparent reason.

The official report claimed that they'd uncovered a plot to arm the prisoners to fight against the government. In reality, we knew it to be a lesson to teach us that rebellion of any kind meant death, that there was no chance of rescue from either the free world or our God, that we stood alone against the powerful forces of the regime.

As my first Christmas in prison drew near, the guards grew more surly. One guard vowed, "We will knock the Christmas out of you before you leave here."

Any mention of the Christian holiday could bring about a beating or stabbing. It was as if Christmas and the celebration of the birth of Christ embodied the collective spiritual faith of the Cuban Christians and must be defeated. Yet we were not deterred. As much as our enemy made Christmas a symbol, so did we. We would enjoy a Christmas "dinner" in spite of our situation.

For weeks before the holiday arrived, the inmates saved bits of their already meager daily rations. Sick or weakened prisoners who had been placed on special prescription diets hoarded eggs and bread scraps. On Christmas day, we pooled our precious resources, mixing the old bread scraps with the yokes and beaten egg whites—we had no way to cook or bake.

Before enjoying our Christmas pudding, we huddled together and bowed our heads to pray. My eyes misted over as each of the brothers in Christ whispered his Christmas prayer—humble words from peasants and scholars alike, yet each prayer held a special meaning for us.

Outside the prison, the Christmas celebration also came under attack by the Castro regime. No one could buy a Christmas tree, though some families made a tree out of broomsticks and wire, then hung their homemade decorations on it. Those caught with one of these makeshift trees or celebrating Christmas with a traditional feast were interrogated and penalized. If the police suspected that a party was in progress, they would burst into the home and accuse the partiers of trading on the black market or theft, crimes punishable by imprisonment.

However, most Christians had little problem as far as the feast went, since the $9.60 a month food allowance almost guaranteed that a family could not have a decent meal, let alone a holiday feast.

In the prison we prayed for our families and longed to be with them to celebrate the Christmas event. I remembered Christmases past with Yraida and with my family as a child in San Germán. How happy we were. Somehow I knew that while we were separated in body, we could always be together in our thoughts. The holiday glow we'd experienced on the twenty-fifth lingered throughout the rest of the year.

With the arrival of the new year, the prison tempo changed—and the trials began.

One after another, prisoners were removed from their cells for their "court appearances." I knew my turn would soon arrive, and I knew that the outcome of the trial had already been determined. Nothing I might say would change it. Eighty-two prisoners before me were found guilty of committing crimes against the state and sentenced accordingly. I became case number eighty-three.

I couldn't allow myself to hope that I would be treated fairly, that my case would receive an honest hearing, anymore than any of the other prisoners I'd listened to. This mockery of justice would but formalize the decree passed nearly a year earlier at G-2 Headquarters. I remembered, all too well, the interrogation officer's pronouncement: "You will prefer dying, because those dead are better off than you will be. I'm going to sentence you to twenty years."

When my turn came, a military guard led me to the courtroom inside the La Cabaña fortress. The sight of khaki and brass met my eyes as I stepped inside the courtroom. All regulation army—the presiding judge, an army captain, the prosecuting attorney, a first lieutenant. Even the female court stenographer was a lieutenant in the army.

My guard led me to a bench on the left side of the room and ordered me to sit beside an army lieutenant, complete with black boots, black beret, black belt, and a black conscience. "Alexander, I am Lieutenant Cebreco. I have been appointed to represent you. I will be your defense attorney."

I smiled awkwardly. "Thank you, but I don't know you. I don't really want you to represent me."

Cebreco rose menacingly to his feet, his face flushed with indignation.

The judge overheard our exchange. "Recluso [which means "prisoner"], are you a lawyer?" It was more a statement of intimidation than a question. "And even if you were, Cebreco is the one the court has appointed to your case!"

I clamped my jaw shut and stared straight ahead. I saw the complexion of the situation more clearly. Instead of having a defense attorney to represent me, I had two prosecuting attorneys.

After the judge called the courtroom to order and read the list of crimes I had supposedly committed, I was called onto the stand.

The prosecuting attorney stood beside his desk holding a sheaf of official-looking documents in his hand. "According to our records, you conspired to place a bomb in President Fidel Castro's plane in 1963. What do you have to say about that?"

"In 1963?" I asked. "I admit to being both a spiritual and a physical being, but as yet have never managed to be in two different places at the same time."

The prosecutor scowled. "Explain yourself."

"If you check your prison records, sir," I said, "you will see that I have been detained by the military since February of last year, 1962, and you say that this year, 1963, I plotted to put a bomb in Castro's plane?"

The prosecutor turned to the judge and requested a short recess, which he granted. After a few minutes the trial resumed, with the prosecuting attorney continuing his case as if the time discrepancy had never been mentioned.

The attorney explained for the court just where the plane had been, where the soldiers guarding it had stood, and just how I supposedly planned to plant the bomb. "Is that not how it happened, Mr. Alexander?"

"Sir, if what you say is true, if the nose of the plane was guarded by a sergeant, each wing guarded by a soldier, and headquarters is at the tail, how could I have gotten anywhere near the plane?"

The prosecuting attorney dismissed my question with a wave of the hand. "You watched and waited until the soldiers weren't looking. In a moment." He snapped his fingers. "In a moment, you could do it."

"But, sir, surely you can see that—"

The judge pounded his fist on his desk. "Shut up, you nigger!" Then, regaining his composure, he leaned back in his chair, put his feet up on the desk, and pretended to sleep.

Stunned, I stared up into the distorted face of the white Communist judge seated before me. Never in my entire life had I experienced the cold hatred of racial persecution. I remembered how, years earlier, a friend of mine, Luna Laera, had argued that the only way a black man could get a decent education in Cuba was by serving in the army long enough to have the government pay for it.

The prosecuting attorney strode over to where I stood and grinned into my face. "We took you off the tree, we cut off your tail, and we dressed you. And now you are against us."

The racial slur that I was no more than a monkey came through all too clearly. I stared straight into my accuser's eyes and replied, "All you have taken from me is the banana in my hands," meaning they had starved me.

The judge snapped awake and snarled, "Can't any of you shut him up?"

Chastised by his commanding officer, the prosecutor swung his arm with all the force he could muster and backhanded me across the mouth, then returned to his seat.

My head reeled and my cheek stung from the sudden slap. My lawyer strutted across the front of the room, then began his defense.

"Sir," he addressed the judge, "seeing that my client is obviously guilty of all charges made against him by the state, be merciful. He well deserves to sacrifice his life for what he did. Instead, as a member of this merciful court, I am going to request that he receive only twenty years of hard labor for his crimes against the state."

The judge nodded in agreement. "So be it. Humberto Noble Alexander, you have been tried and convicted of conspiring to assassinate President Fidel Castro, of aiding and abetting the flight of counterrevolutionaries, and the most serious crime of all—distributing opium to the people of Cuba. I now sentence you to serve twenty years of hard labor under severe conditions." The judge's gavel echoed off the back wall.

How ironic, I thought, as I waited to be removed from the courtroom, for my enemies to declare that my most serious crime against the state wasn't my supposed attempt on their revered leader's life but preaching the gospel of Jesus Christ. Incredible! The thought overwhelmed me. My eyes filled with tears, and a grin tugged at the corners of my mouth as a wellspring of joy rose up inside me.

God had blessed me with a sacred privilege far beyond any I could have imagined. If ever before I'd questioned the wisdom of the choices I'd made that led to my arrest, my eyes were now opened. I was not suffering unjustly for mistakes I was falsely accused of making, but for the gospel of Jesus Christ. From the quizzical look the defense attorney gave me, my smile must have broken through in spite of my efforts to conceal it. I thanked God for revealing the truth of my situation to me.

I remembered the words of the apostle Peter. "What glory is it, if, when ye be buffeted for your faults, ye shall take it patiently? but if, when ye do well, and suffer for it, ye take it patiently, this is acceptable with God. For even hereunto were ye called: because Christ also suffered for us, leaving us an example, that ye should follow his steps" (1 Peter 2:20, 21).

After the trial and sentencing, the guards took me to yard number 1 of gallery 4—a special section of the prison that is completely underground, for hard-core prisoners and those condemned to death by the firing squad. I entered the "cave" through a small gateway and glanced about. The place had two small, well-barred holes for ventilation, one at each end. I moved into the already overcrowded area, wondering how long this place would be my home.

Two days later, the guards informed us that whoever had money could purchase a few extra food items such as bread, sugar, candy, crackers, and cigarettes. In disgust, I watched as my captors haggled with starving men over the prices of the food. "How absolutely crass," I thought. "How typical of their inhumane behavior!" I wasn't surprised, yet I wondered at what point a guard traded his humanity and compassion for the few extra pesos the government might throw his way.

To Fidel's Treasure Island

My trial was one of many. A number of my Christian brothers, including Antonio, were tried the same day, and we were all confined to the "cave" that night. We continued our plans for worship and witnessing in this new place without a break.

One night I fell asleep on my bunk, contented with the progress we had made and eager to put our plans into motion. I don't know how long I slept before we were startled awake by blinding lights and soldiers carrying megaphones and rifles, shouting directly into our faces.

"Everybody on your feet! Pack up your belongings. You are being transferred to the Isle of Pines. You have five minutes to get in line, and three have already passed!"

"What's happening?" I wondered. "Where are they taking us?"

Additional soldiers, with trained dogs leashed to one hand and a weapon in the other, scattered throughout the room. Whether the armed men were angry at us or angry for having their good night's sleep disturbed, I had no idea, but angry they were. Cries of pain mingled with the bone-shattering thuds of army boots kicking against fragile rib cages, of prisoners being stabbed or beaten with the shouting soldiers' long military rifles.

Dazed, we scrambled to our feet. Any hope we might have had of saving our precious Bible faded as the ranking officers stood at key positions that gave them full view of the entire cell and its inhabitants.

I glanced toward the spot where we'd hidden a Bible, then toward Antonio. Reading my thoughts, he shook his head a trifle and looked away. We all scurried back to our bunks to collect what pitiful belongings we had before the soldiers marched us out into the night. The guards continued to prod and beat us with their rifle butts as we climbed into a small pickup truck that was waiting by the gate. They jammed us all into the back of the truck and drove us to the gate, where a refrigerated eighteen-wheeler semi-truck sat waiting. The words "Highway Hauling" were painted on the side. From the outside, no one would ever guess that the semitruck was hauling human flesh.

The soldiers' abuse continued until all fifty of us were on board. When the truck's double doors swung shut, the soldiers also closed the air vents. The atmosphere began to smell stale, and some of the prisoners complained of feeling lightheaded. They pounded on the walls of the truck, begging for fresh air. Two of my brothers in Christ, Bairon Miguel and Heriberto del Cristo, collapsed.

To survive the mindless tortures inflicted, a prisoner learns to block out the atrocities and pain by entering a semi-conscious state. His motions take on a zombielike existence. For the Christian, prayer is a way of escape—not for deliverance as much as communion with the Saviour. It's like transcending to a higher plane. Injuries still occur. The pain is still there, but it becomes tolerable.

After a two-and-a-half-hour wait, our truck started moving. In a very short time, the truck stopped and the double doors flew open. I instantly filled my lungs with the cool morning air.

An officer stuck his head in the trailer and barked, "You have three minutes to get out of there, and two have already passed, so make it snappy!"

We tumbled out of the trailer. Those who fell or stumbled were prodded to their feet by the point of a soldier's bayonet. The soldiers hustled us into a circle and told us to sit on the asphalt roadway. The soldiers, along with a number of trained German shepherd dogs, surrounded us. "If anyone moves," the officer in charge ordered, "shoot them all!"

Early morning light replaced the shadows of night. Without being obvious, I glanced about the circle. When I made eye contact with Antonio, he nodded slightly. I nodded back. I looked beyond the circle to the surrounding terrain. We were at a military airport.

The tropical sun climbed higher in the sky. Hour after hour, we sat under the intense midday sun. The pitch and tar surface beneath us grew hot to the touch. I ached to move, to find a more comfortable position in which to sit, but dared not.

We were given no food or water the entire day. One after another, the prisoners, suffering from malnutrition and dehydration and being unaccustomed to direct sunlight, fainted. Only twenty of our group survived.

This agony went on until four in the afternoon, when our plane arrived. We boarded and were instructed to sit along one side of the airplane in a lotus position. The seats had been removed. Six of the soldiers positioned themselves near the cockpit door, and four occupied the other side of the fuselage. "You are to look down at the floor at all times," the officer in charge ordered. "Whoever lifts his head for any reason—shoot him! Is that understood?"

I don't know what he thought we might do. We were so emaciated and dehydrated from the day's heat that any strength or desire we might have had to fight back had been drained from us. Most of us were fighting just to remain conscious. Perhaps their fears had to do with a new member of our group, a former pilot, an officer in Batista's army, who had been sentenced to thirty years of hard labor.

For the next hour and a half, the officer continued inflicting his verbal abuse on us. "You are taking a one-way trip—to the Isle of Pines. There you will be forced to earn your keep through hard labor. You will work in the marble quarries or in the fields until you drop dead!"

Toward dark, our plane finally lifted off. Under the constant threat of death, the thirty-minute flight seemed more like an eternity. I recalled all I had heard about the Stalinist-modeled labor camp, known as the "Siberia of Cuba," where more than 10,000 prisoners were forced to work in marble quarries and agricultural camps under the most brutal conditions.

The Isle of Pines is about ninety miles southeast of Havana, the capital of Cuba. It is believed to have been the setting for Robert Louis Stevenson's famous adventure story, *Treasure Island*. The wooded island was famous for its game fishing and outdoor recreation. In 1932, General Gerardo Machado, president of Cuba at the time, built a model prison so large that it was believed to be unfillable. When questioned, the president unknowingly prophesied, "One of these days a mad man will come and fill it."

I never imagined, when I learned of the model prison, that it would one day be my home. I knew that the prison itself sprawled over several acres of former swampland, a gigantic square resting on concrete and steel struts. But I would soon learn much, much more than I ever cared to know.

The change in the hum of the plane's engines brought me back to my current situation. The plane tilted as it made its approach for landing. Sitting beneath a small window, I could see out of the corner of my eye. A cloud of dust and small pebbles flew into the air behind us as our wheels touched down. The plane stopped at the end of the runway.

Two officers opened the plane's side doors. This was when I discovered Bairon Miguel's comatose body. I shook my head at the useless waste of human life. Tears stung my cheeks until I remembered that for my brother Bairon, the battle was over. The next voice he'd hear would not express a Cuban guard's profanity but the gentle words, "Arise, ye that sleep in the dust . . ."

Lying beside Bairon on the floor of the airplane was the unconscious form of another prisoner. When Antonio stooped to help him, one of the guards shouted for us to get moving.

As I emerged into the dusk, another officer, the political instructor—every flight has one—shouted, "Go take a bag." He pointed to a stack of canvas bags lying on the roadway. "And get on that truck. Make it snappy!"

I joined the line of prisoners stumbling through a long corridor of shouting soldiers and barking police dogs to the waiting vehicles. The trucks had no stairs to help us climb aboard. Instead, the soldiers with their bayoneted rifles "helped" anyone who couldn't quite make it. All the while, the officer in charge continued to prod us on with, "Hurry up! We haven't all day. Make it snappy!"

Once we were on board, the officer instructed the soldiers to shoot anyone who made the slightest move. We arrived at the prison complex minutes later. From the outside, it resembled a large, fenced-in high school.

Inside the walls we found an extremely sophisticated, high-security prison, where 6,000 or more inmates lived in four circular buildings that were built like giant silos. These were creatively called circular number 1, number 2, number 3, and number 4. Other buildings included the dining room, the main headquarters, the hospital, and the receiving pavilion. In the middle of the area was the "transportation square," where prisoners were loaded each morning and unloaded each evening after working all day as slaves.

A double row of barbed wire fences surrounded the complex. Police dogs that could leap the fences patrolled the area between them. Eight gray-and-black guard towers perched on stilted legs, like monsters from outer space, surveyed the prison grounds.

The trucks stopped in front of the reception pavilion, a square one-story building, where we were unloaded. By now it was suppertime. Curious drawn faces stared out at us from the next building—the dining hall. One by one, a corporal called out each of our names.

"Humberto Noble Alexander," he announced. I walked across to the open door and stood in front of him until he checked me off his list.

Upon entering the reception pavilion, I walked down a long hallway to a large, partially empty room that would soon house 850 men. At one end of the room was a shower and beside it a hole in the floor for a toilet. There was also a sink with a faucet. It was the sink and faucet that classed the Isle of Pines prison as a top-notch prison!

We were ordered to strip naked and face the walls. Immediately, the soldiers searched as well as beat us. Why the beating? It's just routine for all who go to the model prison on the Isle of Pines.

The kitchen sent our food over to the receiving pavilion. The only difference I could see between the food they were serving and what we'd eaten at the other prison was that this cornmeal had more protein floating on top of it. While the other prisoners ate their worm-filled mush, I found a quiet corner of the room. Soon the last beam of sunlight disappeared from the sky outside. Since there were no lights in our quarters, I fell asleep. This area of concrete would be my bed for the next fifteen days.

The next morning, at 4:00 a.m., several loudspeakers jolted me awake with a tooth-rattling trumpet rendition of the national anthem. Added to the trumpets was an orchestra composed only of cymbals. I could have yelled at the top of my lungs, and the person standing next to me would never have heard me.

When the anthem ended, our prison walls shook with the thunder of running guards waving flashlights and shouting for everyone to awaken, as if anyone could have still been asleep!

The guards shined their flashlights in each of our eyes as they took their morning head count. Water pipes sputtered and gurgled back to life as the main valve was turned back on. My first day at the Isle of Pines had begun.

My stomach growled. Then I remembered why. I hadn't eaten anything for twenty-four hours. I could hear my fellow prisoners moving about, forming the morning breakfast line as I fell to my knees for my morning prayer.

"Thank You, Father," I began, "that I am alive this morning. I feel reborn." As I prayed, I remembered that I had just completed my second year in prison.

On our fifteenth day of confinement in the pavilion, I was taken to circular number 4. Each of these tanklike buildings, designed to hold 930 men, often held 1,500 or more. Each circular had six stories with ninety-three cells. The inhabitable cells were supposed to have two canvas berths attached to each wall. However, in most cases, either the ropes that supported the berths were missing or the canvas bed was missing. Seldom could an entire bed be assembled.

In the center of these silos was a tower where guards could sit and watch every prisoner at all times, and above the guard tower was a skylight. On every floor, three cells acted as sewers. The waste products of six thousand men funneled down to an open cesspool behind the encampment.

The inmates on the Isle of Pines could hardly be considered flesh-and-blood humans. They were more like living skeletons. The skin on some of the men's bodies grew so dark and wrinkled that it resembled cheap leather. Others grew so pale that it seemed their bodies contained no blood at all. Many couldn't remain standing throughout the repeated daily roll calls. I soon learned why. Just to stay alive at this Cuban Siberia was a daily struggle.

Each day began at 4:00 a.m. After the morning count we marched to the ground floor, then to the dining room. Breakfast consisted of a small cup of diluted coffee or sugared water and a slice of bread so thin one could see through it. Since I did not drink coffee, I often did without.

At 12:30 p.m. we ate one-third of a condensed milk tin of either macaroni or cornmeal, always without seasoning and always in less than appetizing condition. Between 4:30 and 6:00 p.m., a recount was taken, and supper, consisting of a couple of

Spanish roots floating in hot water, was served. On Sundays they added a few chunks of boiled fish or a potato to the hot water. The prison chefs varied our diet occasionally with boiled rice and rotten beans—a humanitarian gesture to relieve prison boredom, no doubt.

Moving into a new cellblock was an interesting experience. First, one had to find a vacant area—territory that hadn't yet been occupied. This was important, since territory was about all most prisoners could call their own. A new prisoner usually had to barter for a spot. Cigarettes, money, cigars, and medicine made the most desirable transactions.

At circular number 4 I walked about looking for a cell in which to reside, when I noticed a group of prisoners glancing at me, then whispering among themselves. Then I overheard what they were saying! "The pastor from La Cabaña came."

I wondered whether having my reputation precede me would prove to be good or bad, but I didn't have long to find out. Two strangers walked up to me as I prepared to climb the stairs to the sixth floor.

"Excuse me, sir," one of the prisoners began, "my name is Rosendo Martinez, and this is Abelardo Marquez."

After I introduced myself, Rosendo smiled and said, "We know all about you. You are the preacher from La Cabaña." Obviously, the two men had come to check me out. They represented a group of nondenominational Christians in the prison block. Immediately the bonds of Christian love formed between us.

"Don't move into one of the cells on level six," Abelardo warned. "There are no handrails on the stairs to keep you from falling off, and you need to climb up and down them five or six times each day just for your basic necessities." The men urged me to join them on level two in cell 79. It took me no time at all to settle into my new surroundings.

After answering all their questions, it was my turn. "Is there any way to get into any of the other circulars?" I asked.

They shook their heads. "Not that we know of."

I thought for a moment, then asked, "Are there any Bibles here?"

The two men glanced, first one direction, then the other. Rosendo touched his finger to his lips.

"Sh," he cautioned, "if the word got out . . ." He glanced about nervously.

Abelardo drew me closer. "When the prison was first built, a church was erected between circular 3 and the receiving pavilion," he explained. "During Batista's administration, different denominations held services there each Sunday, but when Castro came to power the church was bulldozed down. In the rubble, I found this." With utmost tenderness, he withdrew a sheaf of tattered pages from beneath his worn garments. Carefully he smoothed the treasured pages.

"This is all we have of God's Word," he whispered, "Matthew and Luke, bits and pieces of Paul's epistles, and Isaiah through Malachi."

I felt a rush of tears. Just the sight of this precious treasure left me momentarily speechless. With this tattered Bible, my mission for God would be able to continue.

I could tell that my new cellmates were as eager as I to begin our Bible study. We began with the Gospels. We decided to begin our witnessing program in circular number 4. Each morning, we would have worship together, just the three of us, until a prisoner named Gregorio Rubio joined us. Gradually our number increased. Our cell became a place of refuge from the drudgery of prison life. Though we were men of many faiths attending the same services, we established a motto: "It doesn't matter what church you belong to if we are all in Calvary. If your heart is like mine, give me your hand, and you shall be my brother."

At sunset, we held another service. Men whose backgrounds varied from highly educated doctors and engineers to lowly peasants who had never attended school came to worship. Some came from a desire to develop their own spiritual devotion. Others attended the meetings out of curiosity, liked what they heard, and returned. Twice a day, clean, clear notes of praise filled circular number 4 as we lifted our voices in song. In an environment accustomed to cursing and pain, the sweet beauty of Christian hymns acted as a magnet to the soul-starved inmates. Within a few days, our small cell could hold no more.

This disturbed the guards in the tower. They didn't like not being able to see each prisoner at all times. One day their agitation erupted.

"Clear the cell," one guard snarled from his elevated post. To ensure that his order would be carried out, he took aim at the group and fired. Bullets ricocheted off the concrete walls, converting shards of concrete into dangerous shrapnel that injured a number of men. But we continued to hold our services. Instead of driving the worshipers away, the guards' harassment acted as a lure. More and more prisoners flocked to our cell.

Fearful of insurrection, the guards reported our meetings to headquarters, and I was called in to explain my actions. When I refused to discontinue the religious meetings, the commanding officer, Captain Bernardo, shouted and cursed, threatened and bullied, but to no avail. I refused to discontinue holding our services.

"You think you have the best of me?" he snorted. "In a very few days the problem will solve itself. You won't have the time or the energy for this foolishness." With a wave of his hand, he ordered, "Guard, take him back to his cell."

The Caribbean Killing Fields

A guard marched me back to circular number 4. When I reported the commanding officer's ominous threat to my cellmates, a nagging question hung, unspoken, among us. What else could our captors do to us? How much more miserable could they possibly make our lives? All too soon we discovered the answers to those questions and a whole lot more.

I thought it odd when they fed us roast chicken, until the prison underground passed on the word—a heavy rain shower had flooded a large chicken farm in the area, and many chickens had drowned. Instead of throwing the putrefied poultry away, the prison cooks roasted the birds for the prisoners. The following morning we had milk, or at least what appeared to be milk. It was a powdered mixture, rehydrated, that was usually fed to calves and pigs.

Two days later, the guards gave us new yellow uniforms and high-top work boots. The uniforms, hated by the civilians outside of the prison itself, would forever classify us as political prisoners. The soldiers cut off our hair and made us pose for mug shots. We later learned that the prison security officer sent a lock of each prisoner's hair along with his picture to other Communist countries for their records. From that day on, to Cuban officials, Humberto Noble Alexander ceased to exist. Number 30,954 took his place.

Later that night we listened to, then passed on the latest news through the prison underground. Using all 6,000 prisoners at the Isle of Pines Prison, the officials would initiate the Camilo Cienfuego Plan—a plan to break the prisoners' morale and exploit the island's productivity through the use of slave labor.

The Camilo Cienfuego Plan originated with a pilot program called the Morejon Plan, named after its founder, a tough sergeant who treated his soldiers so brutally that he established a reputation for being the worst slave driver in the Cuban military system. Morejon had randomly picked 300 prisoners and ordered his soldiers to march them to the fields and work them until they dropped where they stood. The slightest delay in carrying out an order resulted in the prisoner's death.

Out of the 300 men destined to be executed, only twelve were actually killed. Two hundred and eighty-eight prisoners worked straight through without weakening, and of that number, 250 pretended to be "re-educated." At the end of ninety days, only one man had refused to accept re-education. The central committee considered the pilot project a huge success and promoted Morejon to first lieutenant. In 1964, the committee decided to adopt Morejon's plan for all 6,000 prisoners at the Isle of Pines, renaming it the Camilo Cienfuego Plan.

There was a touch of irony in naming the slave labor program after Camilo Cienfuego. Cienfuego had been a famous commander under Castro. During the revolution, he fought bravely against Batista's government, earning the title of chief of the Revolutionary Army. When the new government decided to strip all former soldiers and officers of all their rights, Commander Cienfuego, along with a number of other career military men, protested this as grossly unfair.

"If we don't want to use them in the new army, fine. Retire them. But many of these men have been in the army for more than twenty years. They deserve better treatment," Cienfuego argued. "I cannot deprive them of what is theirs."

When another high-ranking officer, Commander Hubert Matos, chose to resign from the revolution because of the unfairness, Cienfuego was ordered to arrest him. He flew his private plane to Matos's estate in Camaguey, but after a short conversation, Cienfuego chose not to arrest the man. The popular saying that "the revolution is a monster that devours its sons" proved true, for Commander Cienfuego never returned home. His plane disappeared mysteriously, and he was reported dead. Years later, the man who championed fairness in the new government was "honored" as a hero by having Castro's twentieth-century slave labor plan named after him. And the Isle of Pines became its testing ground.

The next morning at 4:00, the gallery lights flashed on, and the guards shouted at us to get up. I stumbled to my feet, dressed, and fell into place in line. After roll call, the guards ordered us to breakfast, where we were again given a portion of the milk mixture.

I had just finished eating my bowl of gruel when I heard them call out my block number—block number 8. For reasons unknown even to me, I began softly humming the words to the hymn "When the Roll Is Called Up Yonder." I chuckled, then snapped back to attention, since those who hesitated or forgot their numbers suffered the unpleasant consequences of a rifle butt alongside the head or a bayonet stab in the thigh.

The guards herded us into trucks like cattle and drove us to a field of elephant grass. Before we disembarked, a smaller truck filled with soldiers drove up behind us. The soldiers took their posts along the perimeter of the field. The sergeant in command, Luis Sanchez, ordered a corporal to open the doors to our vehicle. The farmer in whose field we were to work that day stood off to one side as the prisoners climbed out of the trucks and fell into line to be counted. After the count, the soldiers walked down the line handing out machetes. When the sergeant ran out of machetes, he informed the rest of the prisoners that they would roll the grass cut by the first prisoners into bales for the farmer to use as hay.

The sergeant oversaw the work in the field and told the soldiers when to beat, stab, shoot, or kill a prisoner. Occasionally during the day one soldier or another would hide behind a bundle of hay to harass us with his rifle as we worked. We quickly learned that any change in the guards' routine sooner or later meant trouble.

At times, when prisoners were allowed to either write or receive mail from their families, the sergeant also spent part of his day sitting under a nearby tree reading the letters and deciding whether or not they'd ever be delivered.

Each day, we worked until noon, whereupon Sergeant Sanchez blew a whistle to announce lunch. One by one, the line of prisoners inched past an inspection point, where a corporal handed each of us a metal plate, and the next soldier plopped a glob of sickly white mush onto the plate. I took my food, walked to the spot where the guard indicated, and sat down to stare at the strange-looking stuff I was supposed to eat. To eat the unflavored, overcooked mush, one had to cut into it like pudding.

The prisoners were not allowed to talk with one another, but my neighbor hissed, "What's this stuff supposed to be?"

"I think it's macaroni," I whispered, barely moving my lips. "At least it looks like macaroni, I think."

At the end of the break, the sergeant sounded his whistle, and we lined up for a head count. Once certain that none of the prisoners had escaped during the break, the sergeant ordered us back to work.

The stifling afternoon sun beat down relentlessly on our sweating bodies, causing our backs to burn and blister. Weakened by malnutrition and torture, the prisoners hacked away at the elephant grass until 7:30 or 8:00 at night.

Before returning to the prison compound, the guards conducted another head count in the field and a final roll call back in the prison courtyard. About 10:00 p.m., we straggled to our cells for a short night's sleep.

The first night, I lay awake on my cot for hours. My unused muscles screamed from the abuse I'd given them that day. However, sore, aching muscles were not what kept me from sleeping. Concern over breaking the Sabbath did.

While I didn't mind working from Monday to Thursday in the fields, as a Seventh-day Adventist I knew I couldn't go to work on Friday since Sabbath would begin at sundown, long before I returned to the prison. I knew I had to do something, but what? Who could I confide in? Spies and prison stool pigeons might overhear us speaking, which would get both me and the person to whom I confided in trouble.

The second night, I again struggled with my problem. Should I go to the fields anyway? What would happen if I didn't go, if I refused? I felt weak, vulnerable, and so alone. Yet I knew what I must do.

I worked from Monday through Thursday as required. When the block left for the fields on Friday morning, I melted into the shadows of my cell and waited. For reasons I did not know, a few other prisoners also chose to stay behind.

"Are you sick?" some of the prisoners inquired.

"No," I replied, not volunteering any more information than necessary.

"You'll get yourself in serious trouble," another prisoner warned.

"I'm sure I am in serious trouble already," I answered.

At first, nothing happened. No guards shouted, no dogs threatened to attack, nothing. Around 9:30, two officers appeared in the gallery and went from cell to cell, questioning each of the prisoners who had remained behind. In a short time, they strode into my cell.

"Why are you in today?" one asked.

"Do you have a medical permit?" the other inquired.

"Are you summoned to the administration office?"

"Are you working in the circular?"

Their questions followed one another with machine-gun speed and precision.

At the end of the questioning, a special lieutenant entered my cell and barked, "Number 30,954, I am from the Department of Interior Discipline. You will come with me." He took me outside the building, where I joined a number of other prisoners who had failed to show up for roll call that morning. At gunpoint, he and his armed henchmen marched us to the "lake"—the prison's open sewer. At the edge, he ordered us to halt.

"For not showing up for work this morning, you have been assigned to cut the grass growing *inside* the pond," the lieutenant informed us, his lip curling into a sneer. "Guards, throw them into the water."

Two guards picked me up by my arms and legs, then heaved me into the air. I hit the putrid water with a splash. Sinking beneath the surface, I scrambled for a footing on the slime-encrusted bottom. Finally I managed to swim close enough to the edge that I could get a footing.

Nausea from the fumes that emanated from the excrement and other rotting debris engulfed me. I floundered about in the water, trying to escape, but there was no escape. Guards with their rifles pointed lined the edge of the pond, daring us to even try to climb out.

I raised my eyes toward heaven and prayed, "Please, Lord, save me. I can't stand it any longer! How long can I possibly survive?" I fought to keep my chin elevated so as not to allow the filth to enter my mouth. I grew tired from the constant battle to maintain my footing. Many of my fellow sufferers gave up trying and later died from terrible infections. One of my very special friends, Samuel Vidahuereta, contracted an infection and died a week later. "For You, Lord. I will fight to stay alive for You. But why, Lord? Where are You in all of this?" I cried.

God heard me. Immediately following my prayer, my eyes focused on a plant, a lily plant, with a bud growing on the surface of the water beside my face. Fascinated, I watched the bud of the lily plant respond to the morning sunlight. Slowly, with the grace of a ballet dancer, the blossom opened into a pure white lily. "A white lily in this filth," I thought. "Impossible! How could any living thing that pure and white come out of this filthy muck?"

At that moment, the promise found in Hebrews 13:5 flashed into my mind. "I will never leave you nor forsake you." Where was my God? I had asked. Suddenly, I knew that my God stood right beside me, there in the sewage. Trying to picture the Creator of the universe enduring this quagmire of filth *with* me, for me—the thought overwhelmed and humbled me. Three hours later, the lieutenant ordered the prisoners removed from the cesspool.

"This is only a small taste of what will happen to you if you decide to be a goldbrick again! Next time it may be a beating or even a bullet," he warned before marching us back to our circulars.

Heavy of heart, I returned to my cell and considered my fate. The father of lies bombarded my mind with the lieutenant's dire warnings, tempting me to give in to the pressure. The crafty demon devised dozens of ways I could go to the fields in the morning without actually working.

Sabbath had always been the joy of my week, but tomorrow would be a trial instead of a delight. Regardless of Satan's temptations, I saw no options. I would have to disobey again and suffer the consequences of my decision. I would not, I could not, violate my Sabbath.

The day passed. The other prisoners who had gone to the fields returned. After learning of my fate, they drew apart, knowing I would probably repeat the violation in the morning.

Would this be my last night on earth, I wondered, as I lay staring into the darkness of my cell. After facing an irate officer in the morning, would the next face I saw be that of Jesus, my Lord?

Outside, I could hear tiny raindrops hitting the circular's tin roof. Throughout the night, the raindrops grew in number and size, developing into a heavy downpour. From my melancholy state, it was as if all of heaven were weeping with me. I reminded God of His promise about not allowing us to be tempted beyond what we can bear, about providing a way of escape. My mood finally lifted somewhat, allowing me to fall asleep.

Four a.m. arrived with the glare of the lights and the blare of the megaphones. I got up, dressed, and fell into the breakfast line, where, zombielike, we proceeded through pouring rain to the ground floor. I glanced up at the dark, heavy clouds filling the sky.

"Maybe they won't make us go out in this weather," the prisoner next to me suggested.

I shrugged my shoulders. I doubted that our tormentors had that much compassion. Yet, in spite of myself, a spark of hope danced in my mind. Could the rain be the way of escape the Lord had sent for me this morning?

We'd barely finished our breakfast when the public address system sprang to life. "Block numbers 1, 2, and 3 line up at the transportation area." "No luck," I thought. The slave drivers would force the slaves to slog through the mud and pouring rain.

The voice called out the next three blocks—4, 5, and 6. I held my breath. They would be calling my block number at any moment. This would be my last chance to change my mind. No, I couldn't reconsider. There was no turning back. After all I'd already been through, I couldn't weaken now. "Blocks 7, 8, and 9 . . ." I sat, rooted to my bunk. A fellow Sabbath keeper, Rosendo Valdes, sat beside me. "Come on," he coaxed, "act intelligently about this. Go to the fields. God will understand and forgive you."

I shook my head No.

Reluctantly, he glanced at me once, then hurried to take his place for roll call. I listened as the officer checked off the numbers of each of my fellow prisoners. My fingers dug into my flesh as I awaited my fate. And it wasn't long in coming. His voice boomed over the public address system. "Where is 3-0-9-5-4? 3-0-9-5-4!" The officer continued taking roll as I waited in my cell. I knew that hiding was useless. Sooner or later, they'd find me and I would suffer the consequences. So I just waited.

The sergeant stormed into my cell, yelling, "Look here, 3-0-9-5-4! You have held up the block for nearly an hour. That is sabotage to the plan, and you will pay for it!" Then as an afterthought, he added, "Why are you not in roll call?"

"I am not going to work today," I answered in as calm a voice as I could muster.

He eyed me critically. "Are you sick?"

I looked him in the eye. "No, sir, but according to my faith I cannot work today, sergeant."

"Well," the soldier snarled, grabbing me by the arm, "I have a chief, and he says to take you to the field."

"Sergeant, I have another Chief, and He says, 'Remember the Sabbath day to keep it holy. Six days shalt thou labor and do all thy work . . .'"

"So you are not going out?"

I shook my head. "That's it. You have said it." I realized that with those words I had probably signed my death warrant.

The sergeant turned abruptly and walked out of the cell. A few minutes later, he returned with a stern-faced captain.

"So, you are not going to work," the captain barked. "Are you fomenting a strike?"

"No, sir," I replied, "I told your sergeant that I was not going to work today."

The captain glanced at the sergeant, then back to me. "Why?"

"Because, sir, I am a Seventh-day Adventist, as you can see on my chart."

The captain's face softened somewhat; his stance became less threatening.

"Look, I don't want any problem in this block," he explained. "I am going to be considerate with you. I will take you to the field, but you won't have to work."

"That's fine, captain, but I am not going out today," I reiterated in a pleasant, yet firm voice.

He scowled for a moment, then tried again. "Let's do something else. I'll take you to the field and give you a pail. When your mates are thirsty, you can give them water to drink. That's charity, right?"

I shook my head slowly. "I am not going out today."

The captain resumed his threatening stance. "Number 3-0-9-5-4, it won't be as easy as yesterday for you."

"Easy," I thought. "You call yesterday easy?"

When I didn't reply, the captain shrugged his shoulders. "Well, you have asked for it." The two soldiers walked out of my cell.

An hour later the captain returned, along with a lieutenant and two other officers. "Number 3-0-9-5-4," the lieutenant said, "you will come with us. You will be an example for any other prisoners who might be scheming to strike or to sabotage the success of the program."

The officer and the two soldiers under his command took me out into the center of the circular near the base of the tower. The three men each carried a length of electrical cable. The end of each had been splayed into three parts. They turned me to face the tower. I heard the zing of the cables as the officers snapped them through the air. The cables lashed across my back. I fell to the ground. Again and again, the cables ripped at my flesh. When I fainted from the pain, one of the soldiers dumped a bucket of water on me to revive me.

When I came to, the captain asked, "Are you going to work?"

"Not today," I gasped.

Three times the cables whipped across my flesh. Three times I passed out from the pain, only to be revived with a bucket of water. Three times the officer inquired if I would now go to work. Each time, I thought I would die right there on the concrete.

After the fourth beating, the officer again asked, "Are you going to work today?"

"No," I said, unable to speak above a whisper. "Just kill me and be finished with it."

"Is that what you want—to be a martyr?" He strode past my head, then back again. "We are not that foolish!"

The officer turned to the other men and snapped, "He is insane, a fanatic!" With that he turned on his heels and left.

As I lay in a pool of my own blood, I did not know whether I would live or die. I could not see beyond my pain. After a few minutes, some of the braver inmates sneaked over to me and carried me to my cell.

I did not know then that the agony I suffered would ease the way for my brothers who would come to accept the Sabbath day as holy. The guards would call them "one of Noble's people," and leave them in on the Sabbath. But the guards had it all wrong. They were not Noble's people, they were God's.

Two days later a guard took me to headquarters, where they shaved, fingerprinted, and reclassified me. "Your number has been changed from 30,954 to 31,450," the prison commander informed me. "You have been reclassified as a dangerous religious fanatic. You and your equally fanatical friends will be transferred to circular number 2." Strutting across his office, the commander turned, tucked his thumbs in the waistband of his trousers, and wagged his head confidently. "We will win, you know. Sooner or later, we always do. We will break up your cult once and for all."

Living Beyond Fear

The guards marched me to the new circular the next day. When I entered the area, I was horrified. Psychotic murderers and the mentally ill mixed freely within the circular—so freely, in fact, that I was even allowed to choose my own place to sleep! At first I wondered what God's purpose might be in having me moved to these new and highly dangerous quarters. However, the answer soon became apparent. Since the inmates of this circular were considered hopelessly insane, the prison guards were not as diligent to suppress errant behavior, and this meant that Christians could practice their religion more freely without suffering persecution. This move proved to be one of God's greatest blessings!

News of my arrival swept from cell to cell, along with the reason I'd been transferred—my refusal to work on the Sabbath. Within the hour, three inmates sought me out. "We're here because we're Christians too," they said, and suggested that I choose a bunk in their cell.

We banded together for strength. Seventh-day Adventist, Baptist, Catholic, Presbyterian—labels didn't matter in prison. There, in the most disgusting of Communist prison conditions, Christ's church was unified; we were one. Before many days passed, the guards brought Antonio and a few of the brothers from the other circular to join us. We praised God that night for the special gift He'd given us—one another. We knew it was a gift from God because the prison officials were not out to do us any favors.

While many other prison inmates broke their own limbs or amputated their own fingers to avoid going into the fields for fear of never returning, God's children claimed the promise of 1 Corinthians 10:13: God is faithful and will not let you be tempted beyond what you can bear. But when you are tempted, He will also provide a way out so that you can stand under it.

Each week I refused to work during the Sabbath hours. The results of that decision varied. Some weeks my captors would beat me for resisting. Other weeks, for no apparent reason, my resistance would be ignored.

While our continued resistance in the face of persecution was a witness to our fellow prisoners, we also witnessed in other ways. Caring for the sick, sharing our daily food ration with the elderly and the frail, encouraging and praying with inmates who had lost hope, these acts of service drew our fellow prisoners' attention. Just being kind to one another caused us to stand out from the rest of the population.

Yet we wanted to do more. We decided to conduct clandestine church services. We wondered what we had that the other prisoners might want or need. After praying about it, we decided to teach classes. One of our group knew French, another English. I knew algebra. We would teach these ordinary classes, and in the process, we would also teach about God and His love.

It worked. One by one they came, men haunted by memories of the past and devoid of a future. Whether lured by a compassionate smile, a kind deed, or out of hatred for our common enemy, the prisoners came week after week, month after month. Our numbers grew. The strength and focus of Christians united mocked the entire Communistic prison system—a system designed to isolate and break a man's resistance until he submitted to complete mind control.

At every opportunity we witnessed, even to prison officials during interrogation sessions. Once, after a long and frustrating session, a prison officer drew his pistol and said, "I don't care if you are a reverend, you can't talk religion here!" To make his message clear, he shot me in my right hand and leg. As I crumpled to the floor, he added, "Next time, I will shoot you in the mouth."

I knew he uttered no idle threat; he had done so to another minister. The officials beat us; offered bribes; quarantined us and our "disease"; they divided and separated us in hopes of diluting our evangelical fervor. Yet the gospel of Jesus Christ could not be contained.

The design of the prison complex itself defeated their efforts. Each circular contained 1,000 to 1,500 prisoners and functioned as a small town. As with any small town, gossip traveled at remarkable speeds from one end to the other, easily leaping apparently impossible barriers into the other circulars. And just as religious persecution caused the believers of the early Christian church to spread the gospel of Jesus Christ throughout the then-known world, so the punishments designed by our jailers to destroy the growth of Christianity at the Isle of Pines actually spread the good news to the other circulars. Within two years, our little congregation grew to ninety-five. We held baptismal classes, formed a choir, conducted special meetings for the younger prisoners, and even organized a church board! And all of this was made possible by the fact that we were supposedly insane, and therefore our activities didn't *have* to be curtailed as much. For once in my life I was glad to be considered insane!

We had access to a Bible that had been smuggled in to us, and from this we made handwritten copies of the portions we used in our classes. Our paper supply was limited to the back sides of cigarette packs and other scraps that came our way.

One evening after the members of the baptismal class had returned to their own cells, Antonio and I hurried to put away all evidence of the meeting.

I removed a chip of broken cement block from behind his bunk, slid a copy of our handwritten Bible segments into its hiding place, then replaced the chip. "So many of the baptismal class are ready now. If only we could find a way to baptize them, especially Brother Balbon."

"I know." Antonio sauntered over to the doorway to be certain none of the guards were close enough to overhear our conversation. "Balbon learned just today that he's to be transferred back to the main island."

I nodded. "And who knows if there'll be a pastor or a Christian community in the prison where he's sent?"

"Well," Antonio admitted, "God knows. If God wants Brother Balbon baptized before being transferred, he'll be baptized, right?"

"How did choir practice go tonight?" I asked. "Will they be ready to sing at Brother Balbon's farewell service?"

Our choir, called "The Young People's Club," sang for our church services, for the Friday night youth meetings, for the farewell service of a brother being transferred or released, and for any other special occasions the church family might organize. Songs like "This world is not my home, I'm just a passing through" and "Trust and obey, for there's no other way" take on a unique poignancy when echoing in four-part harmony off stark, gray prison walls.

The official overall work routine remained the same. Each morning after roll call, the soldiers drove the prisoners to their assigned post. Paranoid because of previous successful escapes, the prison officials prevented either guards or civilians from becoming too acquainted with any of us by varying our daily work assignments.

Regardless of age, all the prisoners were expected to do the same amount of work. Some days I cut elephant grass for cattle fodder or weeded gardens. Other times, I picked grapefruit or oranges. Occasionally a team of us strung barbed wire on cattle ranches, fencing it by acres. But the hardest work detail to pull was the marble quarry. Instead of a machete, we swung a twenty-four-pound sledge hammer from sunrise till night, breaking stones. The higher the sun climbed, the hotter it pounded down onto our bare backs and the hotter the rocks grew beneath our feet, turning the marble quarry into a massive oven. Spots danced before our eyes for hours at a time from the sun's reflection on the marble boulders.

One morning, Vaquerito, the chief of block number 8, took us to a field near a town we prisoners called Moscow because a large number of atheists and socialists lived there. The first rays of sunlight broke over the horizon as Vaquerito finished the field roll call and strutted the length of the prison line. While we had no respect for the cocky little block chief whose name meant "little cowboy," we feared him. He worked hard to earn his reputation as the meanest, nastiest, most heartless of the block chiefs. He instructed the guards to hand out the machetes and ordered us to cut and gather fodder for the cattle near the village.

While the morning routine hadn't varied from all the other mornings in the fields, something didn't feel right to me. First, the guards hovered close to the prisoners instead of along the outer perimeter of the field. Second, one out of every four soldiers held a Belgian automatic rifle. The rest of the soldiers held the customary Russian AK-47 rifles. All the guards shifted their weapons about uneasily, as if poised for danger.

The prisoners formed the usual line across one end of the field, and we began cutting wide swaths of hay with our machetes. We'd moved a quarter of the way across the field when a few of us noticed that Seruto, a young Christian brother from our group, lagged behind the work line. Before any of us could inconspicuously draw it to his attention, the soldier nearest him shouted.

"Hey! You there!" He called Seruto's number. "You are dropping behind the other workers. You plan to escape, perhaps?"

Startled out of his thoughts, Seruto hastily replied, "No, no."

Tension crackled in the cool morning air. While the rest of us continued working, we inched closer in an effort to shorten the gap and tighten the line of workers around him. By doing so, we hoped to protect him from any violent outburst.

Without warning, our guards plowed into us, beating us with our own machetes and their rifle butts. The blows landed on our heads, shoulders, and bare backs. We struggled to continue working and still maintain our tightly formed pack. Above the brutal frenzy, we heard Vaquerito shout "Fire!" Instantly, the field turned into a battleground. Shouts, screams, the ra-ti-tat-tat of machine-gun fire, and the zing of rifle bullets erupted from everywhere. Prisoners fell flat on the ground; others scattered to the shelter of the closest tree or hay bale to avoid being shot. One of the ranking officers ran to the radio in the truck and called for help. The shooting frenzy continued until additional G-2 forces arrived.

The shooting halted as quickly as it had begun. Brother Seruto had been shot in the leg. Vaquerito inspected the injury and ordered that Seruto be transferred to the hospital. The soldiers loaded Seruto onto the back of a pickup truck and drove him away. Later we learned that on the way to the hospital, Vaquerito took out his fury over the day's outrage by shooting Seruto in the neck. The shot paralyzed the young man, leaving him a quadriplegic.

I marveled at the useless travesty—a young man in the prime of his manhood, reduced to a helpless, paralyzed form of humanity, unable to perform even the simplest bodily functions for himself. How could any of this be used to the honor and glory of God?

The second officer in command of our block ordered us to line up again for roll call. When he was satisfied that no one had escaped in the confusion, he shouted, "Everyone into the trucks. You are being moved."

After a short ride, we arrived at the edge of a plowed field where we were instructed to walk down the long furrows, pulling weeds. The field rested in a green valley surrounded on three sides by hills. Spring and summer's heavy showers had filled the riverbeds, which produced incredibly blue lakes in the region. From where I stood I could see some of these lakes and rivers flowing toward Bibijaqua Beach on the ocean, thirty miles away.

The beauty of the scene stole my breath away. I'd seen so much ugliness and pain that I'd almost forgotten how lovely the natural world could be when turned over to the Creator. In spite of the morning's travesty, my spirits lifted. As I yanked the weeds from the furrows, I whispered the words of Psalm 148: "Praise ye the Lord. Praise ye the Lord from the heavens: praise him in the heights. Praise ye him, all his angels: praise ye him, all his hosts. . . . Mountains, and all hills; fruitful trees, and all cedars."

Lunchtime arrived. Brother Balbon and I huddled together to eat and to discuss the day's events. Our conversation switched to his desire to be baptized.

"I am ready to be baptized now," Brother Balbon reminded me.

"There must be a way, brother," I assured him. "The Lord must have a way."

While we talked, more time passed than we realized. We failed to hear the order to fall in for roll call. Suddenly the shadow of a guard loomed over us. "Didn't you hear the order to fall in?" he shouted, aiming his rifle at us threateningly. "You are all trying to escape!"

Startled, I looked up at the snarling corporal. "Who? Us?"

"Yes! The block was called to line up, and you are all still sitting here, idle. Shove off." He waved his rifle in the direction he intended us to go.

We hopped to our feet and hurried into place. When the sergeant finished the after-lunch roll call, he stopped in front of where we stood at attention. "Corporal," he snapped at the guard by his side, "take these men over to that lake." He pointed to the deepest lake in the tiny valley. "Let them weed the grass there."

"With what tools?" the guard asked.

The sergeant arched one eyebrow in disdain. "With their hands, and don't lose any more time! If they refuse to work or try to escape, you have a rifle. Use it!" He would make an example of us.

The rest of the prisoners watched as the corporal marched us across a road to the lake. As we stepped into the icy waters, I thought, "Why not baptize Brother Balbon here?" I glanced over at my brother in Christ and grinned. Reading my thoughts, he grinned back. "The Lord works in mysterious ways, His wonders to perform," I said as we waded into the lake. I took Brother Balbon's two hands in my left hand and raised my right hand above his head to pronounce the vow.

The prisoners on shore couldn't hear my words or tell what I was doing. Thinking I was crying for help, they started screaming. The political instructor and the guards ran toward them in an effort to regain order just as I lowered Brother Balbon under the water, then lifted him to his feet. Giddy as schoolboys, we embraced one another with laughter and tears at the irony of the event. Not only had God provided a most beautiful setting for the first prison baptism on the Isle of Pines, He allowed it to happen right there in the faces of our foes! In his attempt to punish us, the political instructor had supplied the answer to our prayers.

The officer in charge ordered us out of the lake while the guards restored order among the rest of the prison block. We joined the line of prisoners as the block officials discussed what to do with us. I knew they were determining my fate. Men had been shot and killed for much less. Yet in spite of my danger, I struggled to swallow a smile. I sneaked a glance at Brother Balbon. His face glowed with happiness too.

The block officers finally came to a decision. The officer in charge ordered all the prisoners onto the trucks to be taken back to the prison. Immediately after the evening meal, a group of the brothers in Christ converged on our cell to learn of the day's events firsthand. We were still sharing the incredible story when a high-ranking officer and two armed guards arrived.

"Balbon, you are being transferred to Cuba," the officer announced, irritation oozing from his every word. "You will collect your personal belongings. The plane is about to leave. Do you know that I have been waiting for you since 1:30 this afternoon?"

Our mouths dropped open in surprise. God had demonstrated His love and His power once again. So far as I could tell, it had been at exactly 1:30 p.m. that I baptized Brother Balbon. Coincidence? Never. God had turned a satanic sequence of brutality—the shooting and paralyzing of Seruto—into a triumph for His cause. The stricken Seruto would probably never learn the full result of the sacrifice he made that day, at least not this side of eternity.

After the guards took Brother Balbon away, our church members gathered to pray for Brother Seruto and to praise God for the day's miracle. We worshiped together until bedtime. The spiritual high we experienced during the next few days revived our spirits. At least, it worked for most of us.

A few days after the shooting of Brother Seruto, one of the brothers named Ariel found Roberto Chavez leaning against the bars of his cell. His dark, penetrating eyes stared out into the night, unseeing; his young, handsome face was frozen into a grimace of despair. Immediately, Ariel recognized the signs. He'd seen the look before on the faces of much older men. Roberto had reached the breaking point—the point where his mind and body refused to endure the extreme abuse any longer. As Ariel approached, Roberto straightened and snapped around, as if shaking himself back to reality.

"Hey, Roberto, what are you doing here all alone? Trying to keep the breeze all to yourself?" Ariel teased, hoping to lighten his spirits.

"No . . . no, brother, I was looking at the sea . . ." His voice drifted off as he turned back toward the window, but not before the friend noted a troubled look in his eyes.

Ariel walked over and placed a hand on Roberto's shoulder. "Roberto, what's going on? Did you receive bad news today? You seem very upset."

Roberto turned back toward his friend and stared for several seconds, then sat down on his makeshift cot. He leaned forward, rested his elbows on his knees, folded his hands in the classic pose for prayer, and blew through his fingers before speaking. When he did speak, his words came out calmly and deliberately. "A few minutes ago I came to the conclusion that it's better to sleep in Jesus than to go on as a slave to these beasts."

Ariel cleared his throat. "Then what do you intend to do?"

"It's simple." Roberto spoke in decisive tones. "Beginning tomorrow, Friday, Roberto Chavez will refuse to work."

Ariel stared at his friend and brother in Christ. The scattering of freckles across Roberto's nose made him appear much younger than his twenty-five years. "Roberto, think about what you are saying. Do you realize what that will mean?"

He nodded his head slowly. "Yes, I know, but I've made up my mind. I'm ready for anything—anything!" Roberto stood, glanced at Ariel, then strode over to the barred window once again. It was as if he could see beyond the prison walls, beyond the horizon, to the shores of the main island—Cuba, his home.

Ariel thought of the many times since his incarceration he had done the very same thing, thought the very same thoughts! "What can I say to change his mind? What hope can I give him beyond the blessed hope of the resurrection?" A flood of helplessness overcame him. There was little to do but leave Roberto to his thoughts and report to the brothers.

At one time or another, we'd all been in Roberto's frame of mind. A small group of us prayed for Roberto during the night. "Lord, give him the strength to resist, to persevere."

As the night deepened, angry black clouds filled the seasonally clear skies. By morning roll call, a fine drizzle fell. The soldiers huddled under heavy cloaks to keep dry while we prisoners shivered in the cold, wet morning air, hugging our light, tattered prison uniforms about us as best we could. Up and down the line, prisoners asked one another, "Where's Roberto? Have you seen Roberto this morning?" I glanced about for him, but could not spot him. In our gaunt, emaciated condition and matching garb, one prisoner looked very much like the next.

Sergeant Giron, the leader of block 19, strutted back and forth in front of the prisoners. Every move he made, every word he uttered, screamed his contempt for us. He considered anyone with a formal education, students and professionals alike, as exploiters of the people. We were an affront to his very being. Beyond his inborn bigotry, he resented us for refusing to integrate into the "glorious revolution."

His high, grating voice screeched at us through his hand-held megaphone. "On the way to the trucks, do not speak to anyone. Nor do I want any salutes. And now, to the trucks. Make it snappy."

Often, when a prisoner spotted a friend from one of the other blocks, he would wave or salute. This Sergeant Giron did not want to happen. As the prisoners hurried to the trucks, the guards watched to be certain we obeyed Sergeant Giron's orders.

Within minutes, the long train of trucks rolled out into the countryside, then down the main street of a small town in the area. As always, the adult residents waved to the anti-Communist freedom fighters behind the soldiers' backs. The children, less timid, threw kisses and waved from the side of the road. Beyond the town, two of the trucks halted at the entrance to a field of pangola grass. The guards immediately climbed out of their vehicles and took their positions. Then Sergeant Giron ordered the prisoners out of the truck.

After roll call, the sergeant shouted, "Go get your picks. These fields must be cleared of all weeds." Reluctantly, all but one of the prisoners picked up a tool and headed for the overgrown field. Instantly I recognized Roberto.

Sergeant Giron snarled at him. "Hey, you! What are you waiting for? Pick that up and start clearing if you don't want—"

"If you want the field cleared, clear it yourself," Roberto interrupted. "I won't pull another weed!"

"What are you saying, you wretched fool?" The other prisoners watched, horrified, as the hated sergeant stormed over to where Roberto stood. "Are you nuts?"

Roberto stared steadily into the officer's startled face. "You heard me. You or your boss can do it. I'm finished."

Before the sergeant could reply, a second prisoner joined Roberto. In a trembling voice, he said, "What Roberto says goes for me too."

Sergeant Giron's face turned purple. He drew his bayonet, then paused. The head of the guard unit stood on a small rise some distance away, watching, but too far away to hear the exchange. Poising his machine gun for action, he strode over to Giron's side. "What's happening here?" he asked.

"Nothing much. These two heroes refuse to work," Giron snarled. "Go order your men to close ranks. We're going to have a party."

The head of the guards carried out his orders. The soldiers took up their rifles, ready to fight. "How brave," I thought. "Fully armed with their Russian and Belgian machine guns and rifles, they would face their enemy—dispirited, starving men armed with their dignity, their morality, their Christianity, and an indomitable determination to die rather than surrender."

When the soldiers halted in front of the sergeant, he ordered the two prisoners to follow him. The rest of us stood by, helpless to prevent the brutality we knew would follow. The remaining officers ordered us back to work. Knowing that no purpose would be served should we refuse, we obeyed.

The day dragged by, and our concern for our two brothers heightened. When we arrived back at the prison compound, we learned from prisoners assigned to the hospital work detail that the guards had dumped Roberto and the other prisoner out of a jeep onto the ground in front of the prison hospital like two sacks of potatoes, their clothing in shreds and stained with their own blood, their flesh lacerated, mangled, and bruised by blows from bayonets and rifle butts. After being given a minimum of first aid, the men were returned in critical condition to their cells and denied any further medical treatment. The warden ordered the prison security officer to lock them in their cells.

As soon as we heard the news, we rushed to their sides to see if there was anything we could do to ease their suffering. Despite his pain and discomfort, Roberto continued his campaign by going on a hunger strike.

"Roberto," I begged, "you must eat something—anything."

He smiled and shook his head. "I will never give up. My brother, my time has come."

"But, but—" I sputtered.

"I have heard that in a few weeks there is to be a general convention," Roberto said. "I hope they'll tell the entire world about the crimes that are being committed here."

One of the brothers shook his head. "No, Roberto! No one cares about us! Give it up."

Roberto's eyes brightened in spite of his bruised, swollen face. "You are wrong, my friend. There's One who cares. He has shown me the way. The acts of the apostles of Jesus Christ are still being written."

We prayed with him and bade him good night, then returned to our cells. Depressed, I couldn't sleep that night, for I knew what would be Roberto's fate. Days passed. Roberto grew steadily weaker. His tormentors' greatest efforts could not change his mind or his course. His reply to their insistence that he eat remained the same. "Man shall not live by bread alone."

We continued to visit him and give him what moral strength we could. Our visits stopped when the warden transferred Roberto to the punishment wing of the prison, where no one could visit him. For those of us who loved him, the days passed agonizingly slowly. A ghostlike presence haunted us. We knew that our friend and brother, Roberto, always so full of life and vitality, lay dying alone.

Prison gossip kept us informed of his condition. In horrible pain, his body cried out for nourishment, yet he refused. Before the end, he could barely lift his arms off the cot, yet his heart continued to beat. Through lips turned violet, he continued to breathe harsh, rasping breaths. His once-bright, intelligent eyes could no longer see. During brief moments of lucidity, a smile filled his face. His determined captors tempted him with succulent morsels of food two or three times a day. The odor of death pervaded the cell.

Finally, Lieutenant Morejon himself visited Roberto's cell. "What are you asking for?" the lieutenant demanded. "What is it you want?"

Roberto moved his lips, but no sound came out. Trying again, with superhuman effort, he whispered, "Lieutenant, what I want are flowers."

"Flowers?" The officer glared at Roberto, flexed his fists in anger, turned on his heels, and stormed out of the cell repeating, "Flowers—flowers—flowers! What I want are flowers! Bah, flowers!"

At daybreak on November 13, the guard found Roberto dead. A peaceful smile softened the harsh lines of starvation and abuse that etched his once-young face. Roberto Chavez had found rest at last. He chose to die rather than allow the "Camilo Cienfuego Hard Labor Plan" to re-educate him into accepting Castro's communism.

University Under Shadows

At the beginning of the great re-education plan, the arrogant Captain Morejon predicted that we would weaken, and he promised a gold medal to anyone who resisted the torture and deprivation he inflicted on us. But his prognosis failed. A year passed, and we were far from begging on bended knee for mercy. Faith had led us all the way. It also kindled his fury.

At the end of the first year, the frustrated Captain Morejon told his men to "do with them as you please. You may kill, stab, beat—do whatever is necessary to implant the red terror in their minds."

Lieutenant Aldama, the political instructor of block number 8, leaned against the wall with his arms folded across his chest as our block sergeant completed the first roll call of the day. After the sergeant stepped aside, Aldama swaggered past the line of prisoners, eyeing each of us individually, as if looking for flickers of defiance or weakness in our eyes.

"You are being transferred from work at La Bibijagua to labor at La Reforma," he informed us. "There the sergeant and I will be able to instruct you without interference from outside block number 8."

We understood his real meaning perfectly well. In spite of their cruelty, the G-2 men treated us better than did the local officers. We were being moved during the day to La Reforma, a work program forty-five miles away that produced citrus fruit, because the G-2 did not supervise that program. The political officer and the sergeant could do anything they wanted, and nobody would be around to interfere or temper the soldiers' ire. We would be totally at the mercy of these men.

The soldiers unleashed their fury upon us almost immediately upon our arrival. The first day of work Corporal Louis

Guesternay, one of the most sadistic of the soldiers, ordered us out into a field to cut grass —with our teeth. Should a prisoner slow down, the soldiers would open fire on him, killing him instantly. For the least excuse, the soldiers would turn the field into a battlefield. Two prisoners, Danny Crespo and Eddy Alvarez, were killed on the first day. The next day a corporal stabbed Julio Tan with his bayonet. After the prisoner fell to the ground, the soldier dug at the wound with his bayonet, opening it further until Julio died from loss of blood.

At La Reforma, about twenty-five of us were assigned to pick tangerines. For starving men to be surrounded by millions of succulent oranges, grapefruit, and tangerines day after day and not be able to lift even one to their lips proved torturous. Since the fruit belonged to "the people," to eat any would be stealing. Anyone caught stealing would be made to pay for his theft—a bloody price indeed. He would either be stabbed with a bayonet or savagely beaten.

There was one significant difference between our former work site and La Reforma a welcome one to us. Here we were able to work side-by-side with civilians. And though we were forbidden to talk to them or they to us, that rule was next to impossible for the guards to enforce in an orchard full of trees. Short of posting a guard beside every prisoner, there was no way they could stop us. We often talked to civilians quite at length.

One day the former owner of the plantation came out to the orchard. Since the revolution ended and Castro came into power, he and his family no longer owned the property but only managed it for the government. They told him that if he refused to work for the good of the state, he would lose his home also.

Glancing both ways, he said, "I am not afraid to speak to you prisoners, but I must be careful lest another civilian or one of the guards should overhear us speaking. I have already been reported to the authorities in the past, so now I too have people checking on me as you do."

He nodded toward a cluster of guards standing at the edge of the grove of trees. "As far as I'm concerned, eat as much fruit as you like. Just don't let the guards catch you, and don't tell them I gave you permission to eat it. I don't want to get into any more trouble."

While I became acquainted with the plantation owner, other prisoners formed friendships with the civilian workers. Carlos

Sanchez, one of our Christian brothers, struck up a friendship with one of the local farm boys. Always enthusiastic about Jesus, Carlos shared his faith with the young man. After a while the boy became interested in learning more.

"You must meet the Pastor," Carlos informed him. He brought the young man to meet me. We chatted for some time regarding the promises in God's Word.

"I have a Bible," the farm boy admitted, "not the whole Bible, but a part of one. You may have it if you like. I can get another on the street."

The next day he handed a brown paper bag with the book inside to Carlos. After glancing about to be certain no one was watching, Carlos thanked the boy, then, checking to be certain they'd not been observed, Carlos buried the package at the edge of the citrus grove.

Unfortunately, someone did overhear the conversation and saw the package. A few days later, the prison commandant ordered the guards to bring Carlos and me to his office. While the commandant questioned us, another officer searched our cells for the package. Neither man learned anything. Instead of following up the questioning with the usual torture, the commandant ordered us back to our cells.

"That's strange," Carlos commented. "No torture? No discipline?"

I shrugged for lack of a better response.

During the week following our questioning, Carlos and I were sent on different work assignments. The next week they reassigned us to the fruit grove where Carlos had hidden the Bible. Upon arriving at the grove, Carlos returned to the spot where he'd hidden the Book. After digging it up, he wrapped it in a scrap of plastic from an empty fertilizer bag. We often used the empty plastic bags as ponchos to protect us from the rains. He slipped the package beneath his shirt and placed his metal dinner plate between the Bible and his shirt.

The prison's political instruction officer had bided his time and won. A guard who had been assigned to watch Carlos immediately reported his actions. Carlos had just hidden his treasure when a sniper shot rang out. Startled, Carlos fell on his face, cutting his lip on a sharp stone. Before I could discover just what had happened, the political instructor rushed forward, shouting and accusing him of trying to escape. The guards scooped Carlos into a truck and drove off in a flurry of gravel while the remaining guards ordered the rest of us back to work. That night, back at the prison, Carlos told us what happened.

The guards drove him to the military hospital and rushed him into the doctor's examining room. Blood had dripped from his cut lip onto his clothing during the frantic ride to the hospital. The minute he arrived in the examination room, the doctor tore the clothing off his body. After checking him all over, the doctor stepped back and asked the political instructor why Carlos had been brought to his office.

"Because we shot him in the chest," the political instructor snarled. "He was trying to escape."

"That's ridiculous!" the atheistic doctor snorted. "We have found no bullet. He is in perfect health. Come and see."

"But the blood—"

The doctor arched his eyebrow in disgust. "You bring a prisoner to the hospital for a cut lip?"

"Impossible!" the political instructor shouted. "I know that my man aimed straight at him. He couldn't have missed!"

The doctor shrugged. "See for yourself."

Determined to justify himself, the political officer picked up the package that had dropped to the floor when Carlos's shirt was torn off. "What is this?"

"I don't know. I am not concerned with packages but with patients."

The political instructor unwrapped the package. Inside he found the Bible, and inside the Bible he found the spent bullet. "Ah-ha!" he exclaimed, holding up the bullet for the doctor to see. "I told you we shot him in the chest."

Timidly, Carlos asked to see the Bible, and strangely, the political officer handed it to him. Carlos opened the Bible and looked through the pages that had been damaged by the bullet. The last damaged page opened onto Psalm 91, and an obvious dimple could be seen in the paper at verse 7: "A thousand shall fall at thy side, and ten thousand at thy right hand; but it shall not come nigh thee."

"Look at this," Carlos said.

The doctor and the political instructor leaned over and looked at the Bible.

"See these holes?" Carlos said, pointing to the damaged pages. "And see this page, where the bullet made a dent?"

The doctor nodded.

"Read those words, right where the dent is," Carlos said.

The doctor read the verse, then handed the Bible to the political instructor. Finally he spoke, his voice filled with wonder. "If ever there was a miracle, this is it. Carlos, today the Bible saved your life, for if the bullet had gone all the way through into your chest, you would be a corpse now."

The doctor kept the bullet and Bible, and from then on, at every opportunity, he would call Carlos in for a checkup and talk to him about God. God had taken another of Satan's dastardly tricks and turned it into a blessing. Again His Word had been vindicated. All things do work together for good to them that love God and are called according to His purpose.

The story of Carlos's miracle spread throughout the prison at record speed. Prisoners who had never shown an interest in anything spiritual showed up for services, hoping to meet Carlos and hear his story. And many of these curiosity seekers met more than the miracle prisoner. They met the Christ behind the miracle. The phenomenal growth of attendance at our religious services forced us to move to the sixth floor. While living on this floor could be hazardous, we had more room in which to conduct our religious meetings since the lower cells could not hold all of us. Here we could worship relatively undisturbed. Some of the church members would stand in the entranceway to the cell so that the guards couldn't see what we were doing during our church services. We even managed to smuggle bread out of the mess hall to use for Communion.

Soon after the incident with Carlos, the prison gossip line informed us that a new prisoner had arrived and would be assigned to our gallery—Marino Boffill. We recognized the name of the former Olympic champion boxer immediately and eagerly awaited his arrival. The story of his arrest and bogus trial had preceded him. While competing in East Germany, Marino had attempted to escape to the West. Caught and shipped back to Cuba, he was tried for crimes against the state and sentenced to ten years of hard labor.

While we didn't know Marino, we eagerly greeted him at the door of the gallery, as we did every new prisoner. The prisoners met him with the usual barrage of questions regarding the outside world. He patiently answered each one. When we finished, he had questions of his own.

Just as the prison gossip told us of Marino's arrival, the story of the Christian prisoner who had been shot in the chest without being wounded had reached him.

"Please," he said, "is it true what I have heard? Did a man get shot, and the Bible saved his life?"

"Yes," I assured him, "it is true."

"Can I meet him?"

Carlos, who had been listening to the exchange, stepped forward. "I am he."

He and Carlos took an instant liking to one another. We invited Marino to join us on the sixth floor. Marino surprised us in many ways. Although he boxed for a living, he was a meek and loving individual who hungered after the truth from God's Word. He became active in the young people's group.

Day after day Marino learned more about God's plan of salvation until he decided to join the baptismal class. While studying for his baptism, he also began preparing to become a lay preacher. His enthusiasm and zeal could not be contained. Four months later, he was one of the candidates for baptism.

By this time, God had provided us with our very own baptismal tank. On the sixth floor of each circular was a water tank made of bricks and cement. Each morning it was filled with water for washing plates and to maintain water when the regular water supply was turned off. Keeping the water clean for a baptism and preventing the guards from observing the ceremony took careful planning. Bathing in the tank elicited a ten-day sentence in the dungeon, and baptizing brought a twenty-one-day sentence. When we were ready to baptize someone, the brothers of the faith would form a line, thus blocking the guards' view of the procedure.

We had scheduled Marino to preach his first sermon on Sunday, the next day after his baptism. The word spread throughout the prison. "Marino Boffill will preach on Sunday!"

Accustomed to public appearances as a boxer, the 300 or so prisoners didn't unnerve him in the slightest. He carried off his sermon on David and Goliath with as much style as any seasoned minister. Marino became an overnight celebrity in the gallery. As the prisoners left level six after the closing song of that first meeting, we heard them promising one another to return the following week to hear Marino speak. The next week more prisoners packed level six. The church grew at an astounding rate.

About this time, the church board decided to organize an in-prison university as a witnessing tool. Upon pooling the talent among our members, we decided that we could teach classes in arithmetic, algebra, geography, history, grammar, English, and French. This way prisoners would come looking for instruction, and, in doing so, perhaps find salvation too. We held the classes in the circular, in the fields, anywhere we had the opportunity.

However, Satan and his cohorts never slept. Headquarters grew worried at the sight of so many covert meetings springing up all over the place. They assigned extra guards to scrutinize and report all of our movements.

One day while we worked in the fields, soldiers searched our cells and confiscated all of the books we'd borrowed in order to copy notes, our carefully hidden Bibles, and hand-printed hymnals. Not only did the books represent hundreds of hours of painstaking labor, but they also represented our entire supply of paper. At the end of the day, we learned of the tragedy. The commandant awaited our arrival.

"You persist in perpetrating these religious myths? One way or another we will stop you!" In his usual flamboyant manner, he announced the names of the church leaders who would be transferred to other security prisons and concentration camps on the island. "We will divide and conquer!"

Divide perhaps, conquer never. We would just have to start all over again. The word of the search and seizure swept through the prison. In the next few evenings, prisoners from all over the gallery arrived on the sixth floor carrying more paper that had been smuggled in to them.

"I don't believe it!" Antonio stared at the stack of paper before him. "Over 5,000 sheets—more than we ever had before. Is God's arm ever too short?"

"No," I replied, "but now comes the hard part—writing out the hymns, the texts, and the lesson books all over again."

"And who knows how long it will be before it is confiscated again," Carlos reminded.

"Ah," Marino interrupted, "this time we must be more careful—and wiser."

In order to replace all that had been lost as quickly as possible, we organized three different copying teams. After returning from the fields at 9:00 p.m., we took quick showers, ate our meals, and copied until the lights went out. In days, we completed the manuscripts and created new hiding places for them. We managed to obtain a few books, which ironically included George Orwell's classical works on totalitarianism, *1984* and *Animal Farm*. Our university doors again opened to our eager students.

The university's curriculum grew with the arrival of José Carreno, a journalism and psychology teacher. We set up a board of education with the following professors:

Pastor H. Noble Alexander—university director, professor of mathematics and algebra.

Pastor Luis Rodriguez—registrar, professor of grammar and oratory.

Deacon José Carreno—professor of journalism, grammar, and poetry.

Deacon Felipe Hernendez—professor of English and French.

Professor Bango—professor of philosophy and humanities.

We taught from memory and from what little we could copy out of contraband books. We no longer trusted our knowledge to books since they could again be confiscated. Whenever written materials fell into our hands, we immediately memorized it word for word. Our students did the same. The written word our enemy could destroy, but word committed to memory was ours to keep forever.

The more the church grew, the more Satan and his Communist cohorts harassed us. During my four years at the Isle of Pines, church attendance grew to more than 200 members. The prison officials felt threatened by the potential power of our organization. At the end of one day in the fields, I noticed the corporal in charge of our brigade standing at the edge of the field, speaking in hushed tones to Aldama, our political adviser. I couldn't make out what they were saying, but I knew their exchange could only mean trouble for one of us prisoners. After they had finished speaking, the two men walked away, in opposite directions. I had just turned my attention back to my task when I heard my number called.

"Number 3-1-4-5-0, come here! We want to speak with you." I turned and saw Aldama gesturing for me to come to him. We had nicknamed Aldama "the grandfather" due to his interrogation techniques. To a prisoner's face, Aldama sympathized and spoke gently and affectionately, but after the prisoner left the office, he'd order that the man be beaten or killed.

"I can't go there," I replied, "because I will be out of the guards' circle of protection."

"But I am calling you!" He elevated his arrogant chin ever so slightly.

"Yes, but the guards don't know that," I argued. "When I step out of the circle, they will shoot at me."

His eyes flashed with anger. "You are not going to obey?"

I shook my head. "On this occasion, I am not. Obeying would cost me my life."

His jaw tightened as he clenched and unclenched his fists. "Your disobedience may cost it!"

I straightened my shoulders and met his gaze. "Well, if you want to kill me, do it here, in the circle—so that you can't say I was trying to escape."

"You think you are smart! I could end it all for you with one bullet!" He paused to regain his composure. "We will discuss this problem further this evening."

When Aldama called me to the edge of the field, the corporal had gone in the opposite direction to alert the sniper to catch me out of the safety zone. The official report would have indicated that I'd been trying to escape. When the Lord revealed their plot to me and I refused to cross the line, their scheme to get rid of me without repercussions failed. They were forced to use an alternate plan.

That evening after the counting, a special guard, Corporal Hienica ("hyena" in English) was ordered to escort me to the dungeon for my disobedience. Escort doesn't adequately describe his task. Corporal Hienica's job was to beat me with a machete or prod me with a bayonet point all the way to the dungeon. The corporal added his own touch to his task. He sang a little Mexican tune that said, "Why are you complaining, you yourself looked for your evil."

Hienica began singing the tune as he prodded me out into the courtyard with his machete. It had begun to rain, so he ordered me to run, but I continued walking at my normal pace. When we stepped inside the dungeon cell, he growled, "You see how I got wet because of you. I told you to run, and you didn't."

"I am not a criminal, so I don't have to run," I answered.

"I suppose that I am the criminal?"

I shrugged. "You said it, not I."

Furious at my audacity, he drew his revolver from his holster and shot me in my right thigh. He turned and walked out of the cell as I fell to the floor. Later, the official report stated that I had tried to wrestle the gun from him, and it accidentally went off. Fortunately for me, the bullet missed my thigh bone, leaving no permanent damage to my leg.

The ninety dungeon cells reflected the brutish, Draconian nature of the prison officials. Eighteen of the cells were "tiger cages," suspended like bird cages. The floor, roof, and walls were all made of three-quarter-inch steel bars. The eighteen "monkey boxes" were so small that the prisoner was forced to remain in a squatting position with the roof touching his head. The eighteen coffinlike "showers" were vertical. In these the prisoner was forced to stand on his toes to avoid stepping on the broken glass and nails partially embedded in the back of the shower stall while droplets of water rhythmically pelted his head. The last thirty-six dungeon cells were solitary confinement rooms. Eighteen had sleeping facilities, and eighteen did not. The eighteen cells with berths were for those prisoners who would spend months in isolation. At one time or another, I experienced all five.

This time I was placed in a cell without a berth for twenty-one days, during which I was not allowed to either shower or shave. Yet even in this pit of degradation, I was not alone. Each evening at sunset, my brothers in Christ stood outside the building that housed the dungeons and called to me, bidding me good night.

When a guard came to release me, I could barely walk, due to my leg wound. I was forced to hop on my good leg back to the circular. When I arrived back at my circular, twenty-five of my brethren welcomed me with a song: "The Fight Is On, O Christian Soldiers."

"Stop singing, or we'll shoot!" the guards in the tower shouted over their bullhorns.

I stood stunned when, instead of obeying the order, other prisoners joined in until more than a hundred voices filled the circular with singing. My heart overflowed with emotion. I tried to choke back my tears, but I could not. The hero's welcome caused me to forget my injured leg. Somehow, I walked across the circular's open area on both legs. The guards could only sit in their towers and glower. They'd been foiled again by the power of Jesus Christ and of Christian solidarity.

The Cuban officials decided that the way to "break the back" of Christianity at the Isle of Pines prison was to transfer various members of the prison church to other prisons in the system. When we first heard the news, we interpreted the move as a tragedy for God's cause. Instead, the dispersion of our brothers to nine different prisons led to the formation of nine new churches. God had a way of turning apparent defeat into overwhelming victory!

Toward the end of 1965, rumors flew through the prison that all political prisoners would be transported back to the main island, and the common prisoners would take our places in the fields. New prisoners also informed us of strong international pressure being applied on the Cuban government because of the death of Chino Atan, a prisoner who had been killed while working in one of the fields. His death occurred when our political instructor and a sergeant ordered us into a field during a thunderstorm. Lightning struck and killed three prisoners, one of whom was Chino Atan. Word leaked out to the international press, stirring up trouble for Castro and his government officials.

When we learned the prisoners would be sent back to the main island, we conducted a work slowdown. Unfortunately, the block sergeants sensed the change and intensified their brutality. These soldiers earned their regular army pay plus two dollars a day for taking us to the fields. They also earned a sack of whatever we were harvesting on the farms along with an extra five dollars and a three-day leave every time one of the prisoners opted for the re-education plan. So it was their goal to make life as intolerable as possible for us in order to convince us to accept the re-education plan. When a sergeant shouted, "Kill!" there would be little hesitation, for if a soldier did not meet his quota, there were dozens more eager to take his place and reap the advantages of the job.

While it was difficult to imagine these bloodthirsty ghouls having families to feed, I could understand the conditions that motivated them. In other places of the world, five dollars might seem like nothing, but in Cuba, where a citizen could only buy

$9.60 worth of goods per month, it was a lot. In addition to the limited purchasing that was allowed, many articles did not arrive in time for the customer to buy them. For instance, the customer might go to the grocery store and request four pounds of rice. The clerk in charge would then ask for his consumer booklet to be certain that it was his turn to get rice. After the clerk validated that it was indeed the customer's turn to get rice, he would inform him that there would be no more rice until the next week. When the customer returned the next week for his four pounds of rice, the clerk would then look at the consumer booklet and say, "Sorry, last week was your turn. You can't have any this week."

Daily, the block officials demanded more and more work out of the inmates. If the prisoners failed to increase their daily quotas sufficiently, beatings and killings occurred. Life in the fields became so unbearable that many inmates mutilated themselves in order to avoid going to work. So each day there were fewer and fewer prisoners to do the same amount of work. As tensions in the fields increased, one accident after another occurred, either to the trucks or to the farm equipment, and at the prison itself. In an effort to break the downward spiral, headquarters developed a new strategy for re-education.

First, they renamed the Isle of Pines "Youth's Island." Youth's Island would serve a double purpose. It would house political prisoners, and it would be used to separate young people from their parents in order to indoctrinate them, all under the guise of education. If a student applied for a scholarship, he would be sent to a training center far from his parents' home in order to isolate him. He would receive free room, board, and education, and his curriculum included work, study, and weaponry—the skillful use of rifles, bayonets, and handguns.

Castro himself welcomed the first 3,000 students to the island, changing the name of the island at that time to Youth's Island in their honor. Barracks were built, along with kitchen facilities. The students, both male and female, were organized into blocks just like the prisoners, and taken to the fields to work. The only difference was that the students had no guards following them.

Unofficially, the Department of Psychology called the plan "The Sex Plan." After being incarcerated for more than three years, the prisoners were to work side by side with the pretty young female students. Surely no normal man could resist such a temptation, they reasoned. And should he succumb, the psychologists knew that, having lost his moral force, he would be putty in the interrogators' hands. With many men, it worked. However, the majority of the brethren resisted, not through their power but through the power of community prayer. When it was obvious to our captors that all those who would weaken had weakened, they reassigned the resisters to other blocks. I was assigned to block number 7, the block that worked in the marble quarry, or "TB pit," as the prisoners called it.

The chief of the block, Lieutenant Rivera, called me into his office.

"You are 31,450?"

"Yes," I answered, "I am Humberto Noble Alexander." The number and the name response supplied the officer with a double identification.

Rivera nodded. His cold, dark, penetrating eyes revealed no sign of human kindness. "If you do not want to work, just tell me," he started. "I will kill you on the spot."

He leaned back on his heels and sized me up. "To begin with, I don't want any preaching here. It's enough with the brainwashing you are carrying on in the circulars." He shook his head in disgust. "I can't understand how Tarrao put up with that!" Tarrao had been the chief of the circulars, or prison director.

"You will work at the quarry beginning tomorrow morning. You are dismissed."

I stared straight ahead. Long ago I had learned not to volunteer information of any kind, never to say No, and not to reveal my true emotions. A guard would knock out one tooth for each No a prisoner uttered. Inside, I shrank from the idea of working at the marble quarry each day from seven in the morning to six at night. During the evening hours, the guards enjoyed harassing the workers by making the prisoners move the stones they'd broken that morning to the opposite side of the quarry, then back again.

It wasn't the extreme hard labor, the sweltering heat, the blinding sunlight reflecting off the white marble, or the sadistic games the guards enjoyed playing. It was fear—the fear of dying from the suffocating marble dust and white lime that polluted every breath inhaled. Inmates who worked in the quarry for any length of time usually died from a horrible lung disease. Would my resolve to survive this nightmare be defeated by marble dust or powdered lime? Would I go out with a gasp or a whimper and never again breathe the sweet perfume of freedom?

Promises Made, Promises Broken

The next morning at the marble quarry, I climbed out of the truck into the sunlight. At the end of the roll call, a guard handed me a pick and sent me to a section of the quarry, where I worked with Isaac de la Campa, a former policeman from Batista's force. As I worked, I glanced about at the blood-stained walls of the quarry where guards had stabbed or shot countless prisoners for whatever minor infractions of the rules they could contrive. "Such a waste of human potential," I thought. "Such wickedness!"

The watchman assigned to take care of the tools secretly kept a herd of small livestock in the quarry, including hens and roosters. During the day, one of his roosters was out parading for a group of hens when a chicken hawk swooped down from the sky. The rooster fell to the ground in a faint. His comb faded to white as if every drop of blood had spilled out of it. The chicken hawk, thinking the rooster was dead, took off again. The rooster remained motionless for five minutes. Once it was certain the hawk was gone, it got up, flapped its wings, and crowed as if saying, "I won!"

I turned toward Isaac and grimaced. "This is a place of terror even for the cock. Even the fowls learn to fear here."

At the end of the day, my throat and lungs ached, the excruciating pain behind my eyes pulsated to the rhythm of my heartbeat, and my arms felt as if they would drop off. The truck bounced over the rough gravel roads on the way back to the prison, giving me time to think. I wondered if I would survive even one week working in the quarry.

That evening the work foreman learned that I had welding and mechanical experience. When I arrived for work on the second day, he reassigned me to weld the broken parts on one of the machines. Unfortunately, the prisoners considered that any who worked as a professional or a tradesman at his skill was aiding the regime. The prison officials understood this, yet they persisted.

"No, I can't," I said. "It has been many years since I did that kind of work."

"Go on," he insisted, "just try. See if you can."

"What if I don't want to try?" I asked.

His lips formed a thin, grim line for a moment; then he answered, "If you refuse, we will consider it as sabotage."

"Well, I am sorry, because if anything went wrong I would be charged with the guilt anyway, so I prefer not to even touch that machine."

Irked by my refusal, he assigned me to the lime pit, the "TB division," as the prisoners called it. There, I, along with a number of other prisoners, shoveled white lime. Without proper safety masks, we inhaled the fine dust particles throughout the day. By the time we arrived back at the prison, we wheezed ourselves to sleep. The lethal combination of severe malnutrition and layers of lime dust in one's lungs made tuberculosis an almost guaranteed fate. Inmate after inmate succumbed to the quarry's exhausting environment and the soldiers' brutality.

The mindless work in the quarry allowed me time to think. As I broke rock, I exercised my memory by reciting Bible texts and singing my way through the church's hymnbook. I carried on long conversations with God and created mental images of my beautiful Yraida. I cannot even guess how many times I relived our wedding day as I labored beneath the stifling tropical sun. The more details I could recall, the less pain I consciously felt. My routine was predictable.

August 3, 1959—our wedding day. Members from the Marianao and Cerro churches packed my mother-in-law's small home to attend our wedding. I remembered the broad smile on Pastor Roberto Acosta's face as he prepared to conduct the ceremony. He later laughed about how sober my face looked as I stood in front of him, waiting for my bride to appear.

"I was afraid you might pass out on me," he joked. "Talk about a frightened groom!"

I tried to remember the names of the four candle bearers and of the little Bible boy. Sometimes the names and faces would surface; other times, my mind refused to cooperate. This scared me. I couldn't allow the devils who held me captive to rob me of my memory!

When my mind went on strike, I would plead with God. "Help me, Father. Help me to hold on to these precious memories."

When my mind cooperated, I continued reliving the wedding ceremony, watching each of the bridal attendants come down the aisle and take their places. I enjoyed a perverse delight in holding off my most vivid memory—my first glimpse of Yraida in her blush pink wedding gown. I gasped at the vision of the beautiful woman soon to be my wife. I could almost feel the texture of my white linen suit as nervously I ran the edges of my sleeves back and forth between my thumbs and fingers.

The word *radiant* couldn't do justice to the glow on her face as she walked down the aisle toward me. I have never seen any woman look so stunningly beautiful. Eagerly I went to meet her, took her arm gently in mine, and turned to face the pastor.

At this point, the shout of a guard often jarred me back to the present. "Stop being a goldbrick, 3-1-4-5-0!"

I hastened to obey, since anything less than instant obedience produced guaranteed violence on the guard's part.

So when the prison authorities announced a visitor's day, I could scarcely keep my mind on anything else—until I learned just what a visit from one's wife, mother, and children entailed. In preparation for the visit, the prisoners would be forced to strip naked, then, in a squatting position, jump so as to be certain they had hidden nothing in their colons that could be smuggled out. With all the other atrocities and violations against our human sensibilities, we could tolerate one more in order to have the privilege of seeing those we loved, until we learned that our visitors would be put through the same ordeal. That's when the prisoners went on strike. After some time, the prison officials agreed to make the inmates go through the body search both going in and coming out rather than subject the visitors to such mistreatment.

The first visiting day will stand out in my memory forever. The pathetic scene in the reception room defied description. Mothers wailed as if they mourned their sons' deaths. Wives and daughters clung to their husbands and fathers. Some fainted at the sight of their loved ones' emaciated bodies. Others had fits of hysteria, while still others quivered uncontrollably in shock, struck speechless by the horror of the moment.

I searched for Yraida, but she failed to come. Something terrible must have happened to her, I reasoned. I knew that my son often suffered from tropical dysentery. Perhaps she or Humberto had taken ill or died or . . . My mind invented every nightmarish fantasy possible. When she didn't appear forty-five days later for the second visiting day, I had to know what was wrong, so I smuggled out a note to her.

On the third visiting day, I entered the reception area terrified that again she would not come. A numbing relief flooded through me when I saw her standing toward the back of the crowd of women. Delighted, I ran to her. Yet even in the first few moments as I approached her, I sensed a strange reserve about her. She's just uncomfortable with the surroundings, I reasoned. After all, what woman with such delicate sensibilities could act natural in such an awkward situation? When she pulled out a cigarette and lighted it, a cacophony of warning bells clanged away in my head.

After she left, a former neighbor of ours visited my cell. "I hate to be the one to tell you this, Noble," he began, "but you have to be strong. My wife told me that Yraida has been seeing an army captain."

"What? I don't believe it!" I shouted, clenching and unclenching my fists. I could feel a raging anger tearing apart my insides. Never a man given to violence, I ached with an unfamiliar urge to punch something, someone, anyone!

I refused to believe it. Other wives might be unfaithful to their imprisoned husbands, but not Yraida. I shook my head violently to rid myself of the mere suggestion.

My neighbor grabbed me by the shoulders, bringing my denial to a sudden halt. "Noble, it's true. She plans to divorce you."

"No! No! No! My Yraida is a good Christian woman. She would never . . ." Noting the pain in my friend's eyes, I paused. Fear engulfed me. I swallowed hard in order to abort the flood of tears threatening to undo me. "I will write to her, and she will deny these charges. You will see how wrong these rumors are," I shouted. Without another word, he turned and left me standing in the middle of my cell.

In the next few days, with the help of a prisoner about to be released, I managed to smuggle a letter out to Yraida. I asked her if what our neighbor said was true. When she replied, she completely denied the entire story. I thought of the words of Proverbs 31:10, 11, "Who can find a virtuous woman? for her price is far above rubies. The heart of her husband doth safely trust in her, so that he shall have no need of spoil." During the weeks that followed, even the work at the marble quarry couldn't get me down. I praised God again and again for my beautiful, faithful wife.

More good news followed Yraida's letter. Through the prison's gossip line we learned that the officials would soon be shipping the political and religious prisoners back to the main island of Cuba. Our exile would soon be over.

At the quarry, we worked with new enthusiasm. No one wanted to die or be killed by a guard's bayonet at the last moment before going home. When one of the other inmates threatened to react to a guard's abuse or to do some other stupid or careless act, the rest of us would stop him with, "It's not worth it. Probably tomorrow, we will go back to Cuba." Unfortunately, it took one year and eight months for the rumor to become a reality. Meanwhile, the guards took advantage of the prisoners' lack of defiance and intensified their brutality.

On Wednesday evening, the night before our scheduled departure, the church family joined for a mass prayer meeting. Each man shared his testimony of his struggle and of a faith triumphant. We sang the words to "Praise Him! Praise Him! Jesus our Blessed Redeemer!" with renewed vigor. The poignant question in the song, "O the Way Is Long and Weary," took on an entirely new meaning as we stood on the brink of our departure. Nationality, religious persuasion, race, and politics dissolved as we formed a giant prayer circle. As brothers in Christ, we were closer than any physical brothers could possibly be.

Angered by our prayer meeting, the prison officials rousted us out of our bunks much earlier than usual the next morning. At the quarry, the guards hurried us to our areas and took count. Then the beating began. At one moment we were standing there listening for our numbers, when suddenly, without warning, the soldiers were beating on us with their rifle butts and bayonets.

The prison officials reserved their harshest brutality for blacks and Americans—blacks because the revolution had come to emancipate them, and by refusing to become a part of the revolution we were ungrateful, and Americans because, as imperialists, they intended to stifle the revolution.

The lieutenant gave an order for the guards to beat Larry Lunt, an American prisoner and a relative of the queen of Belgium. This wealthy Christian gentleman owned a large farm in Pinar del Rio, at the extreme west part of the island of Cuba. The Cuban government confiscated his farm, saying he had aided the rebels, and sentenced him to thirty years of hard labor on the Isle of Pines. Hating the Americans as they did, the guards especially targeted this formerly wealthy "gringo" landowner to suffer their vengeance.

Minutes later, a guard shot another prisoner, Chico Praderas, in the abdomen. Both men lived in spite of the irrational violence unleashed.

One man I will always remember was Elroy Menoya, a former high-ranking officer in Castro's army. When he and fifty of his men questioned the route the revolution was taking, they were taken to prison and charged with conspiring against the revolution. Elroy was assigned to the quarry block. Seldom did a month go by but the guards would lug him back to the circular at night, a bundle of meat and blood. How long would his body be able to absorb the indecent abuse it suffered?

A few days earlier, in one of the fields, a prisoner by the name of Reinaldo Aqui had escaped. The guards hadn't been watching as closely since they knew the inmates would soon be going home. The soldiers ended their unsuccessful search for Reinaldo four days later. Reprimanded by their superiors for their carelessness, the guards were out for blood—our blood.

When the soldiers brought us back to the prison the night after the violence at the quarry, we lined up for counting. The hat fell off of the head of Chino Aqui, Reinaldo's brother. He asked for permission to pick it up, which gave the guards all the excuse for violence they needed. After the officer gave Chino permission to retrieve his hat, Chino stepped out of the lineup, bent down to pick up the hat, and bang! They shot him.

"He planned to escape like his brother. The two of them planned it together," the lieutenant said, defying anyone to disagree. He then gave an order to have the entire block severely beaten. When the soldiers exhausted their pent-up energy and hate, the lieutenant ordered us back to the circular. Three of the brothers lay dead on the cold, stone floor. They paid the price for Reinaldo's escape and for the mass prayer meeting we'd held the night before. The deaths of our brothers in Christ had sullied our anticipated joy over our transfer back to a mainland prison.

"So many deaths—so much waste," I thought. As I considered the possibility of leaving Isle of Pines, I recalled the names and faces of those who would not be leaving with us, those who would remain a part of the island until Jesus' return.

In His Footsteps

The ferryboat whistle blasted, filling my senses with exhilaration and hope. Going home! I was going home. Even having to sit for six hours in one position in the hold of the boat didn't deaden my enthusiasm. I had no idea to what prison I'd be sent or what the living conditions might be like, but it didn't matter. Just being back on the mainland appeared as a sign that I would survive; I would one day be free. While no one dared speak, I could sense the same excitement in the other prisoners as we crowded together inside the hold of the ferry.

When the ferry anchored at Batabano pier outside of the capital city of Havana, the dock was filled with family members of the incoming prisoners straining to see their loved ones and with policemen, trained dogs, and military guards straining equally hard to prevent them from reaching the prisoners. Under strict guard, we boarded the buses. And as always, we sat in the buses for five hours, weak from hunger, thirst, and heat exhaustion. Finally the buses began to roll toward our unknown destiny. One of the drivers made a wrong turn and got lost, along with his cargo of guards, dogs, and prisoners, causing the rest of us to sit for another two hours while the prison officials frantically tried to locate the missing bus. We arrived in the city of Sagua la Grande to a hero's welcome.

Sagua la Grande, an important city in the midsection of the province of Las Villas, is in the mountainous part of Cuba, a natural shelter for many rebels who opposed Castro. When the citizens of the city learned that a contingency of political prisoners was being transferred to Sagua's prison, they flooded the streets. When the drivers tried to park the buses alongside the city streets, the people swarmed the bus, giving us all kinds of goodies—coffee, milk, cookies, candy, etc. The guards on the buses tried to stop them, but short of a massacre, there was little they could do. Finally the chief guard announced, "You may give them whatever you like, just do not board the buses."

By evening the officials decided the people of Sagua's sympathy for us was so great the government could not risk placing us there, so we were transferred to another prison before we even arrived at the first one. We were told that the Sagua Prison was too small to house us. And by ten that night, we arrived at Remedios Prison.

Once we established residence in our new quarters, we began daily worship services. We elected Gerard Alvarez, also known as "the Brother in the Faith," to lead out in our morning worships. Before becoming a Christian, G.G., as he was called, had lived a life of violence as a pimp and loan shark. But in prison he found Jesus Christ and was transformed by the power of God. His natural charisma and his desire to tell others of his new faith made him a perfect candidate to preach God's Word. Before the first week ended, neighboring civilians complained to the guards that our worship services disturbed them. Some of our neighbors worked nights, and our singing didn't allow them to sleep during the day.

The prison director punished the entire religious and political prison population for this infraction. Over the loudspeaker, he announced, "The following rules will be strictly enforced. One, you will be allowed ten minutes to eat your supper. Two, you will appear well dressed in the dining room. Three, you cannot speak to anyone. Four, you cannot sit until everyone at your table is in place, and then you must sit in the same sequence you arrived at the table. And five, you must remain seated until everyone is finished or the ten minutes has expired."

The punishment came when the dining room official began counting the ten minutes with the first table to begin eating instead of the last. This meant the majority of prisoners would either need to wolf their food down almost without chewing or go hungry, since no food could be removed from the area.

One morning they served boiled fish, a real treat. The fish contained lots of tiny bones that needed to be removed before eating it. We had managed to eat less than half of our allotment when the departure bell rang. Angry and starving, every prisoner in the room picked up his metal plate. Fish and fish bones flew in every direction. Some overturned their plates on top of the tables while others dumped the food onto the floor. A few of the bravest prisoners flung the fish against the dining room walls in protest.

Before the last piece of fish had slid down the wall onto the floor, a troop of soldiers, their rifles and bayonets leveled for action, burst into the building, shouting and beating anyone in their way. Brutally, they cleared the dining room.

Early the next morning three buses waited in the prison courtyard to take us and our meager belongings to other prisons. When the officials announced that we were being moved to another prison, we church members stuck together, knowing it would improve our chances of being housed in the same prison units. After searching each of us thoroughly, the guards ordered us to board the buses. "What happened in Sagua la Grande will never happen again," the officer in charge announced. "We will not allow anyone the opportunity to manifest his sympathies for you traitors of the state again."

Once on board, we waited to depart. All day long we waited, until ten o'clock that evening. Finally the drivers started the engines, and we left Remedios Prison behind for an unknown destination—fifty-nine days after our arrival from Isle of Pines.

We arrived at La Cabaña Prison eight hours later, suffering from the effects of heat exhaustion, hunger, and extreme tiredness. The new prison guards eyed us as we climbed off the buses the way hungry wolves might inspect a flock of sheep. Before leaving Remedios Prison, the members of the church had schemed a way to be together at the new prison. Our plan worked. We were assigned to the same gallery—patio number 2. News of our arrival preceded us, for as we entered patio number 2, the inmates in the different galleries surrounding the yard began singing in Spanish the words, "In hardships and struggles, the church always continues . . ."

This show of defiance infuriated the La Cabaña officials, since they had declared that the prisoners could not talk to one another, let alone sing. They assigned a special force to each gallery to ensure that no one spoke a word.

It took some adjustment to get acquainted with the unique problems of living at La Cabaña. The lack of sufficient food was the biggest problem. Second, with 200 prisoners housed in a gallery designed for eighty-six, personalities could not help but

clash regularly. The third adjustment came from a lack of sufficient restroom facilities and the common bathing area in the
yard that served all the surrounding galleries. The showers consisted of a long half-inch pipe that ran the length of a wall.
Smaller quarter-inch pipes protruded at appropriate intervals
from the larger pipe. These were the shower heads.

One faucet, operated by a guard, controlled the water's flow.
Soon after our arrival at La Cabaña, we learned exactly how the
showers worked. The gallery door swung open, and one of the
prison guards entered, whereupon, according to the rule, all of
the prisoners snapped to attention. The arrival of a guard usually meant trouble—either someone would be beaten or taken to
interrogation—but this time the soldier stepped inside the gallery and shouted, "Prepare for a shower."

Immediately, other guards swung the door wide open, and the
inmates dashed for the showers.

"Run, Noble," one of my friends whispered.

The instant the gate swung open, the guard operating the
faucet turned on the water and began timing the shower.

Bewildered, I looked about at the chaos. There was no privacy
and no time to prepare. It had been three or four days since I'd
been allowed to bathe, so I hurried into the fray. I had just
soaped up when the guard turned off the water. All I could do
was dry off and return to my gallery, worse than before. For
some reason, the guards did this for entertainment. The ill treatment of prisoners operated much like a musical scale, with each
gallery officer striving to inflict the highest note of discomfort
and misery possible on his charges. For all their variations to the
beatings, starvations, and humiliation, our captors never seemed
to run out of new ideas to make our lives miserable.

One morning, three days after they shuffled us from one section of the prison to another, we were conducting morning worship when a colonel, two commanders, and three captains entered patio number 2 and called the gallery directors and the
prisoners' elected representatives to the administrative offices.
We knew that one way or another, such a visit could only spell
trouble for us.

When our elected representative returned from this meeting,
he announced, "The prison officials have decided to allow your
families to visit you for your monthly visit. They may bring to

you a package of supplies weighing up to thirty-five pounds. This parcel may include three books from the approved list, writing paper, pencils . . ." He continued reading the list of approved items. Those of us who had been incarcerated for any length of time at all listened in skeptical disbelief, suspicious of their act of apparent kindness.

The visiting day proved to be all the officials promised. Yraida arrived in the large visitors' gallery, prepared by her brother to seduce me into the re-education plan. An officer sat off to one side listening as she skillfully wove her spell over me—taunting, teasing, tantalizing my senses, using my love for her as the weapon to catch and destroy me.

"Oh, God," I prayed, observing the lovely woman offering herself to me, "how can I resist?" Suddenly, as if startled awake, I realized what was happening, and with the realization came the strength to resist. "Yraida," I said, grasping her by the shoulders and holding her at arm's length, "I would prefer death before accepting what you offer!"

For an instant, pain over what we'd lost and anger at being scorned flitted across her face, but then a haughty pride settled in. She withdrew from my grasp and lifted her chin defiantly. "I have no more time to lose. You can continue to follow those people in there if you wish." She paused to change tactics. "Other Christian brothers have accepted the proposal. Are you better than them? They realize they have a duty to support their wives and kids; they know their duty."

Her accusations punched me in the softest portions of my heritage—a male's duty to support his family. Regaining my composure, I replied, "Yes, they know their duties, but I know mine. They are frustrated with their decision; I am not. They betrayed their God, but I will not betray mine!"

I had barely finished speaking when the officer listening to our conversation declared, "Your visit is over."

Uncertain I'd heard him correctly, I asked, "Is the visiting period up?"

"No, he replied, "only your visit is over."

Yraida stood up, glanced at me one more time, turned on her heel, and left the room.

When our guests left, Colonel Lemus, the prison director, assembled the prisoners and collected their gift parcels before they had even been opened. "By order of the Minister of the Interior, there are going to be some changes made—to be announced at a future date. To receive your gifts, you must agree to our conditions, and there must be a marked improvement in your behavior." The visit had proved to be a trap for all of us, a moment of pleasure to cling to, with promises of more to come if we cooperated with the military.

The conditions involved turning in our yellow uniforms that identified us as political prisoners for the blue uniforms worn by the common criminals. All of us immediately recognized the significance of the change in uniforms. It had developed out of an interesting history.

The color-coding of military uniforms had begun years earlier when Cuba gained its independence from Spain. The system's popularity died out for a time, until the government rewrote the country's constitution in 1940. At that time, it was decided to have the police force wear blue, the navy white, and the army yellow. During the 1953 rebellion, the Rural Police and the regular army had carried out most of the action, so when Castro gained control of the country in 1959, his revenge against the two branches of the military was to designate that their once-proud uniforms be worn by prisoners—blue by the common criminals and yellow by the political prisoners. The new army wore olive green.

At first the citizens of Cuba hated the prisoners who wore yellow. It was a symbol of rebellion. The revolutionary government hadn't been in charge long, however, before the people's attitude changed. The prisoners became instant heroes, and their yellow uniforms became badges of honor. Whenever the prison officials transferred one of the political prisoners to a new prison or to a hospital, he received the civilians' concern instead of their scorn.

It was only a matter of time before this growing tide of sympathy both angered and worried the Minister of the Interior and the Central Committee members. To avoid a riot or further civil disobedience, they decided to dress all the prisoners in the blue uniforms of the common prisoners.

The next morning, a fleet of trucks arrived carrying bundles of blue uniforms as well as eighty extra soldiers. I, along with the rest of the prison population, eyed the uniforms being unloaded with disgust. Obviously, the prison director expected trouble from the political and religious prisoners. Besides bringing in extra troops, he arranged for the prisoners to run a gauntlet of soldiers wielding bayonets, clubs, chains, and segments of iron pipes. He announced that at the end of the gauntlet, we would have a choice. We could enter cell number 9, remove our yellow uniforms, and take two blue uniforms, or we could enter cell number 7 and remove our yellow uniforms. All of us would be required to leave the cell clad in nothing but our underwear.

Of course, anyone who chose to wear the prison blues would give justification for his incarceration. He would be classified as a common thief, rapist, or murderer. Being religious or political dissenters set us apart, and we could not afford to lose that distinction. Of the political prisoners who ran the gauntlet and shed their uniforms, 850 chose not to wear the blues. Angry with our strong show of defiance, the captain in charge corralled all of us into two galleries that had been stripped of bunks or furniture of any kind—850 men in a space built to house eighty-six! Those who found a spot where they could sit down on the cold granite floor considered themselves lucky. In order to give everyone a chance to rest, we established a four-hour sleep rotation.

The prison officials gave us time to wear down from lack of sleep and from starvation before they began the next phase of their inquisition. Total compliance became a matter of honor for our interrogators. One by one, the guards led each of us from the gallery to the interrogation rooms, where an army officer waited, determined to break our wills.

"Alexander," the captain demanded when I appeared, "why must you be so belligerent and unreasonable? Must you challenge everything we do?"

"I am not a common prisoner."

The captain slammed his fist on the desktop. "You defy us and the revolution! The revolution is good, and you are wrong! Wrong! Wrong!"

Silently, I stared straight ahead. Nothing I could say would make any difference.

Suddenly he leaped up from the desk, grabbed for my throat, and pushed me backward. My head slammed against the concrete cinder blocks with such force that shooting stars flashed around in my head.

"Admit it!" he screamed. "Admit that you are wrong and the great revolution is right!"

I tried to turn my head to indicate my disagreement, when his fist crunched against my nose. I felt a snap; then blood spurted out all over his uniform and my bare chest. He shoved me backward once more and walked away in disgust.

"Get him out of here," the captain ordered the guard. "The miserable *plantado* [one who has been firmly planted—political prisoners who defied the government's "re-education efforts]!"

Back at the gallery, the guards continued the verbal and physical abuse. "You are a *plantado*. You do not deserve to wear clothing given you by the revolution."

Faint from the pain in my head and the loss of blood, I asked to see a doctor.

"A doctor?" The guard laughed. "*Plantados* do not deserve medical treatment. Nor will you be allowed books to read, letters from family, or monthly visitation privileges any longer—unless, of course, you . . ."

My fellow prisoners didn't wait for the end of his speech. We'd heard it so often in the past. They led me to an open spot on the floor where I could lie down and try to stop the bleeding. The last scrap of dignity had been removed from us when we chose to remain firm to what we believed. We would show them, we decided. *Plantados*? Yes, we would be *plantados*. We would defy their attempts at "re-education." For the next seventeen years I wore nothing but underwear.

The prison officials counted on the crushing summer heat, the human odors from so many men living in such close quarters, and the gnawing hunger to wear us down. Instead, after the first few days, we adjusted to our new environment by setting up rules that would enable us to live together in an orderly fashion. We elected a gallery elder to maintain order.

It has been said that in the time of trouble God's people will cling more to God. During our times of trouble, when we had no religious materials whatsoever, this was also true. The inmates flocked together to worship, to learn more of the Bible, to sing hymns, and to pray. A core of us spent every spare minute of our time orally training the new converts.

Our enemies bided their time. Winter would soon arrive. Lack of proper food, lack of clothing—we would weaken. "You will soon be begging us on your knees to 're-educate' you!" our guards chided.

As if our tormentors had satanic powers that could control the weather, the winter temperatures dropped to unbelievable lows—50°, 40°, and into the thirties (Fahrenheit). Prisoners and soldiers alike suffered in the unusual cold, and the *plantados* suffered the worst.

"I can't go on," one young man whispered through clenched teeth. "I'm so cold."

"I know, brother," one of the church elders assured him. "But together we can make it—together."

"I—I—I am not so sure about that," the younger man replied, glancing out into the yard, where a group of soldiers stood warming their hands over an open fire. "Maybe I could . . . just for a short time . . ." His words drifted off longingly.

"Yes," another prisoner answered, his voice quivering from weakness as well as from the cold. "Only until spring; then we could change our minds."

"No," the elder argued, "you will not be allowed to rescind your confession. Please, stand firm. We can make it together."

Conversations such as this occurred more and more frequently as the temperatures continued to drop, until they reached the incredible, all-time low of 3°C (about 38°F).

The criminal prisoners had quite a bit more freedom than the political prisoners. Among other things, since they were housed in a different part of the prison, they were issued daily newspapers to read. However, the prisoners between the two sections quickly established a highly efficient system for smuggling papers from them to us.

Not only did these newspapers provide us with some contact with the outside world; they also provided us with warmth.

We stuffed old newspapers around the cracks of the door to cut down on the cold breezes blowing through the cells. The prison director ordered that nothing could cover the prison doors, yet we persisted. Each morning, the guards scooped up the newspapers, claiming that they blocked their view of our activities. Ironically, this move worked against the government's plan instead of for it, implanting steel in the backbones of the *plantados* who had been seriously considering accepting the government's "re-education" plan in exchange for warmth and clothing. The Spirit of God drew us closer together.

It is amazing just how much of one's body a handkerchief can cover, how much heat one human body expels, the warmth one can receive from a single roll of toilet tissue. Each morning, the guards searched our cells and removed anything we might have used for survival the previous night. They would then use whatever they found to warm themselves.

When we refused to give in or to die, the officials intensified their efforts by removing the only personal freedom we had left, our sleep. They installed loudspeakers at the gates to our gallery. Every two hours throughout the night, the loudspeakers roared to life to the tune of an ancient folk song that claimed, "More than a thousand years, many more, you'll have to wait. I do not know if eternity will have an end . . ."

A string of propaganda from the health department followed. "Prisoners in such undernourished condition, sleeping on the floor, will catch colds. Untreated, these colds can very easily become tuberculosis. With the loss of blood, you will become anemic. If this anemia continues, you will contract leukemia. The government docs not want this to happen to you. But you have a free will. If you accept the government's plan, you are accepting life; if you reject our offer, you are choosing a slow but sure death."

Many good men believed the government's propaganda and gave in. As they fell away, those remaining pressed together. Night after night, for more than two months, the routine continued. Life grew more impossible with each passing day. Something had to be done—but what? What could a bunch of starving, half-naked political castoffs do to put pressure on the Cuban prison officials, who seemingly held all the cards?

Life in the House of the Dead

The loudspeakers broke into my sleep again. The lack of sleep drained all of us of our energies. "Something has to be done," I decided, "but what? What could we do? What advantage do we have over our tormentors?" The only thing we had that we refused to give them was our cooperation. I realized that for some reason, getting the political prisoners to conform to the "re-education" program was vital to their happiness, maybe even important to their prestige and career advancement in Fidel Castro's new government.

The text of Matthew 5:6 came to my mind. "Blessed are they which do hunger and thirst after righteousness: for they shall be filled." A food strike! That just might be the answer. We certainly wouldn't be missing much pleasure by denying ourselves the paltry meals now offered. Before I could share my idea with anyone else, another brother suggested the same thing, and another, and another. Spontaneously, a large number of us had come up with the same decision at the same time. We presented the idea to the rest of the inmates, warned them of the possible consequences, and took a vote. Ninety-three percent of the group agreed—the next morning we would begin our strike.

We listened for the telltale squeak of the metal-wheeled cart that delivered our food since we no longer were allowed to take our meals in the dining room used by the common prisoners. A hush fell over the gallery as the soldier pushing the food cart neared our gallery. We watched the door open. The breakfast of the day consisted of brown sugar dissolved in hot water and bread sliced so thin that one could literally see through it.

The soldier called out, "Come for your breakfast."

No one answered.

"Whoever wants breakfast, come and get it now," the kitchen sergeant roared. "The rest will be going back."

Again no one spoke.

Rafael Alzamora, the inmate in charge of distributing our meals, stepped forward. "They don't want it."

"What about you?" the soldier asked.

"Neither do I."

"Is this a strike?"

Rafael paused a moment and lifted one eyebrow a trifle. "It could be—everything depends on you all."

The sergeant's eyes narrowed as he glared about the gallery at the stone-faced prisoners. "Do you know the consequences?" He left without waiting for an answer. During the next few hours we sang together and prayed.

At nine o'clock the soldier returned with our lunch and with his sergeant, a short, stocky, red-faced man who apparently was unaccustomed to being opposed. This time I was the group's spokesman. As the soldier and I went through the same dialogue we'd had at breakfast, he flew into a rage, shouting over and over again, "This is a strike! This is a strike! This is a strike!" Throwing his hat on the floor, he jumped up and down on it like a spoiled child throwing a temper tantrum.

The sergeant was required to report a food strike to the main office, and that meant trouble. And trouble in the prison meant all military personnel would be on twenty-four-hour call—all leaves canceled.

Supper arrived with the same result. Each time a meal arrived during the next three days, more prison officials came to witness our rebellion and to scream and threaten us. After venting their anger, the officers turned on their heels and left.

On the fourth day, the guards no longer brought the usual prison food but the much more tempting fare fed to the guards. They placed the better food by our door so we could see and smell it. When we refused to weaken, they carted it off to the dining room. That night, we had just begun our evening worship when the loudspeakers came on.

"Your attention please, your attention please, to all the inmates on strike in yard number 2. This is counsel from the Health Department of the Interior Ministry. After three days on strike, your metabolism can be changed. If you are fat, your body will sustain itself from that source. If you aren't, your body will begin stripping nourishment from your stomach. Your gastric fluids will eat away at the walls of your stomach, producing ulcers, cancer, and other such diseases. The loss of vitality will make it impossible for you to ever recover."

Pound after pound—as we lost physical strength, we gained spiritual strength. We recited the words of Paul in 2 Corinthians 4:16-18: "For which cause we faint not; but though our outward man perish, yet the inward man is renewed day by day. For our light affliction, which is but for a moment, worketh for us a far more exceeding and eternal weight of glory; while we look not at the things which are seen, but at the things which are not seen: for the things which are seen are temporal; but the things which are not seen are eternal."

We fortified our spiritual strength with prayer as our physical muscles deteriorated from starvation, and we were busy using our intellectual muscles to alert others to our plight. Understanding the Cuban Communist party's desire for good press, we devised a prison postal service. We wrote letters to organizations like the International Red Cross and Amnesty International using the inside of cigarette packs and other scraps of paper. We bored a hole in each of our walls, then passed a long black cord from one gallery to the next all the way to patio number 1 in yard 4. Then we folded our letters into small rectangles, hung them on the cord, and slid them to prisoners who were about to be released, who, in turn, smuggled them out of the prison. By the time the prison officials discovered our communication line and emptied out the cells on either side of ours, the letters were well on their way to their intended destination.

On the thirteenth day, a number of officers of different ranks conducted an inspection. Some of our weaker brethren accepted the uniform and the "re-education" program and were immediately transferred to other prisons. When the military brass had concluded their inspection, Colonel Pacheco, the commanding officer in charge, snarled, "These prisoners are getting nourishment from some unknown source. Otherwise, they'd be dead by now!"

He then ordered that two soldiers be stationed inside each gallery to discover just who might be smuggling in food for us. Their presence hampered our conversations. We could no longer discuss our problems with one another. However, we continued holding our prayer meetings in front of them, praying, singing, and reciting Bible texts. When Colonel Pacheco checked back with his men, one of the soldiers admitted that Someone was entering the cell regularly.

"I haven't seen Him, but this Man, Jesus, comes every evening at sunset," the soldier explained. "The prisoners form a circle around Him and call to Him. I think He must be the one bringing them food since I sometimes hear them saying, 'Thank You, Jesus.'"

We chuckled to ourselves, understanding just how the soldier could come up with such a conclusion—Jesus is a very common name for males in the Spanish culture.

On day fifteen, Colonel Pacheco ordered the soldiers to shoot us if we conducted any more general worships. To avoid unnecessary problems, we conducted our worships by dividing into small groups of three or four scattered about the gallery.

The next morning, Colonel Pacheco, along with Vice-Colonel Ofarril and other high-ranking officers, entered our gallery. After the guards gathered us together, Vice-Colonel Ofarril took charge.

"I don't know what is happening to all of you. We offered you visiting privileges, and you blew it. We were willing to supply you with the new blue uniforms so you could continue having normal visiting rights, and you refused to accept them." He sighed a deep sigh of disgust. "It's your turn now. Here is Colonel Pacheco. Tell him what you want."

The officers scanned the group of silent prisoners. No one budged.

Vice-Colonel Ofarril attacked our spirituality. "You say you are religious and political prisoners, not common criminals, but you are nothing. You have no discipline. If you had a bit of . . . not instruction, but education, at least, you would answer me." Waving his hand in frustration, he added, "Even a bunch of dogs would bark when spoken to. You are nothing more than dead bodies."

At this point, one of the political prisoners, Francisco Rodriguez, answered, "You are right, because even dogs at their masters' homes are treated better than we are treated in this country."

Ofarril glared at Francisco. "We have done all we can within our power to help you."

"Then, perhaps, it is not you who are treating us worse than animals; it is your government headed by Fidel Castro!"

Ofarril doubled up his fists and lunged at Francisco, but the other officers stepped between him and the prisoner.

Francisco threw another slur at the vice-colonel, and Ofarril struggled to break free of his men's hold. "Let me at 'im. I'm gonna jam those words down your throat, Rodriguez!"

Accustomed to having their word be law to the prisoners, all the officers found it more and more difficult to restrain themselves. Ofarril and Francisco continued their verbal battle, inciting both the prisoners and the officers to the point of riot—all except Colonel Pacheco, who remained cool and detached from the action.

Just before the gallery broke into a major fistfight, Colonel Pacheco turned to Ofarril. "Ofarril, you can leave now. I will see about this from here on out."

Fire flashed in Ofarril's eyes. For a moment, he looked as if he might take on the colonel himself. Instead, he regained his military stance, snapped to attention, saluted, and left.

Turning to Francisco, Pacheco said, "All of this could have been avoided. I came to give you a list of concessions." His soothing voice and sympathy-filled eyes fooled many of the younger prisoners.

"If you will recant from the strike and change your attitude, I will reinstate your medical assistance and your visiting privileges. I will see to it that you receive better food and television twice a week, and I will consider whatever other improvements you might suggest." Young and gullible, many of the prisoners believed him and were transferred from our group. Later we learned that one step after another, each of them had eventually denied their faith in God and had accepted the re-education plan completely.

Eight-hundred and thirty remained faithful. On the seventeenth, the piped-in water was turned off. We had no water for either the restroom or for drinking. Some inmates began losing their hair, yet they persisted. After our prison postal service ended, we developed a new plan. We folded our letters into tiny rectangles as before, then made a rubber slingshot to shoot them across the walls. Beyond the concrete walls, relatives of the prisoners gathered each day, trying to gain permission to visit their loved ones. They used bribery, sex, and threats to accomplish their goals and were only too willing to pass on our letters to the proper organizations.

On day twenty of our hunger strike, shortly after two o'clock, 200 soldiers marched into yard number 2. While they herded many of us out into the yard, the commanding officer ordered other prisoners to stay behind and watch as the soldiers searched the galleries, even tearing up portions of the floor. They were searching for a radio. Somehow, word of our hunger strike had leaked out to the International Red Cross—how, the prison officials did not know. The Red Cross authorities demanded to speak with us, but the revolutionary government refused. The Department of the Interior for the Revolution decided that the protesters were holding out because we had somehow discovered that the Red Cross and Amnesty International were inquiring about us, hence the source of our moral strength—or as they saw it, our stubbornness.

In the days that followed, the prison officials rounded up our family members and brought them to the prison without our knowledge. The officers told our loved ones about the hunger strike. "They are being totally unreasonable. They don't want to see you. We offered to allow you to visit them, but they didn't accept our offer. They desire to be masters for the Imperialists," the prison commander lied. "The Revolutionary government has gone the second mile with them, sending for you to see if you can talk some sense into them. See these clothes here?" They were the clothes we had been wearing when arrested, or so a prisoner who worked in the military laundry told us later.

"We are willing to give them a five-day pass to go home with you if only they will say Yes. I know you don't believe us, but if you want, you may send them a note. We will give it to your relative."

One relative asked, "How can we know that they have received it?"

"We will allow them to answer it," the officer explained. The prisoners' families had no idea how deceitful and devilish these officers were. Many believed the lies and began writing notes. The guards read each note, and if the prisoner didn't answer the way the officials wanted, they would write their own answers in the prisoner's name, giving false answers. We longed to see our loved ones but not on those conditions. After the military officers set the stage for their charade, the guards led us into a small room where our families waited.

I watched a friend's agonizing struggle as his wife knelt before him, pleading with him to give in. "Take the five-day pass. Come home with me. If you don't," she screamed, "I will kill myself."

All the while, the officer sat off to one side at a table, watching and sneering as if to say, "With this one, it will work."

My friend weakened and took the five-day pass. When he returned to the prison, he discovered that the strike had ended the very next day after he left.

We learned later that news of the strike had filtered out of the prison and out of Cuba. The international press reported it around the world, thus discrediting the Cuban Communist regime. The Cuban government received orders from Russia to end the strike. Was it possible that the monster Fidel Castro had created might be forced by international opinion to change its image, to develop a face of humanity?

As with most bureaucracies, blame for the strike filtered down the ranks, resting finally on the prison director. The Minister of the Interior removed the prison director from office and placed another man in command. The new prison director immediately restored proper medical aid, family visits, and books to read. Later we learned that the deposed director had a nervous breakdown and has since required years of psychiatric treatment.

Almost immediately they enriched our diet. With our relatives' visit pending, the new director wanted to be certain we looked vigorously healthy. One of the most popular additives to our food was brewer's yeast to quickly add the much-needed weight to our skeletons. The new director also wished to improve the prison's overall image by bringing in beds, mattresses, pillows, and sheets for us to use.

While we wanted to see our loved ones, we didn't relish the idea of visiting them while wearing only underpants. That's when we got the idea to make Bermuda shorts and shirts out of our sheets. We viewed our tailoring project quite proudly when we finished. We felt respectable again.

The first visit after the strike will always be poignant to me. We assembled in patio number 2, family and prisoners alike, and conducted a mass praise service. Tears flowed uncontrolled and words failed as we raised our voices together singing hymns such as "Amazing Grace" and "Old Hundredth." After our worship service we broke off into smaller family groups to hear about all the precious moments we'd missed since we'd been imprisoned, about the loss of favorite uncles, aunts, or grandparents, and the births of new family members who we might never meet. Our time together ended all too quickly. We kissed goodbye and promised to meet again in a month. Even life at La Cabaña could be tolerated knowing that just thirty days hence I'd be allowed to see friends and family again and to hear news from the outside world.

The visits came to an end after only a few short months. Early one February morning, a voice over the loudspeakers awakened us from sleep by calling out a list of names—mine among them. "What do they want me for now?" I wondered. I searched through my memory to discover something I might have done wrong, but nothing came to mind. I didn't have long to wait.

After breakfast, a lieutenant and his aide strode up to the gallery and unlocked the door. "Humberto Noble Alexander, collect your belongings immediately. You are being transferred to another prison."

Belongings? What belongings? While I wrapped my few possessions into my spare homemade shirt and tied it shut, my brothers in Christ formed a prayer circle one last time. I looked around the circle of fellow sufferers and swallowed hard to choke back my tears. We'd been through so much. Shoulder to shoulder, we'd sung hymns of praise; we'd prayed for strength; we'd shivered in the cold; and we'd almost starved together. I could feel their love giving me courage to face whatever might lie ahead for me.

The closeness we shared in that prison cell transcended religion, race, or political persuasion. These men were my family. I looked into individual faces as we embraced for the last time. Would we meet again this side of eternity? Perhaps some would, but not all.

"Come on, Alexander, move out," the lieutenant growled.

I turned to leave, glanced into his dark, emotionless eyes, and wondered, "Can he really be so hard, so devoid of humanity as to feel nothing?"

They marched us out into the courtyard and loaded us into cellular trucks similar to dog carriers. A guard loaded four of us into one of the cages and locked the door. More prisoners filled the other four cages. The driver and a soldier occupied the front seat. In the middle seat, a corporal kept watch over the prisoners. Unknown to us, they had laced our morning rations with Ipeca, a product that produces nausea, vomiting, diarrhea, and headaches.

After thirty hours, the trucks rolled to a stop at Boniato Prison. Boniato Prison had a reputation as the worst prison in Cuba. Like in the Nazi prison camps during World War II, Boniato's prison officials conducted experiments on the prisoners. They collected data on how long the human body could survive, first without food, and later, as the prisoners weakened, without water, before dying.

Weak and dehydrated from the medicine we'd been given and lame from our cramped quarters, we staggered out of our cages to face the prison keeper and his staff. The prison guards looked us over as if we were merchandise in the marketplace.

"Well, boys," the prison keeper curled his lip into a snarl, "you are in Boniato now. So forget all the benefits you enjoyed at La Cabaña. Here you will earn privilege according to your actions."

We understood. All the glorious promises made after our hunger strike would not be fulfilled. The monster of Communism had not changed its nature. The fiend had only masked its evil long enough to allow the international community time to forget and move on to a new cause.

The location of the Boniato Prison, in a small valley surrounded by hills, guaranteed our torturers complete privacy as they carried out their atrocities on the inmates. The prison compound contained five two-story buildings, each divided into four pavilions.

Armed guards marched me to pavilion 5-C. Inside the iron-barred gates, a long hallway stretched out before us. Thirty-nine solid steel doors lined each side of the corridor. They took me to cell number 26. I waited while one of the guards hauled out a giant ring of keys from his pocket, unlocked the padlock, and slid the iron bar back. The second guard pulled open the door and pushed me roughly inside. The quarter-inch iron door clanged shut behind me, followed by the grating sound of metal sliding against metal and the click of a padlock snapping shut. The cell, about five feet by ten feet, had one lightbulb hanging from the ceiling. It was controlled from the office. When the officer so chose, it was daytime, and when he wanted it to be night, it was night. By turning the switch, the light would go from dim to bright, brighter, and brightest, to complete darkness.

There were two sleeping berths in the cell, an upper and a lower one. In the back corner of the cell, a young man cringed against the wall in a tight fetal position.

"Stay away," he whimpered. "Don't hurt me."

"I am not here to hurt you," I assured him, glancing around at the sparse conditions. "It looks like we are going to be cellmates for a while. My name is Alexander—Noble Alexander."

Cautiously, he began to unwind his body, his dark-ringed, hollowed-out eyes sizing me up.

"So," I dropped my pack and glanced around the cell, "which bunk do you prefer, upper or lower?"

He glanced toward the lower canvas.

"Fine." I picked up my bundle and placed it on the canvas that would be mine. "Uh, what do you want me to call you, friend? What's your name?"

He scowled as if trying to decide just how far to trust me. "Calixto Orihuela," he mumbled, curling himself into a ball on his own bed.

In the next few days, Calixto revealed more about himself. He said he'd been arrested for being a rebel leader's aide and condemned to die. He watched as the firing squad executed two of his fellow aides. Then, a last-minute reprieve commuted all three of their sentences to thirty years. Unfortunately, two of them had already been executed. However, seeing his friends die and the torture he endured during the next few days caused his mind to snap. At times he was lucid and reasonable, but at other times he would lie on his bunk, his eyes wide open, and stare at the ceiling without saying a word. When in this state, sometimes he would neither sleep nor speak for weeks at a time. The only food he'd eat I had to force upon him. And there were times when he'd rage out of control.

Calixto needed my constant attention—my nursing skills—when he drifted out of reality or out of control, and my pastoral skills when he was conscious of his surroundings. But it was the work of the Holy Spirit that, in time, caused him to accept Jesus as his Saviour.

My first day at Boniato began at 6:00 a.m. with the first counting. Any prisoner who did not instantly jump to his feet when the whistle sounded was beaten severely and given no medical care. Following the counting, a troop of soldiers marched into the hallway, the doors swung open, and each prisoner received a beating. They repeated the routine at six that evening, and each morning and evening for the next month.

Our cell had a small window on the back wall. The windows in the other cells had been covered with iron sheeting, so when our captors discovered our luxury, they moved Calixto and me to a new pavilion and a new dungeon. In this pavilion, each iron door along the corridors had a small window cut into it through which our meals were passed. Since we were locked up twenty-four hours a day, the window became my pulpit. Through this narrow slot I preached the Word of God. Each morning and evening the faces of prisoners praising God could be seen pressing against their doors. On the Sabbath, we conducted a general service, and on Sunday, a class in Bible history. Those of us who knew texts from God's Word would recite a text, and the converts would repeat the text after us. A new church began to grow.

La Cabaña, the Isle of Pines, Remedios, Boniato—each prison had its own hellish identifying feature, much like an individual's fingerprints. However, the worst torture I experienced came while at Boniato—not from the prison officials or their sadistic guards, but from my precious Yraida. It was here, in 1972, that our divorce became final. Up until the news of the final decree arrived, I refused to believe that my beautiful wife, the mother of my son, would really go through with such an action. In her divorce action, she claimed I had tried to "assassinate her prime minister." While divorce is common in many prisoners' lives, I didn't believe it could happen to me. After all, I was a Christian; Yraida was a Christian; Christians do not divorce. They stay married for life.

"This can't be happening!" I shouted at my friends. "The Communists must be forcing her to say these things. Or maybe it's all a trick to destroy me." I grasped at every straw I could imagine to negate the truthfulness of the divorce decree. I had to believe that she still loved me; I had to!

"The divorce is real," my friends argued. "You are a fool if you do not believe it."

The older prisoners understood how a fellow inmate reacts to the news of a pending divorce or the announcement of one's death sentence. He either sinks into deep depression and possible suicide or lashes out in defiance. Either reaction can and will destroy him.

"Leave me alone," I snarled at my brothers in Christ. "I just want to be alone!"

"No, Noble," my friends insisted, "we are staying right with you through this. We love you, and it isn't safe for you to be alone right now."

I tried to argue. I wanted to fight someone—preferably a guard. Death and danger had lost their bite for me. A soldier's bullet would ease the gut-wrenching pain I felt deep inside my soul. "Why go on living? I've lost my wife, my son—everything! My only remaining family live more than a thousand miles away in another country, and I may never see them again anyway."

As time went on, we were allowed more and more to be together outside of our cells. My friends stayed constantly by my side, even as I sank into a depression, deeper than any I'd ever experienced. Life in the tiger cage, in the marble quarry, in the cesspool, or in the dungeons had been nothing compared to the despair I felt at this time. "How will I survive? Why would I want to survive?" I asked myself. Yet slowly I began to realize that while my earthly family had been removed from me, I had a host of brothers, not given by a father and mother, but by God.

A gentle touch on the shoulder, a sympathetic smile, a pat on the back, eased the agony. And when compassion failed to get through, they resorted to mocking. "You will let the Communist monsters win in the end? What kind of man are you, anyway? Where is that strength you've always preached about? Come on, Pastor, pull yourself together!"

Rolando Fuentes, the head deacon, forced me to see my duty. "Pastor, stop thinking about Yraida. Come, do your duty for us before you lose it all."

Somehow the mention of my nickname—Pastor—reminded me of my calling. Daily, the guards brought in new prisoners. These men hungered after the hope the gospel could give them. Worse yet, lately it seemed that the Castro regime had run out of adults and had taken to arresting children barely in their teens. The guards claimed they'd been arrested for petty thievery—something I doubted. I felt a special mission to these confused and frightened young men. Also, the prisoners I counseled and prayed with, who teetered on the brink of a decision for Christ, were watching to see if my faith would see me through.

I remembered the promises of Psalm 27:10-14 and the faithful examples of Hebrews 11, especially verses 33-37. I realized I had to rise above my grief, or my ministry to these men would be lost. If the "pastor's" faith failed during times of trouble, how could they trust theirs to see them through their times of trouble?

The Family

Ghosts of Yraida and my lost love haunted my dreams. I had to know. I had to find out for myself, I decided, just why she had divorced me. I smuggled a note out to her demanding to know her reasons. Her reply ripped me apart.

"Noble, I couldn't wait any longer. If you do not wish to accept the re-education plan, then neither our son nor I are going to put up with your stubbornness any longer. You have to choose," she wrote. "I have stopped attending church, and your son is now a member of the Youth Communist Party—a pioneer for Castro. I have become acquainted with a considerate man, an army captain. He has asked me to marry him, and I have accepted."

I read her letter over and over again. It seemed so unreal. My thoughts drifted back to the day we met at the Marianao church at choir rehearsal—December 28, 1958. Instantly attracted to her vivaciousness and her obvious spirit, I had wrestled with my thoughts that night. Could this be the woman God intended for me? I invited her out on a date; she brought her sister along. The more we dated during the next few months, the more certain I was that Yraida was the woman I would spend the rest of my life loving. We were married on August 3, 1959. And now, thirteen years later, I must somehow let her go.

In my reply to her letter, I tried to explain why I could not conform to the re-education plan, why I must remain a *plantado*. I ended the letter with, "I prefer my Jesus to silver or gold, I prefer to serve Him to endless gold."

My prison family sustained me throughout my crisis. Claiming the promise that Jesus made as He ascended into heaven, "Lo, I am with you always," I moved zombielike through the prison's daily round of torment. Whenever I threatened to break or slip backward, a brother was always there to prod me out of my despair. Slowly I recovered. The work of the infant church at Boniato forced me back to life. The church became my wife and my son.

About this time I met Andres Gomez, a lawyer and former ambassador to a number of Latin American countries. When Fidel Castro won the revolution, Brother Andres was sent to France as the Cuban ambassador. As the Cuban government took on an uncomfortably reddish hue, Andres and others of his colleagues who had been exiled to Europe conspired to invade Cuba and retake it.

In 1961, before the Bay of Pigs invasion, Andres traveled to the United States, then secretly entered Cuba in order to pave the way for the invasion. Caught, tried, and sentenced to death by a firing squad, Andres awaited his fate. When the news of his sentence leaked out to other countries, the presidents of the countries where he'd served over the years appealed his death decree. The resulting pressure caused the Central Committee to change his sentence to thirty years of hard labor.

During the war for independence against Spain between 1895 and 1902, Andres's grandfather, Maximo Gomez, had been the leader of the Cuban struggle. Maximo would have been the first Cuban president, but when asked to assume the position, he declined with the words, "It is my work to emancipate, not govern."

Andres was a sincere Christian gentleman who had been educated in Catholic schools of his homeland. He and I began holding religious services back to back. I would preach to the Protestant prisoners, and he would preach to the Catholics. Our worship services attracted the attention of the prison director. Certain that one or more of the inmates in our unit had smuggled in a Bible, he ordered a search-and-destroy mission. The soldiers found no Bibles. Furious, the director announced over the loudspeakers, "You will pay, you know, for every action brings a reaction."

When the director discovered that some of the worship leaders did not eat pork, he went to the nearest farm and bought a number of sick pigs that the farmer had intended to destroy. For two meals a day, the cook served pork for us to eat. Those who chose to eat the diseased flesh took sick and were given no medical attention, while those of us who did not eat the meat grew weaker from starvation.

"What would God have of us?" a new convert shouted in frustration. "Would He have us starve to death? Will that honor Him?" Other inmates joined in.

I had no answers. What did God want? Would this be the end of us? Would all our vows to stay alive until we again lived in freedom be nothing more than the hysterical wish of defiant children? I sympathized with their distress, especially with the younger ones. I had been young at the time of my arrest, but I had aged quickly. I could hardly remember what it felt like to be young and free. Would I ever feel that way again?

"Pastor," Enrique Correa, one of the older prisoners, interrupted my musings. "What we need here is a morale booster, don't you think? I have an idea."

"Yes?"

"Look," he reasoned, "we have all come from different backgrounds. We each have different surnames, yet we are living together under one roof as one family."

"True."

"Perhaps we need to get better acquainted. Let's learn all that we can about one another," he suggested. "We can teach one another about our occupations, our trades, our individual talents and proficiencies—whatever skills we possess—kind of like we did at the Isle of Pines with our university. Then, when we are finally released, we will be knowledgeable in all sorts of topics."

Seven of us decided to begin a program called *La Familia*—"The Family." A brother named Estaban Kaisser had an astounding memory, truly blessed of God, and a talent for public speaking. A former boxing promoter, Estaban could give a blow-by-blow account of the bouts of every Cuban champion and his challengers. We elected Brother Estaban to be our group historian.

Pastor Luis Rodriguez, who still remains in prison in Cuba today, taught homiletics; José Carreno taught journalism. An engineer, Arnaldo Mangado, taught chemistry, and Aldo Cabrera instructed us in health and temperance. We studied agriculture under the tutelage of Pablo Avilis, and we spent many hours enjoying the talents of Mario del Toro, a professional entertainer. Andres Gomez acted as a lawyer for the group.

On the first day of the week, each of the teachers taught us for a half hour to forty-five minutes. We would memorize their lectures word for word. Occasionally, when we managed to find a scrap of paper, we wrote down everything we could remember. The various courses of study lifted our depression, eased our boredom, and kept our minds from deteriorating.

Up to this point, I had never seen anyone die of starvation. Once witnessed, the memory would stay with me forever. Men's bodies swelled beyond recognition. The first to die was our historian, Esteban. Two days later, Israel Martinez, the youngest in our section, succumbed. By this time another prisoner, J. C. Correno, had swollen to where he resembled a monster from an old Hollywood movie. We stood helplessly by as J. C. grew more and more grotesque. Finally his body began to release the water buildup. In twenty-four hours he lost fifty pounds, yet he lived.

The guards from our pavilion reported our deteriorating condition to the prison director. Concerned with his own image as prison commandant and fearing the possibility of adverse information leaking to the international press, the director sent three officers to question us and to give us a physical examination. The officers didn't waste time with the prisoners who were already too weak. They left them to die. They examined and questioned the rest of us, trying to make us promise that we would cease to worship. A few desperate men chose not to suffer any longer and betrayed their ideals. These men were instantly removed from our midst. What happened to them after they left us, I do not know. I do know, however, that it was with sadness, not censure, that we said farewell. No one can be truly certain of his faith and his endurance until he is forced to test them.

We who continued to resist were transferred to an isolation ward. The reason? Preparing to hold the first congress of the Communist party of Cuba, the Central Committee was afraid that our hunger strike might unmask the carefully designed façade they wished to present to the world community.

A special detachment of soldiers guarded our section of the prison to prevent any unauthorized communication from escaping to the outside world. Instead of taking us to the general prison clinic to visit the doctors, the doctors came to our dungeon to examine us. They immediately began pumping all kinds of nutrients into us to build up our systems in record time. But it didn't work. At the same time that the prison director ordered a medical dispensary to be set up on one side of our holding area so he could report to the Central Committee that we were being properly cared for, he also arranged that a special kitchen be set up across from our cell. From that kitchen, our captors piped carbon monoxide and other poisonous gases into our cells. When we complained, the captain shrugged, then assured us that they were searching for better quarters.

During the hunger strike and the months that followed, our once-robust church dwindled in number to less than thirty. I knew from Scripture that "many would fall away," not by the will of the Lord, but by the will of the individuals themselves. Even the strongest lights were not immune, including brothers we had thought to be the very pillars supporting God's church in exile. These capitulations filled us witn astonishment, then an over-whelming sadness, which lasted for days. Yet we continued to worship regardless of the opposition.

One evening as we gathered in the center of the gallery for worship, a guard sat in the sniper's cage counting the number of prisoners attending the meeting. We had just finished singing the opening hymn, "Trust and Obey," when a soldier appeared at the gallery door.

"All of you cult members, get out here and line up!" he ordered.

We glanced at one another, then down at the floor. We knew what would follow his command—we would be taken to the dungeon for punishment.

Since I had been leading out in the worship service, I led the way out into the courtyard. The others followed. Once outside, we waited as the soldier took count.

"There are only twenty of you here," he announced. "I counted thirty of you in there. Where are the other ten?"

I gazed down at my feet, then across the prison yard at the far wall to avoid catching the soldier's eye—all the while praying that God would give me strength for the trial to come. I knew that the inmates surrounding me were doing exactly the same thing. By now every prisoner who was not a part of the unfolding drama in the courtyard stood in the gallery, watching.

Marching back and forth in front of us, he shouted again, "Where are the other ten prisoners who attended your meeting?"

The soldier knew, and we knew, that no one would betray a fellow inmate to an officer. If ten of our number had managed to fade into the shadows unnoticed, we would not be the ones to squeal on them. Any inmate who "stool pigeoned" on a fellow prisoner would at least be shunned by the entire prison community for the rest of his prison stay or perhaps even killed in his sleep. Only the Christian community would accept a prisoner who foolishly confided in a guard, yet even the brothers would be careful with what they said while they were around him.

The soldier paced back and forth again, waving his rifle threateningly before our faces. "If those ten inmates do not appear immediately, I am going to chastise the entire gallery! You will be placed in the dungeon."

Now we had a serious problem. While no one would report a brother, neither did anyone want to be beaten or put in the dungeon for another prisoner's infraction of the rules—especially those prisoners who had no interest in Christianity.

"Look!" The guard stopped in front of me, his face inches from mine. "You and your cult are being unreasonable and bringing nothing but trouble to the rest of the prisoners in the gallery. You may say that it is the guards who are harassing you, but you are bringing the trouble on yourselves when you break the prison rules. Why do you continue to do it?"

Staring straight ahead, I continued to pray.

At that moment, as if touched by the Holy Spirit, an inmate who had never once attended a meeting or showed any interest at all in Christianity walked over to where we stood. "I am one of the thirty men, sir," he announced.

A second inmate, also not of the church family, joined us, a third, a fourth, a fifth, and so on until more than fifty prisoners insisted they'd attended the meeting. The guard's face reddened with the addition of each prisoner. Now the problem the guard had tried to cause for us became an even larger problem for him. With only ninety dungeon cells and forty already occupied, he had no place to put us all. Even if they cleared the entire dungeon, there would not be room for everyone!

Furious, frustrated, and frightened at the situation he'd provoked, the soldier went to find his superior officer and never returned.

The inmates who came to our rescue started attending the daily worship services, doubling and tripling our numbers. While the ten who faded into the shadows never returned, more than fifty stepped in to take their places. In the weeks to come, when I thought of the brothers who fell by the wayside, I would also remember the message in Revelation 3:11 about those who may take our places and receive our crowns. And while I felt sadness for my brothers who turned away, I knew I could trust the promise in Romans 8:28 that "all things work together for good to them that love God."

During one of our numerous hunger strikes, a guard marched me to one of the main offices and told me to enter. Expecting the worst, I opened the door and walked in. An officer sat to one side of the room. Suddenly I stopped short and stared in disbelief. There, on the far side of the small cubicle, sat my ex-wife, Yraida, holding a small boy on her lap. She stared back in shock. Her face reddened as her gaze scanned my scarred, emaciated body, clad only in undershorts.

Suddenly I remembered my lack of clothing and blushed uncomfortably. "What are you doing here?" I asked.

"Are you not ashamed to be like that?" She waved her hand toward the brief clothing I wore.

I straightened noticeably. "I am not like that!" I said, emphasizing the word *that* in the same way she had. "It is your people who keep me like that!"

Flustered, yet indignant, she changed her attack. "Just why did you send for me—being in that condition? I am remarried, and this is our son. What if he tells his father that I went to see a naked man?"

"I didn't send for you." I fought to control the anger seeping into my voice. "Your people did all of this. The last person I expected to meet when I opened that door was you. I thought they were taking me to be questioned by the officer or something."

The officer, seeing our annoyance with one another, realized the error and stood up. "This visit is canceled." Turning to the guard who had brought me to the office, he ordered, "Take Alexander back to his department."

I later learned that Yraida had been sent for, along with the relatives of other strikers, in hopes of breaking the strike. Unfortunately for the prison officials, they didn't know of our divorce and her subsequent remarriage, so their plan backfired.

Back in my cell, I couldn't help but compare my memories of the gentle, loving Yraida I'd married with the angry, frustrated woman I had met in the office. It was true. Everyone was a victim of the Communist monster. No one could escape.

While some dreams were shattered, God fulfilled others. Two Adventist pastors came to visit me and Dr. Pedro de Armas, a former Cuban Adventist church official who was in the same prison with me, though on a different floor. News of the church that had been raised up in the prison had reached beyond the prison walls, and a number of my brothers in Christ made arrangements for these three ministers to ordain me. The biggest obstacle was that I lived on the fourth floor, and Dr. de Armas lived on the first floor. This meant we had different visiting hours. I arranged with the guards to go out during the first-floor visiting hours, and the guards, thinking my desire to speak with non-*plantados* might mean I was weakening, gave their permission.

I stepped up to Pastor de Armas and introduced myself. He, in turn, introduced me to the other two ministers. For a few minutes they quizzed me about my prison ministry. They spoke of Matthias in Acts 1:24, 25 and of 2 Corinthians 3:1-6, then ordained me as a minister of the gospel of the Seventh-day Adventist Church.

A joy like I'd never experienced before engulfed me. Though it had taken many years, the dreams of my youth were fulfilled. Noting my excitement, Pastor de Armas warned, "The service will need to be confirmed by the conference to become official. I'll get word to you when your ordination becomes official."

In spite of the necessary delay, I couldn't contain my joy. Whenever I'd imagined my ordination service, I'd pictured it occurring at a large church gathering, never inside a prison! Two weeks later, the guards herded all of us out into the prison yard for a cell search. From across the yard, Pastor de Armas signaled to me. My ordination had been confirmed! I am certain that my smile of joy assured him that I'd received and understood his message.

Waiting for Eternity

To foster love and squelch hate must be the second most challenging battle a Christian has to fight while incarcerated in a Cuban prison—the first being to stay alive. One of the champions of love was Sergio Bravo, a young prisoner of slight build and as agile as a professional athlete. He made it his daily mission to spread the principle of love triumphing over hate to anyone who would listen. "You can rise above your natural human passions in your service for Christ," he claimed—not a simple task while living in an environment of deprivation, wanton cruelty, and brutish torment.

Sergio lived on the fifth floor of circular number 3. Somehow he had managed to have a small Bible the size of a pack of cigarettes smuggled in to him. The treasure of his life, he guarded the book carefully. When not using it, he hid it in a hole he'd dug into the concrete wall next to his bunk. The book had survived a number of searches.

Early one morning, the dreaded warning echoed throughout the gallery: "The guards are coming! Inspection." Startled awake, Sergio leaped from his bunk to his feet. As he rushed to the door of his cell, he noticed that the guard tower was opened. From his vantage point he also saw something else that made his blood run cold. On each side of the entrance to the gallery, the guards had built two parallel walls of sandbags. Behind the bags, soldiers waited with machine guns and rifles.

"Everybody out!" an officer shouted over the public address system. "Inspection! Everybody out!" At the same time, a company of soldiers bounded up the stairs. Already, guards were prodding prisoners with their bayonets toward the corridor of death that led to the courtyard. Once within shooting range of the guards behind the sandbag walls, the prisoners ran for their lives into the courtyard amid volleys of bullets. Many fell, wounded.

There had been a successful prison break—the nightmare of every inmate—and every officer from the prison director down to the lowest-ranking guard was out for blood. Furious at the damage to their reputations for operating a "tight ship," they wanted revenge.

Sergio ran down the steps three at a time. When he reached the fourth level, he realized that he'd left his Bible under his pillow the night before instead of replacing it in the wall. The guards would definitely find it if he left it there, but if he returned for it, he would receive additional blows for exiting so slowly. He decided it would be worth the extra pain. He bounded up the stairs and down the corridor to his cell. Twelve more steps, and he entered his cell. His heart pounding, he gasped for breath as he slipped the Bible into its protective spot. Congratulating himself for keeping it out of their reach, he ran from the cell. Alone in the hall, he raced the race of his lifetime down the stairs. The guards took aim and fired at him as if hunting a wild deer. Two bullets in his lower left leg sent him crashing to the floor. He left a trail of blood behind as two guards dragged him from the gallery.

At the hospital, the doctor on duty examined Sergio's injured leg, then conferred with other members of the surgical staff. The doctor turned back to Sergio and in a cold, matter-of-fact voice announced, "I could remove the bullet and restore your leg, but frankly, it would take more time and more medicine than I think it is worth. You have a choice, Bravo. Either allow me to amputate your leg or bleed to death—which will it be?" In his pain-wracked condition, Sergio agreed to the amputation. He survived, minus his right leg. When he returned to the gallery, Sergio continued preaching his message of love, not only with his words, but by his actions.

Another man known in the gallery for his compassion was Pastor Gerardo Alvarez, though very few of those who knew him knew his real name. Instead, they knew him as the Brother of the Faith. A local elder, Gerardo had consecrated his life to the propagation of the Word of God. Even the nonbelievers saw Christ in the way he lived. And, like Sergio, Gerardo made it his mission to teach us to love and not hate our enemies.

An older man with white hair, Gerardo arrived at Boniato Prison along with hundreds of other prisoners and was confined to an already-overcrowded gallery. He made his bed on the concrete floor beneath another prisoner's bunk. Each night, soldiers removed prisoners from the galleries, took them out to the firing wall, and shot them. We who remained heard the centuries-old cries of "Viva, Cristo el Rey!" ("Long live Christ the King!") before the rifle shots. Then—silence.

During these terrible moments, while we shook with fear, Gerardo would move about the gallery laying a friendly hand on a quivering shoulder, repeating the soothing words, "Let not your heart be troubled. Our beloved brother is asleep in Jesus." He helped prisoners prepare to meet their deaths with courage, to look forward to the resurrection. Wherever he went, whatever life he touched, Gerardo left behind a trace of his faith, his optimism and peace.

During the day, when the galleries were open, he moved from section to section searching out the sick. He shared his meager food with them, washed their clothes, and did whatever possible to ease their misery. At worship time, Gerardo became militant in his zeal.

Berth by berth, this white-haired saint invited each inmate to attend the meeting. "Come on," he'd say as he pulled them from their beds or lifted them from the floor, "Jesus is calling."

When a prisoner hesitated, Gerardo would urge, "I am waiting for you to begin the worship." No one could tell this loving man No. He preached with a primitive beauty and possessed a magnetic charm that drew people to him. His Christ-centered message gave many Christian men the strength to resist falling into the enemy's ranks or being devoured by the cancer of hate.

One day the prison director assembled the prisoners in our gallery. "It seems that you are not carrying out the re-education plan," he bellowed. "This we cannot allow." Then he called in a garrison of special soldiers trained to most effectively use the bayonet, the electric cane, clubs, and chains. A shower of blows fell on our heads and backs. Unified by fear, we felt one another's pain.

One Friday evening as we were returning from a long, hard day working in a mosquito-infested swamp, we staggered back toward our circular. The seasonal storm clouds threatened above our heads, and the sergeant in charge screamed at us to run. Exhausted, undernourished, and sick with all kinds of diseases, we could barely walk, let alone run.

"It is going to rain. Run!" he shouted, prodding the first man in line with the tip of his bayonet. Barely able to lift one foot in front of the other, the lead man stumbled forward, and the rest of us followed.

"Run, I said." We tried to accommodate his command, but our efforts fell short of his expectations.

Furious, he screamed at us. "Hurry up, you miserable worms!"

The chief of the block whipped out his machete and began beating us and shouting for the other soldiers to do the same. The political instructor gave a signal, which unleashed the specially trained soldiers on us like a pack of hungry wolves. The shouting and cursing drew the attention of the prisoners in circulars 2 and 3. They gathered to watch.

As the crippling blows fell, one of the prisoners in the line lifted his hands and his eyes toward heaven, and in a calm, clear voice, said, "Father, forgive them for they do not know what they are doing."

No evidence of pain could be seen on his face. This infuriated his torturers all the more. The sergeant ripped the prisoner's shirt from his back; then with a vengeance driven by insane savagery, four of the soldiers beat the man to his knees. Blood flowed from his lacerated back, yet he remained with his eyes gazing heavenward, as if he could see beyond his drab prison surroundings, as if he stood before the very throne of God. The entire prison population watched as this giant of a man, Gerardo, prayed for his enemies even as they beat him.

The old prisoner's hat fell to the ground. A hush echoed throughout the area at the sight of the prisoner's full head of white hair—Gerardo, Brother of the Faith. Then he fainted. Two soldiers picked him up and carried him to his circular, where they left him without any medical attention.

Even before the riot, a natural animosity existed between the soldiers and the prison population. With the soldiers' attitudes ranging from surly (those who disliked their assignment at the prison) to sadistic (those who relished inflicting pain), any attempt at friendliness on the part of a guard would automatically be suspect. And any overture a prisoner might make toward a guard would label the prisoner as an informer— a death knell. A strong sense of justice exists behind iron bars. Even with those imprisoned for theft, murder, and other legitimate crimes, the prison officials committed the ultimate injustice when they refused to set free the prisoner who had completed his sentence. Usually when asked, the guard would say, "I have to wait for notification from the head office." So was the story of Brother Cordero.

On September 10, 1972, the last day of his ten-year prison term, they took Brother Cordero to the Piner del Rios Court, where Cuban officials tried and convicted him of trumped-up charges in order to keep him in prison.

Later that day, the guard opened the gate to our gallery and led the sallow, gaunt prisoner down the narrow hall. Faces pressed against the barred windows in the iron doors to see who the prisoner might be.

"It's Cordero!" The whispered news traveled the length of the corridor faster than the prisoner and his jailer ever could.

A second message followed the first. "He's passed into eternity"—an expression that meant one's release date had come and gone, and he had not been freed. It meant he probably never would be freed. Always there would be other excuses, other accusations that would keep him a prisoner.

The guard opened cell number 12, and Cordero stepped inside. The door clanged shut behind him. He removed his shirt and walked toward the barred window. Only slight cracks between the welded iron sheeting and the concrete walls allowed ventilation or light to enter the cell. Peering through the tiny crack, he stared out into the prison courtyard until the glaring yard lights replaced the setting sun.

He told the brothers later that as he stood watching the day disappear, the day when he should have been set free, he thought of the beatings he'd endured over the last ten years, of the maggot-ridden food he'd been forced to eat, of the humiliations and deprivations inflicted on him almost daily. "What hope do I have," he wondered, "of ever being freed? How can I continue to live, knowing that my days will be filled with more of the same treatment? I must do something—anything!"

Two days later a prison official stopped outside Cordero's cell and called his name: "Cordero Rodriguez." The officer, his voice terse and abrupt, never glanced up from the piece of paper he held in his hand.

"It's me," Cordero replied.

The officer ordered the gallery guard to open the door. Immediately the guard obeyed. The door swung open, and Cordero came out. "Follow me," the officer said.

Cordero followed the soldier down the corridor and out of the gallery. Upon reaching headquarters, the officer took Cordero directly to the prison director's office, where the director ordered him to sit down. A group of soldiers stepped into the room behind Cordero, then closed the office door.

The director leaned back in his desk chair, folded his hands on his stomach, and mockingly said, "From today forward, you are no longer to be classed as a political prisoner. You are now considered a common prisoner."

Cordero leaped to his feet. "No!" he shouted. "You can't—"

He didn't have time to finish his statement before the soldiers behind him grabbed him and began beating him. Cordero fought, but the unequal numbers and his weakened physical condition defeated him. Once they'd subdued the prisoner, the guards forcibly dressed him in the blues of the common prisoner. To prevent him from removing the uniform, they bound his hands, then took him to gallery number 5 at the far end of the prison compound, a gallery constructed entirely underground.

Upon reaching the damp and humid cell that was to become Cordero's new home, the guards untied his hands. The prisoner immediately shed the hated garment. The common prisoners couldn't understand why he would do such a thing—their mentality was so totally different from that of the political prisoner jailed because of his principles instead of for his greed.

Water dripped constantly down on Cordero from the ceiling. Never cleaned or aired, everything in the cell was coated with grease, dirt, and mold. The temperatures climbed higher in Cordero's cell since it was located next to the kitchen facilities.

Cordero decided to go on a hunger strike. At best, he might be able to demand better treatment, and at worst he might die. At the same time, he wondered if the worst that could happen was really the worst. He spent eleven days on his hunger strike, but ended it when he realized that it would do no good. The common prisoners could not understand him, and it did nothing to strengthen the brethren. After beating him for not eating and for not wearing the uniform, the guards stripped him of his underwear and moved him to section 4, which was close to us. We devised a method of communication between our sections, which allowed us to "speak" with him daily.

Early in the morning, one year after Cordero's sham trial, an officer announced, "I have come to inform you of your sentence." The officer eyed Cordero strangely as he spoke. He had lost so much weight during the year since the officer had last seen him that his chest and clavicle had formed one pointed bow, like a boat under construction. He stared out of deep brown, sunken eyes. His pale, emaciated skin stretched leatherlike across his jutting bones. He was a walking skeleton.

"Ah, yes," Cordero whispered, his heartbeat accelerating with a glimmer of hope, "the sentence."

Apparently unnerved by the prisoner's condition, the officer snapped, "It's two years," then wheeled about and marched doubletime from the gallery.

Months later, the prison officials moved Cordero to the "charity dungeon"—a euphemism for the most filthy, despicable dungeon in the prison complex. He had just settled in when another officer informed him that there had been a mistake. "Your sentence is three years."

From that moment on, Cordero realized that he would never leave the prison alive. His captors had no intention of ever setting him free. He would spend the rest of his life living from year to year, only to have his sentence increased. Originally he had been jailed for giving food to a rebel. Since then, his "crimes" varied from participating in hunger strikes to being discovered hiding a piece of paper in his shoe.

A simple peasant who had spent his youth working on a tobacco plantation, he knew that his only hope of survival was to get reinstated as a political prisoner. While he had been incarcerated with us, he'd learned grammar, algebra, arithmetic, and the gospel of Christ, which he believed with all his heart.

Each Christian must face Calvary. Solitary confinement was Cordero's. As days, weeks, and months passed, he reflected on all he'd learned since his imprisonment began. The more he thought of his mates, the more he craved their companionship and their support. He needed the compassion and understanding he'd found in the presence of the saints.

One day, he came to a decision. He would go on strike again, demanding to be reclassified as a political prisoner. Already weakened by two earlier hunger strikes, his body slowly disinte-grated into a bony frame, wrapped in a pale, smelly layer of wrinkled skin. He never made it back to our gallery. He entered the shadow of death on May 21, 1975.

Brothers in Christ

My second stay at La Cabaña Prison lasted less than a year, when they moved me to building number 2 at "Combinado del Este Prison"—the Eastern Combined Prison. This prison contained more than 7,000 inmates, all unshaven, with missing teeth, and as hollowed-eyed as I'd seen in my former prisons. As I stared at their emaciated bodies, I wasn't aware of how closely I resembled my brothers.

The prison was called the "combined" prison because beside the prefabricated prison housing the government operated a factory. Slave labor from the prison produced steel and concrete forms used in the building of additional prison complexes being erected in the surrounding hills. When it rained, the prefabricated units leaked like they were made of Swiss cheese. When it rained, it poured inside, and when the rain stopped, the ceiling continued to drip.

Would Castro and his henchmen be satisfied when they'd imprisoned all Cubans, I wondered one morning as I studied the jumble of gray buildings scattered across the terrain. When the heroes of the revolution ran out of native blood to feed their fiendish machine of destruction, where would they turn next—Mexico? The Bahamas? The United States?

Combinado del Este Prison was considered a show prison—one where foreign delegations were taken on scenic-cruise bus tours. Communist propagandists had learned to "play" the gullible foreigners—tell them what they wanted them to hear, show them what they wanted them to see, and send them home to herald the advances of the great proletarian society. When a group of journalists and other international dignitaries came through, the prison officials handpicked inmates involved in the re-education plan to dress in basketball uniforms and play on the court outside the buildings. After the visitors left, the "basketball team" returned their uniforms and returned to their cells.

My nickname "the Pastor" and my reputation for building up churches had preceded me here. Many of my earlier prison mates greeted me when I arrived. They invited me to join them on the fourth floor. Before long we were operating a full-scale religious education program.

Combinado del Este had an advantage over the earlier prisons I'd been in, an advantage conducive to worship. Also, by this time, we'd grown wiser in our worship habits. On each floor, a laundry room sat next to the dining rooms, and here we conducted our worship services, Catholics, Baptists, Pentecostals, and Adventists alike. We established a Christian Watch Team. While one group worshiped, members of the Watch Team acted as "door keepers for the house of the Lord" to warn us of the approach of the guards. This way we aided and supported one another.

Our fortune improved when a visitor smuggled a small transistor radio into the prison. This gave us access to news from the world beyond. When a rat bit Everett Jackson, an American journalist, and the prison medical team couldn't stop the bleeding, they transferred him to a civilian hospital in Havana. When he returned, he had more good news. "Today, I met two American prisoners at the hospital," he said. "They're great. You're going to love them as much as I."

Americans! One of the *plantados'* most effective routes for sending out information! The next two weeks dragged by until I began to doubt that the men would ever arrive at Combinado. I spent more time thinking of my mother and my sister Paulina living in Salem, Massachusetts, than I had in all the years previous. I had been able to smuggle out an occasional letter to them over the years to let them know I was still alive, and they'd managed to send a few notes back to me. How I wanted to talk with these men, to learn more about my mother's adopted country, where the government stood politically, and, though I dared not even hope, what might be done to initiate my release.

One Sunday night, while I led the congregation in singing "At the Cross," our song leader, Luis Gallo, stood in the back of the room, shadowing a stranger so that the guards would not notice him. The stranger, tall, lean, and looking totally American, watched and listened to the congregation sing. Whispers traveled to the front of the room: "It's the American."

The instant Tom's eyes met mine, a bond of friendship was formed. The congregation stopped singing as I rushed back to greet our visitor. We embraced one another as if we'd been friends for many years. The program planned for that evening's worship service shifted. Everyone wanted to hear what this former Los Angeles schoolteacher had to say about the world beyond the cold, gray walls of our existence.

Tom told us how he had learned about our church family. "We learned that some Cuban Christians and political prisoners lived on the fourth floor," he said. "One morning I heard some of you singing. Thirty or forty male voices powerfully penetrated the sordid prison atmosphere. It was as if you were singing of victory, of hope in Jesus." He swallowed hard before continuing his story. "Immediately I wanted to go to the fourth floor. I knew that my brothers were there—my family. And I had heard that a pastor was there among the believers."

Everett Jackson had told Tom White and Mel Bailey, the second American, how eager the other believers and I were to meet them, so that Sunday evening he decided to attend our church on the fourth floor.

"How did you get up here?" I asked.

"On the dumbwaiter," he replied. An ancient, creaking, grease-coated elevator carried food up to and garbage down from the upper floors.

"Oh, you can't come up that way again," Luis warned. "The cable has broken twice; you could be killed! When the time comes for another visit, we'll find another way to move you."

"You are the pastor?" Tom asked.

"Yes, and you are one of the Americans arrested for dropping religious literature on Cuba's mainland?"

"How did you know about the tracts we dropped?" Tom and Mel had crashed in Manzanillo after scattering their cargo across Camaguey province, more than 200 miles from Combinado del Este Prison.

"We have been reading your tracts," I explained. "The first week of June some were passed into the prison. We all read them." I beamed with pleasure at the surprise registered on his face.

"But the first week in June was only a few days after we crashed. How did the tracts reach the prison so fast?"

Not able to comprehend the miraculous workings of the Holy Spirit, I shrugged. "And you have been in Havana?" I urged.

He nodded his head.

"How are things there with the churches?"

"A Captain Santos, you know him?"

A murmur passed through the men assembled there. We all knew Captain Santos.

"Well, after more than a hundred hours of playing cat and mouse with me in and out of the interrogation room, the captain took Mel and me, in separate cars, along with an entourage of secret police, of course, on a two-hour tour of the churches in Havana. He hoped to convince us that the people of Cuba enjoyed religious freedom," Tom explained. "First, the driver took us to a large Catholic cathedral near the ocean in West Havana."

"Yes," I answered, "I know the one."

"Iron bars have been welded over the doors and windows, and eight-foot bars blocked the sidewalk that led to the front door. The captain, in an effort to save face, made an excuse about it not being time for Mass. Then he snapped at the driver."

Tom told about visiting another cathedral with six or seven people inside, and two more with less than twenty in each. At a Baptist church, the sign had fallen off into the shrubbery, and stairs had been erected in the main entry. A woman carrying some sacks came up to the "church" in the middle of what Santos said was a church service and walked up the stairs. It was an apartment house. The embarrassed captain shrugged and uttered something like, "It's big enough to be an apartment house." Tom told of one church the government had converted into a wholesale depot.

"The Adventist church," I urged, "what about the Adventist church?"

Tom shook his head sadly. "No one was there since it was Sunday, but metal plates were welded over the windows, and a large padlock secured the front door."

I paused for a moment. The weight of this news deadened my usual joy. My brothers and sisters, where were they? Had many of my Christian family fallen away now that they had no place to worship?

Tom then told us about the mango incident. "During one of the interrogations, I told Captain Santos about the wife of a friend who recently visited Cuba and purchased mangoes for the enormous sum of two days' wages. I had heard that the government exported so much of the mango crop that there were none left for the people. A short time later the captain took me for a walk in Havana—one of his propaganda tours. A woman carrying a fishnet bag holding six or seven big, ripe mangoes passed us on the street. Captain Santos pointed at the woman and exclaimed, 'Wow! Would you look at those mangoes!' A few seconds later, one of the guards did the same.

"I had a hard time trying to keep a straight face. It was so obvious that the whole drama was just that—theater. Then, before the captain could whisk me back into the automobile, a second woman, not a part of the captain's scheme, overheard the conversation and saw the fruit. Eager to get a few pieces of fruit for herself, she rushed to get into the mango line, but of course there were none available."

We laughed along with Tom. Anytime we could poke fun at our captors, we enjoyed ourselves immensely. Later Captain Santos arranged to have mangoes delivered to Tom's and Mel's individual prison cells. Amazed at the sight of the mangoes, the guards peered into both of the cells and kept asking how the Americans enjoyed the fruit.

Each of us then shared *our* prison experiences with the American. We told about the times in La Cabaña Prison when the guards had opened fire on our prayer circles. "We continued praying and singing as the bullets and shrapnel embedded in our flesh," I said, laughing. "We weren't about to let those hoodlums interrupt our worship service."

Tom looked at me quizzically. How could I explain that my laughter was due to joy, not humor?

"Sometimes one or another of the worshipers would break and run, but he'd come back. And always the guards would beat on us, but we continued our worship. As you have already learned, Christians behind prison bars can truly relate to 'the fellowship of his sufferings' that the apostle Paul speaks of in Philippians 3:10."

From that evening on, Tom and Mel attended as many Sunday worship services as possible. The prison officials had sectioned off a special area on the fourth floor of building 2, on the extreme right-hand side of the building, for foreign prisoners. We *plantados* lived on the fourth floor at the extreme left side of our building, which faced building 2. Re-educated prisoners and the common prisoners occupied the other floors in both buildings. Though two galleries and a dining room separated us from the Americans, we could sneak across the dining room at lunchtime while the guards checked the food. When the guard turned his back, we would slip inside one of the other galleries, then return when that gallery came out for supper. For a few months, before the guards confiscated Tom's contraband transistor radio, he and I huddled by the wall every day to listen to Voice of America and to a Christian radio station in Ecuador. The radio operators on those stations will never know, this side of eternity, how much they encouraged the lost souls in Castro's prison.

Out in the prison yard, we would communicate with hand signals in order to keep one another informed between visits. Since the constant presence of guards restricted verbal communication, we developed a silent code: the letter A was a hand on the head; the hand passed over the face was B; the thumb and forefinger to the mouth was C, D was the clenched fist, and so on.

One evening, in one of the galleries where sixty-five old prisoners who were paralyzed or too sick to leave their beds lived, Tom and I were just setting up our "pulpit" (a bedsheet covering a board), when a guard named Pedro burst into the cell.

"Tom White," he shouted. "I know he's in here! I saw him enter the gallery." The inmates, acting as a well-trained unit, shoved Tom onto a top bunk and threw a sheet over his head.

"All right, where is he? Where is the American?" Pedro demanded. "I know you have him here."

Suspicious, Pedro walked about the cell, then paused beside one of the bunks. The guard rested his hand on a bunk as his fingers tapped out his frustration. Pedro's gaze swept the room as he asked a few more questions. The inmates either shrugged or answered his questions with a joke. Infuriated, Pedro stomped out of the cell, unaware that his fingers had been inches from Tom's frozen body!

One of the brothers checked to be certain the guard had left the area before I removed the sheet from Tom's body and returned to the task of preparing the pulpit for the evening meeting. Taking their hymnals from their hiding places, the inmates began singing. As usual, we felt a surge of power and strength as we sang—uniting our voices in Christ. I looked over at Tom as we sang. His eyes brimmed with tears. He too was experiencing the love, the compassion, and the oneness that occur when Christians praise God together.

Following my sermon, I asked if anyone had any special requests for prayer. The inmates prayed for others, not themselves. Most requested prayers for family members. Some prayed for their beloved Cuba and for the United States. After prayer we returned to our own separate cells.

One Sunday, after the church service, Tom stopped me, Rosendo Valdes, Tony Padilla, and Alfredo Cadoval at the doorway.

"You know, brothers," he said, "we should conduct a Communion service."

I sighed and shook my head. "Tell me, how would we get any bread out of the dining room? That guard is always watching."

The guards delivered our food to the dining room on their time schedule. Supper was often served at 1:00 p.m., and nothing more would be served until 7:00 the next morning—eighteen hours later. The prison officials stringently enforced their rule against removing food from the mess hall by placing a guard at the door to check as we exited.

"Well," Tom drawled in his typical American style, "where there's a will, there's a way. Why don't you all see what you can do at this end, and I'll see what I can do at mine."

After Tom left, we discussed his proposal.

"He's right," Tony admitted. "There must be a way!"

I glanced toward Rosendo. "What do you think?"

"There just might be . . ." Rosendo smiled. "Diversionary tactics!"

"Yeah! Some of us could attract the guard's attention while others smuggled out enough bread for the Communion service." Alfredo's eyes glistened with the spirit of adventure.

I nodded and stroked my chin. "You know, you might be on to something."

"The other day when those two guys started shoving one another, the guard at the door went to break it up," Tony suggested. "That's it, a fight gets them every time! Rosendo, Alfredo, and I—the three of us—we can begin arguing. Jesus Sanchez can help you do your part, Pastor."

Sanchez agreed. The five of us discussed our plan at length. Any time a prisoner claimed or even insinuated that the other might be an informant, a fight would break out. That would be our strategy. When the bell rang for the midday meal, we marched into the mess hall, sat down, and ate a small portion of our food allotment. One after another, the four conspirators slipped pieces of their bread to me.

When I had all of the bread hidden, I signaled the others. Jesus Sanchez immediately stood up and left the dining room. Rosendo shouted at Alfredo. "I saw you talking to the guard. What were you doing, informing on someone?"

Alfredo leaped to his feet and leaned across the table. "Don't you accuse me of being a stool pigeon."

"Hey, man," Tony interrupted, "you're wrong. Alfredo would never squeal on an inmate."

"Oh, yeah?"

"Yeah!" Their voices grew louder and louder until everyone in the mess hall craned their necks to see and hear the altercation.

The guard at the door eyed the shouting men for a few moments, then leaped into the fray.

"All right, you guys, we'll have no fistfights on my shift."

All eyes watched to see if the three angry men would back off or challenge the guard. No one noticed when I stepped over to an open window where Jesus Sanchez stood waiting and handed him my package. Once Sanchez disappeared from view, the three men bowed their heads in humility. Satisfied that he'd cowered them into submission, the guard shouted a few epithets their way, then strutted back to his post by the door.

Tears of joy and victory flowed between us as we celebrated the Communion supper together.

Several months later, the Cuban officials allowed Tom's mother to visit him in prison and bring him a pair of spectacles to replace the ones he'd broken in the plane crash. He learned from her and through the prison grapevine of a huge international campaign being conducted by important United States government officials and religious leaders. Knowing the Cuban Communists' insatiable craving for acceptance by the international community, such a movement could work.

All of us decided we needed to pray for Tom White's and Mel Bailey's release. The Americans asked us to pray daily up to and including a certain date. If God hadn't answered our prayers by then, they were committed to accepting their imprisonment at Combinado del Este Prison as His will.

The day before we were scheduled to stop praying, the prison grapevine reported that the two Americans had been called to the prison director's office. When we assembled in the prison courtyard for counting that evening, Tom signaled to me that he and Mel would be leaving soon.

Tom and Mel found a way to slip up to the fourth floor before leaving. I choked back the tears as we shared our last worship service together. The steel bonds of love between us had been forged in the furnaces of tribulation. I wondered if I would ever see them again, this side of heaven.

"I won't forget you. And I will do everything I can to press for your release, my brother. The world will know!" Tom placed his Bible in my hands.

During my prison stay, a French pilot gave me an old Esterbrook fountain pen. I treasured the pen almost as much as I did the portions of Scripture I had painstakingly hand copied. I reached in my pocket, withdrew the pen, and handed it to Tom. In the future, I would write my letters with one of the handmade pens the inmates crafted out of the stainless steel rods discarded on the prison grounds.

"Tom, I know that if I keep this pen in here I will eventually lose it," I said. "So take it for me until we meet again. Here, take a copy of our hymnal with you and guard it with your life."

He chuckled and stuffed it in his socks. "Don't worry, Noble. I'll get them both out." That night Tom prepared a hidden compartment in his shoes so he could take my treasures with him.

Mel embraced me, then pressed pictures of his wife and children into my hand. I understood the sentiment of his gesture.

In a Place Without a Soul

I treasured Tom's Bible, not only as the Word of God and as a reminder of our friendship, but because of the hope it represented—the hope of eventually being released. Just knowing that people on the outside knew of our plight brought satisfaction. It also increased my determination to come out of the experience alive.

Our church at Combinado del Este continued to grow—a blatant affront to the Communist officials, who repeatedly vowed to wipe all evidence of Christianity from Cuba and, in time, from the world. Since we represented the "evidence" of their failure, the prison officials, incited by satanic agencies, intensified their vigilance. Our skills at "hide-and-seek" with God's Word and with our homemade hymnals improved. This ghoulish game took on higher stakes when the prison director upped the punishment for being caught with contraband literature.

As much as I treasured Tom's Bible, it was made to be shared. So in spite of the threat, we regularly passed it from cell to cell. We tried to protect ourselves and the Book from detection, but as Christians, we had little protection against prison informers. The inherent nature of a Christian is to accept other people unconditionally and to trust them. So it was inevitable that, while we won a few, sooner or later we would also lose a few.

One morning a unit of guards led by Lieutenant Nuarlart, the officer in charge of the re-education program, announced a surprise inspection. He and the guards searched through our gallery from six in the morning till two in the afternoon. Normally when they searched, they emptied the cell of all inmates before looking for papers and books. This time they had each prisoner empty his belongings onto his bunk. Then a special officer went through

159

each man's belongings while we watched. Three other military men searched the rest of the cell.

When one found something, he asked, "Whose is this?" If the owner didn't claim the item, the entire gallery would be punished. So when one of the men found the Bible and took it to the lieutenant, I didn't hesitate to claim the book. I didn't want the entire gallery chastised because of me.

"You all continue to smuggle things in here." He shook his finger in my face. "You will all reap what you sow!" They continued with the search. When they finished ransacking our cells, I was summoned to the office.

"Alexander, you will spend the next thirty days in the box, considering your crime," the lieutenant told me. My thirty-day sentence stretched into ninety before they released me.

The "box," or "drawer," as it was sometimes called, resembled a coffin. It had an opening at each end for ventilation, and the opening at one end was larger so that meals could be passed inside. The box measured about seven feet long. The floor was about three feet wide, and it was probably a little over three feet high. There was also an opening on one end at the bottom of the box, and the box was slanted toward that end so that our sewage would run out. Each box was large enough, by our tormentors' definition, to accommodate six men squatting side by side.

The guard opened the box and ordered me to climb inside. I obeyed.

"Squat!" the guard ordered. I joined my brothers, Antonio Diaz and Rafael Pacheco. Three more prisoners were squeezed into the already uncomfortable space beside us. I lowered myself to my haunches, and the lid slammed down, leaving the six of us in total darkness. Our nights and our days blended into one. When the guard brought the hot sugar water and the thin slices of bread, we counted it as morning. When we heard the guards taking roll, we assumed it was time for evening worship.

There in the perpetual darkness, we conducted our own worships. We shared our hope for freedom. We talked about what we would do when freed. We discussed the story of Job and retold the story of Jeremiah in the pit and Paul in the Roman jail.

We prayed for the three other prisoners who endured this heinous punishment without hope. Around the clock, they ranted and shouted obscenities at their persecutors. But at worship time, when we began singing our evening hymn, "Now the day is over—night is drawing nigh—," they calmed down long enough to allow us a few hours of sleep.

Along with the hymn, I recited a poem I composed after entering the box. Translated into English, it said:

> Slowly Cuba's sun is setting,
> O'er Bonita's hills far away,
> Filling all the cells with sorrow,
> And the end of a sad day.
> Now let all lift up our forehead,
> As men forged in fear,
> Bringing joy to those among us,
> With the blessed Christian hope.

While the routine made the long hours endurable, the first few minutes in the box produced sheer pain. I knew what to expect. Our cramped muscles tightened. Our veins and arteries ceased transmitting blood to our feet and lower legs. We ached to stretch our arms and legs, to arch our backs, to breathe fresh, clean air into our constricted lungs. Claustrophobia set in. My imagination ran wild—what if they leave me in here forever? What if I die here?

I remembered when a Brother Calsadilla spent an entire year in the box. It took him six months to learn to walk again. Would I leave the "box" a cripple for six months, perhaps for the rest of my life? I reminded myself that even here in this compartment of horrors, I was still in God's hands. I kept telling myself that the God I served walked amidst the flames with His children, He walked among the lions, and He endured the pain of Calvary all alone for me. I tried to picture Him cramped into a squatting position beside me.

The muscles in my legs and haunches knotted. I tried to shift my weight a bit in order to relieve the pain, but I couldn't. We were too tightly packed into the box. I could feel the blood vessels in my knees and ankles constrict. I thought that once the numbness set in, maybe the pain would lessen. Instead it intensified. In desperation, I prayed the promises found in God's Word. I prayed for strength to endure. Again and again I repeated the words, "He who endures unto the end will receive a crown of life."

Since I couldn't physically escape my confinement, I willed my mind to leave my pain-racked body for the private world of my childhood. My thoughts went back to the friend who first introduced me to Christ. Rolando Claxton was his name; we played ball together.

For some reason, my mind went back to a particular day. Rolando came over to my house and knocked on the door. "Hey, Noble, wanna bat a few?" he said.

"Sure," I replied as I grabbed my ball and bat. "And pitch it over the plate this time, OK?" We walked out to a vacant lot, and I took the bat first.

"Think you can hit it if I pitch it right?" Rolando joked, throwing his best curve toward me. He laughed as the ball zinged squarely over the plate before the bat had left my shoulder.

"I wasn't ready," I protested feebly.

After a few pitches, I connected, sending a fly ball high and to the left field. "Hey, you're not bad, Alexander," Rolando admitted. "A couple of us guys are forming a team. Wanna join?"

"Sure!" Like any fifteen-year-old boy, I leaped at the chance. My best childhood friend, Orlando Mondosa, had joined Batista's army in order to secure a college degree, and I missed the camaraderie we'd enjoyed. I had no way of knowing then just how much that one decision would affect my entire life. I got along with the other team members from the start. We won a few and lost a few. The only consistency our team exhibited was that we never played baseball on Saturday. When I asked why, Rolando told me that most of the team members belonged to the Seventh-day Adventist Church. "We go to church on Saturday," he explained.

"On Saturday?" I asked incredulously. I'd never heard of such a church. Everyone I knew worshiped on Sunday at the local Catholic church. I pondered this strange bit of information for some time—especially on Saturday afternoons, when I found myself totally alone with nothing to do and no one with whom to do it.

One particular Saturday afternoon, after I'd exhausted all my usual Saturday activities, feeling bored and restless, I wandered over to Rolando's house, hoping he'd be around so we could at least talk a while or play jacks with his little sister, Martha. Maybe his mom would offer me some of her delicious cookies.

"Seventh-day Adventists have to at least talk and eat cookies on Saturdays," I reasoned.

When I arrived, the Rolando family had company—all the young people from his church. He introduced me to everyone.

"We're playing a game," he explained. "We call it *Trono*—the throne."

I grimaced. The "throne" was a chair in the middle of the circle of people. It looked like a little kid's game to me.

The leader, a person sitting on the chair, called out a letter. "I'm thinking of a person in the Bible whose name begins with the letter *S*. " The rest of the participants then tried to guess who the person might be from the leader's clues. I tried to join in, but I didn't know the names of too many people in the Bible.

We had played *Trono* for some time when a man arrived who my friend, Rolando, introduced as William Burke, a medical student from Jamaica who was selling Christian books in the region during a school break.

After watching us play for a while, William suggested to Rolando, "You should be telling Noble about his soul salvation instead of playing *Trono*." William turned to me. "Are you interested in learning about Christ and what He has done for you?" he asked.

I nodded. Being the odd man out on Saturday mornings wasn't my idea of a good time. I decided to listen to what the man had to say. Following the Bible studies William gave me, I was baptized in 1953.

Squatting there in the box, I felt a warmth flood through me as I visualized the young Jamaican's face. In my imagination, I tried to picture the lake site where I'd been baptized, but the pain in my legs blotted out the image and forced me back to the agony of the present.

Days passed. Finally, after ninety days, the lid to the box flew open, and a guard called our names. I squinted into the sudden flood of light. Two burly guards grabbed my arms and lifted me from the box. I tried to straighten my legs, but they remained frozen in my squatting position. They carried me across the room to an electric bicycle and sat me on the seat. My breath caught in my throat as they straightened my paralyzed legs and strapped my useless feet to the pedals, then turned on the switch. I screamed from the intense pain as the machine forced my legs into motion. At every turn of the wheel, it felt as if my kneecaps would break. I fought to remain conscious throughout the ordeal. The fifteen-minute bike ride seemed like eternity.

The guards deposited me back in my cell with a warning. "The next time you are caught with propaganda, the pain you feel now will be like child's play!" Yet even as they marched out of sight, I knew that sooner or later, I would again be subjected to their tortures, for under no circumstance would I cease witnessing for my God. Witnessing for Him was my power, my strength, my will to go on. I couldn't stop sharing the wonderful story of Jesus and His love anymore than I could willingly stop breathing.

As soon as the pain subsided in my legs, José Rodriguez and two other brothers in Christ, one a physical therapist and the other a sports trainer, set up an exercise program to get me back on my feet. Forty-five days later I could walk without pain. Two months later, a guard caught me with a hymnal and reported me to the prison warden, who sent me to the "shower." This experience was similar to one I had shortly after my imprisonment.

They placed me in a container, similar in size to the "box," where I had to remain on the balls of my feet to avoid having the soles of my feet punctured with nails that protruded up through the floor. As soon as the guards closed the door to the shower, tiny droplets of water dripped one at a time down on my head.

My feet immediately registered the strain of supporting all of my body weight, and at first the water droplets falling on exactly the same spot on my head didn't bother me at all. After a few hours, that changed. Irritated by the steady drip, drip, drip of the water, I tried to move my head. I couldn't. I developed a headache that intensified with every passing hour. A day passed, two days, three—the droplets felt more like a carpenter's hammer pounding away at my skull. After four days in the shower, the size of the "hammer" increased to that of a sledge hammer pounding out my brain.

"How long can I endure this?" I cried to God. I tried to pray, but I couldn't. I thought I would lose my mind. I tried to play the same mental games I'd played so often before in order to block the pain, but the constant pounding broke through even my most persistent memories.

I thought of my mother in the United States. Had my letters reached her? What about Tom White? Had he forgotten? I knew he hadn't, but Satan's demons continued to bombard my fevered brain with doubts and discouragement. His devilish taunts persisted. "Everyone is gone. Everyone has forgotten you. You are dead to society. No one knows or cares about you."

"Lo, I am with you always," I shouted. "Lo, I am with you always!" I couldn't lose it now. No matter what, I had to survive, I just had to survive!

Forty-two days later, the prison director ordered the door to the shower unlatched. He couldn't control the shock that swept across his face. He'd expected to find a raving lunatic. Instead, he saw a prisoner smiling in spite of his pain. While I was certain my smile was more of a grimace, I gasped out a faint, "Praise God."

God and I had won.

Like the madman he'd expected to find, the prison director shouted and flailed his arms about in wild exasperation. "Your life would be so simple if you did not defy me at every turn!"

Again two guards lifted me from my confinement and placed me on the electric bicycle. Again, my body screamed for relief. When they returned me to my cell, the brothers were waiting and ready to serve my needs.

Surrounded by my family in Christ, I still missed my mother and my sister. I kept their memories alive in my mind by writing letters to them—letters that I had no idea whether or not they were ever able to read.

Inside Out

"It's about 2:30," one of my letters began. "Once more in the middle of glaring sunlight, with nothing around me but bars, I have taken the pen which is the only form I have to speak to you . . ."

The letter, dated January 3, 1969, was the last legal letter I sent to my mother.

In the early years of my incarceration, the prison officials allowed me to write to family members. Then I became a *plantado,* and everything changed. My letters, written on the fragile tissue-paper wrapper of Cuban oranges, needed to be smuggled out. While I could no longer receive guests, many of my fellow prisoners could. These guests, strangers at best, risked being caught with contraband to keep our families informed as to our personal condition. Occasionally a prisoner about to be released also would manage to smuggle out our carefully penned letters.

To ensure delivery, we would write the same information a number of times, sending the letters out by many couriers. That way, we believed that at least one copy would make it to its destination. In my letters I would try to maintain a cheerful, positive attitude, regardless of my present condition, always closing with "I, at present, am well, thanks be to the Almighty." I would draw flowers in the margins to brighten it up. I saw no reason to recite my ills and create further stress and pain for those I loved, since there was little they could do.

Whenever the guards discovered one of our "mail routes," we invented a new one. Their control tightened until we were forced to use desperate measures. We folded our letters into tight little rectangles, then wrapped them in three layers of plastic hoarded for the purpose. Then our letters took a circuitous route from prisoner to prisoner and from one section of the prison to the next. On visiting day, the prisoner who would deliver the letter

166

to his visitor would either swallow it or insert it into his colon in order to get through the search.

When the letter reached the dining hall, where the prisoners and the visitors met, the outer plastic covering would be removed, revealing the second layer of clean plastic covering. The visitor would then hide the package in the private areas of his or her body in order to get it out of the dining hall and finally out of Cuba. Once out of Castro's reach, the letter would be opened and sent to its true destination. Anyone caught carrying a letter would be tried as a spy, which carried with it a sentence anywhere from four to thirty years.

Each letter I wrote revived my hopes for freedom. Perhaps this letter would be the trigger that blew a hole in the carefully constructed wall of propaganda Castro and his public relations people had built for the international press. Perhaps this letter would ignite world opinion against the Castro regime and force the Cuban government to release us. And every time, for more than twenty-two years, I hoped, I prayed, and nothing happened. But for us, the last thing we could afford to lose was hope. We had to believe that at any moment something could happen to bring about our release. Faith in God and in our fellow men must be maintained in order to survive.

The Christian prisoners were an affront to Fidel Castro's entire communistic philosophy. Whenever we got news that one of our letters had reached the desk of a U.S. congressman or when some foreign official broadcast our plight over radio or TV, we rejoiced. Inevitably, our interior officer would take offense and increase the level of violence toward us. Instead of becoming depressed because of the increased number of beatings or the intensified harassment, we rejoiced over our successes. Someone outside knew about us; someone cared enough to speak out. We clung to our motto, "We were not born in prison and we are not going to die in prison." Personally, I refused to let Castro and Communism win. I vowed, "I will die free!" Yet all the time, God's grace, God's power, not any strength or power I might have, made it possible for me to fulfill that vow.

Even before my arrest, my mother and my sister Paulina, who lived in Salem, Massachusetts, petitioned government and social agencies to arrange for me to emigrate to the United States. Paulina visited Cuba many times before and after the revolution, trying to arrange for exit visas for Yraida and me. Each time she visited the island, government officials made it more difficult for her to return to the States. On her last visit, in 1959, it took her two months to arrange for her return trip to Massachusetts.

As if prophesying, she warned, "This is no place for you to stay, Noble. You must emigrate before all the escapes are slammed shut."

Castro's takeover gave people an excuse for old enemies to settle old scores. If someone didn't like you, they would accuse you of disloyalty to Castro. You would be taken prisoner, often killed. One day during my sister's visit, guerilla soldiers wielding machine guns rounded up a number of men from our neighborhood. Herded into a truck like cattle, the stunned men did as they were told even though they had no idea what crimes they'd been accused of. Perhaps one of the men sneezed or made some move—no one knew. Suddenly a soldier opened fire, killing seven of the men. Later the bodies were dumped into a common grave.

When Paulina arrived back in the U.S., both she and my mother started campaigning to get Yraida and me out. First, they needed to find a sponsor for us. They appealed to their local church family. Some months before, the church had sponsored a family of East German refugees, but this time the church turned down their request. My mother and my sister weren't asking the church for funds to pay for our trip but simply to sign the sponsor form required by immigration. No amount of pleading would change the church board's mind.

My sister didn't understand their refusal except for the fact that at that time, the people in the United States didn't understand the savagery of the new regime. Many Americans didn't even know where the island of Cuba was located. They thought it was somewhere near Hawaii.

When their pleas fell on deaf ears at their church, Paulina traveled to Mexico City to plead with the Cubans directly. They turned her away. She petitioned the Swiss and the Czechoslovakian embassies and was turned away. In the following months, they heard of my arrest. Their prayers for my release continued.

Paulina stubbornly continued butting against the inertia and reluctance of various government bureaucracies. "What is the reason for his arrest?" she asked of everyone who would listen. "What has he done?"

The official Cuban explanation came through the Czech embassy in Washington, D.C. "Humberto Noble Alexander was sentenced to twenty years in prison in Case 83/1963 for reasons of activities against the security of the state and imperfect homicide," a reference to the presumed plot to assassinate Fidel Castro. The letter went on to acknowledge the irritation my religious persuasion had become to the Cubans. "During his stay in prison," the letter said, "he has maintained a negative and disorderly conduct in all aspects as well as links to terrorist groups." This image did little to encourage support from either the American or the Czechoslovakian governments.

Paulina wrote two letters to Senator Edward Kennedy in 1976 and in 1979. She wrote to her congressman, Michael Harrington, and to his successor, North Shore congressman Nicholas Mavroules, who in turn sought help from the Czechoslovakian government and the U.S. State Department. And she personally badgered the officials at the U.S. State Department.

In 1979, when Castro freed 3,500 prisoners, I was told I would be freed. Even though I didn't fully believe I would be released, I wrote to my mother to share the good news. "I do hope the good Lord will put His hands in and very soon we'll see each other in liberty." But in spite of the international pressure, I was not freed. Czech officials told my mother and sister that I was not released because of my "intransigence."

As a result of the ordeal, my mother became ill, and with each false hope she worsened. I often wondered if I would ever see her alive again on this earth. Repeatedly, the demons of discouragement surrounded me with clouds of despair, only to have the powers of heaven force them back.

Orlando Martinez, a fellow prisoner, was released and made his way to Miami through Costa Rica. He called my mother and sister to tell them that he'd seen me and had seen my name on a list of prisoners to be deported. Their hopes soared again.

On February 3, 1983, my twenty-year prison sentence officially ended. However, I had long since given up hope of being released through the normal means. I'd seen my friends and brothers build their hopes as the day of their release approached, only to have the prison guards shrug their shoulders and say they could do nothing, after which the prison officials would accuse them of new crimes and extend their sentence. I had decided that regardless of the government's inhumanity, God didn't want me to waste unnecessary energy on discouragement. He'd given me a mission, and He expected me to be about His business. So when my supposed release date arrived, my friends actually had to remind me of the fact. The day came and went without my being released—just as I'd expected. I praised God for clouding my memory during the previous months, thus sparing me the hopelessness that so many of my brothers had suffered.

I asked a guard when I would be released now that my sentence had been served, and he replied, "You will not be released until you have been totally re-educated." I am certain he didn't appreciate my reply. I laughed at his audacity, as I had laughed during the twenty years I'd been imprisoned. We prisoners understood the routine all too well. Hostages—Castro used prisoners whose sentences had been served as hostages for negotiation with the United States and other more compassionate countries. He never released a prisoner who hadn't already served his time. With this policy he won both ways: first, he extracted his "pound of flesh" from the prisoner, and second, upon releasing prisoners, he received favorable international press.

In the meantime, Reverend Willis P. Miller, the pastor of the Lafayette Street United Methodist Church in Salem, Massachusetts, visited my mother and sister to discover why they no longer attended the church. When he learned of my plight, he vowed to do all he could to instigate my release.

"I can tell you one thing, Pastor Miller," my sister said. "I know Noble is going to keep on preaching. The only way they'll stop him from doing that is if they kill him."

Along with organizing a prayer group, the minister launched a public campaign for my release. "Through prayer, publicity, and politicalization, we are determined to help obtain the release of this innocent victim of a cruel system," the pastor said. "We solicit the help of others who may be interested in bringing about the release of Brother Alexander."

After Tom White's release, I sent letters to him in Glendale, California, with the request that he forward them to my mother. On September 1, 1983, I wrote two letters to Tom and three to Armando Valladares, a dear friend and a Cuban poet, who had spent twenty-two years himself in Castro's prison. During his imprisonment he had been paralyzed and was now confined to a wheelchair. A French professor who had also been imprisoned for a time agitated for Armando's release. Armando moved to France following his release. When Tom and Armando learned that Rev. Jesse Jackson was one of the Democratic party's presidential candidates for 1984, they both forwarded copies of my letter and my prisoners' list to him along with the following note:

"Dear Rev. Jackson, We have learned that you are going to Cuba. In Combinado del Este Prison, there is a pastor, just like you. He is black, just like you. And he is rotting in Castro's prison because he preaches just like you. See if you can do something for him."

In my letter to my family I had told about the plight of the *plantados*, and I included a list of names of those of us who had completed our sentences but were still being held prisoners. Then I waited, hoped, and continued on with my ministry, not knowing whether any of the copies would ever reach their destination. I still had Bible texts to write out, worships to conduct, classes to teach, and precious souls to prepare for baptism.

Even though I could not know it, beyond those gray, foreboding walls many people *did* know about me. A storm of protest grew from many parts of the world demanding my release. By any law, Cuban or otherwise, I had served my prison term. Guilty or innocent of the charges against me, justice demanded I be set free. In the dark of the night, when I felt surrounded by insanity and the sane world seemed eternities away, I reminded myself over and over again, "I was born free and I will die free."

Even before the prison underground learned of Jackson's intended negotiations with Castro regarding the Americans being held in Cuban prisons, we prisoners knew something big was up. Tension filled the air as rumors about visiting VIPs flew from cell to cell and gallery to gallery.

"Did you know that they have guards out front, painting walls?" one prisoner sneered.

"You're kidding!" I replied, wondering if I'd heard him right. "Guards painting the walls?" This must be something really big if the government was going to the trouble to "whitewash" the walls. Whitewash their lies maybe, but never the prison walls! "Yeah, the walls!" the inmate assured me. "They're painting them green and yellow—only the ones that will be seen, you understand."

"Of course," I chuckled. Aloud I could poke fun at the cosmetic changes taking place and at Castro and his façade of goodwill. Inwardly, my hopes of a possible release grew no matter how hard I tried to convince myself otherwise. And I could tell by looking in the eyes of my fellow *plantados* that they rode the same cruel roller coaster from elation to despair and back again.

More information filtered into the gallery during the day. "The VIP is the American, Rev. Jesse James," a fellow inmate whispered.

"Jesse James, huh—" I grunted. Months earlier, we had all heard of the famous black preacher and politician, Jesse Jackson, and thought of him as kind of a political bandit, hence the nickname, Jesse James.

"So maybe the black preacher is coming here to get another black minister," my friends teased. I laughed along at their chiding, daring not to hope—too much.

Early Tuesday morning, the golden and orange streaks of morning hadn't cleared the horizon before we heard the public address system click on, followed by the usual squawk and screech.

"The following prisoners are to line up," and a list of names was read.

"Oh." One of the *plantados* grunted and turned away. "They're all re-education prisoners."

Despite knowing that my name would not be on the list, I listened.

"You men," the guard explained, "have been chosen to play baseball for our visitors today."

I shook my head in disgust. I knew this routine well. Castro loved baseball, America's favorite sport. Growing up in the Oriente Province, he played with the local team against neighboring towns. And since baseball was one of America's favorite sports, he used it to demonstrate to the visiting VIPs just how successful his "re-education plan" had become. Like trained monkeys, the prisoners played their little game for the VIPs, after which it was back to the cells with the prisoners and back to the mothballs with the uniforms. At the same time, family members of the inmates would be beaten and driven away from the front gate to prevent them from telling the visiting dignitaries of our true condition—that many of them hadn't seen their imprisoned loved ones for five or ten years!

"Now, follow me and make it snappy!" the guard ordered.

I watched the guards lead the "visitor's team," as we called them, out of the gallery, wondering, as I had so often during the last twenty-two years, whether these guards had to go through extensive training to learn how to shout, bellow, bully, and curse. They sounded so much alike. At home, did they shout the same crudities at their wives and children as they shouted at work? I had heard that some practiced what they called a "five-minute hatred" routine.

Those of us not included in the ballgame found places on the upper floors of the gallery where we could watch the game. After a few minutes, the ballplayers ran onto the field, clad in complete regulation baseball uniforms, right down to the striped socks and cleat shoes. The players divided into teams. By the way the guards continued shouting, "Hurry up! Make it snappy!" I assumed that the visiting dignitaries must be arriving momentarily.

When the players took their positions on the field, the lieutenant in charge shouted, "Play ball!" I had to admit that the game looked authentic enough to the unseasoned eye and from a distance. Up close, the visitors would have seen a group of sick, starving men playing out a macabre charade choreographed by a madman. The first batter stepped up to the plate and waited for the pitch. "Strike one!"

On the next pitch, the batter hit a grounder and reached first base. The second batter, then the third and the fourth, took their turns up to bat. The team switched places after the shortstop caught the seventh batter's pop-up. One inning, two innings, three, four, five, six, they played ball. Seventh, eighth, ninth, tenth, they played ball. The fiery, tropical sun lifted off the eastern horizon and climbed into the sky overhead. Sweat poured down their foreheads, necks, and backs, soaking the brand new uniforms, yet they continued to play ball. In spite of the twenty-five-gallon plastic jugs of ice water and lemonade and the box of Spam sandwiches, the players staggered from heat exhaustion. When one fell, another was sent to take his position.

For those of us watching, our earlier envy at getting to play ball soon turned to pity. Exhausted, their necks, faces, and arms reddened, scorched by the sun. Out to the field, chase the ball, catch it, throw it to first, tag the runner—three out and up to bat—again. Hit a fly ball, run to first, get tagged on sec-

ond—three outs and back into the field—again. The teams
played seventy complete innings before a four-car motorcade
entered the prison grounds and cruised by the playing field!

Those of us still watching from the windows craned our necks
to see the procession.

"Jackson's supposed to be in one of those cars," one of the
prisoners near me confided.

The ball teams played on as the VIPs inched by. The moment
the last car disappeared beyond the prison's barbed wire, the
guards called an end to the torturous day at the ballpark.

"That's enough," the lieutenant in charge shouted. "You will
exchange your baseball uniforms for your prison uniforms and
return to your gallery."

The next morning, one of the *plantados* sat watching the
courtyard from our fourth-floor window. "Hey, come look," he
shouted to the rest of us, "they're rounding up all of the American prisoners."

I joined the herd of prisoners at the window to watch the
guards march the Americans from their gallery. In the four
hours that followed, rumors swept through the prison complex
with hurricane fury. "Jesse Jackson is negotiating their release."

"Oh, Father," I prayed as I watched and listened for their
return, "please, could this be the time?" With anguish, I added,
"Not my will, but Thine alone. Amen." As the hours dragged by,
I returned to my bunk, where I could be alone with my thoughts.

Suddenly a shout went up. "They're bringing them back!" Repeated again and again, the cry echoed from one prisoner to the
next and from one gallery to the next. I leaped from my bunk and
rushed to the windows.

As the Americans marched by, their faces glowed with happiness. They grinned toward us and signaled in code, "We are being
released. Probably some of you will be too." We grinned back and
gave a thumbs-up signal that we'd received their message.

My roller-coaster ride took on a note of wild frenzy. All the
while I hoped, I tried to prepare myself for disappointment.

Promise of Freedom

I sat on the edge of my bunk thinking about the day's events and what they might mean for me. I glanced around at my brothers. I knew that our thoughts paralleled one another's. Some men huddled together discussing the good news, while others found a quiet little space to contemplate and digest the changes taking place. Each of us wondered, "Is it only a matter of time and I'll be wearing normal clothes again, eating food not riddled with vermin or rotting with age? Will I be able to walk down a street unshackled; amble along a beach at will; laugh, cry, and celebrate holidays with my family once again?"

The next morning after the guards returned the American prisoners to their cells, a silence fell over our cellblock. A contingency of high-ranking Cuban officers entered the gallery. Stony faced, the top brass of the military's secret service strutted past our cells, eyeing us suspiciously. They'd been sent to check to be certain we had no idea what was about to happen. Five minutes later we snapped to attention at the sudden boom of the public address system. At the same time, General Laeyba, the interior minister, and his staff entered the gallery.

"Guards." The loudspeaker crackled and hissed as the general's aide ordered the guards to open all cell doors in our section. "Assemble the prisoners in front of the laundry room and dining hall," he announced.

We scrambled to obey. Now was not the time to incite a guard to violence—not with the possibility of release within our reach. Wide-eyed and terrified that something might yet go wrong, we stood at attention before the general. My breath caught in my throat as the implications of the general's words sunk into my being.

With all the pomp and authority of the revolution in his voice, the general adjusted his spectacles on the end of his nose, then announced, "You are to be released and deported to the United States. The Cuban government has decided to do this as a humanitarian gesture."

We later learned that when Jesse Jackson finished negotiating for the Americans held in Cuban prisons, he asked about us, the *plantados*. At first the Cuban dictator acted as if he hadn't understood the question clearly. But when Jackson began reading the names, dates, and locations of the *plantados* from the list I'd written, Castro recognized that he could not hide his tyranny from Rev. Jackson and the Western world any longer. So, cloaking his decision in rhetoric, Castro finally agreed to our release as a humanitarian gesture.

A humanitarian gesture to release prisoners who had already completed more than their sentence? I wasn't complaining, just cynical over his word choice. I longed to believe in my good fortune, but I'd been disappointed by many such empty promises over the years. True, this time, the events of the day made it all seem more real than in the past.

I snapped back to attention when the general continued with his instructions. "The water will be turned on to allow you to shower. After you shower, pack your belongings. We will be back for you in two or three hours." The general adjusted his glasses one more time, sniffed disdainfully, then strode out of the gallery, his entourage of officers imitating his style of departure. After the officials disappeared from view, the guards dismissed us.

The water pipes throughout our cellblock gurgled and chugged with the unfamiliar pressure of water surging through them as we dashed for the showers. All along the pipeline, faucets roared to life. At first, the water, red with rust, poured out of the seldom-used pipes. But no one cared or noticed.

"It's happening, Lord," I dared to whisper as the cool, refreshing water cascaded over my sunburned body. "It is really happening." I rushed through my shower and returned to my cell, all the while thinking ahead to the next thing I must do. "My Bible, I can't leave my Bible. The picture Mel gave me of his family—I want to take that with me too." I mentally went through my meager list of belongings as I dressed in a pair of fresh, homemade underwear, my official wardrobe during the last seventeen years.

"I must say goodbye to . . ." And I began thinking of the names of my brothers in Christ whom I needed to speak with before leaving.

Then I mentally listed the names of those whom I'd been studying the Bible with, those who were on the verge of accepting Christ. "And someone will take over running the church . . . perhaps Brother Fernandez or Valdes Cancio. José Carreno or Luis Rodriguez—either would do an excellent job." I had so much to do in the next two hours. I dared not waste a minute.

I had barely returned from my shower when the general and his staff reentered the gallery. "What?" I stood up and turned around at the sound of my name being called over the loudspeaker. It had only been fifteen minutes since they'd left.

"You will now be taken to a room where you will shave and be photographed," the general announced.

It is happening! It is really happening. Reality gripped my heart. What if it was just another game to break our spirit? I immediately pushed that thought aside. I couldn't allow myself to think that way—not now. It had to be real. It just *had* to be.

The general and his subordinate officers led us to the main floor and to a hastily prepared photo studio. Five white shirts, black jackets, and black neckties lay atop a small folding table. "You will take turns shaving, dressing, and having your photo taken. After your picture is taken, remove the garments for the next prisoner," the general explained.

Twenty-six men, varying in size from five feet five inches to more than six feet tall, took their turns wearing the ill-fitting shirts and jackets. No one had bothered to include trousers since we would be photographed only from the chest up. When my turn came, I put on the shirt and buttoned it as best I could since the shirt must have been made for a man with a much slighter build. The jacket, on the other hand, draped across my shoulders like a graduation robe. We laughed good-naturedly at the ludicrous picture we must have created as we shuffled jackets and shirts back and forth. What a bizarre ending to twenty-two years of torture! But at that moment, none of us worried about the cut of a jacket or the width of a tie. We were anticipating the heady thrill of freedom.

After they photographed the last prisoner, a guard collected the clothing and left the room, and a second guard ordered us to follow him. A myriad of thoughts bombarded my mind as I fell into step. What could possibly come next? What other games would they force us to play before we would be totally and irreversibly free men? I swallowed hard to control my excitement.

The hours of that day passed quickly, yet dragged unendingly for me. At nightfall, the guards took twenty of us to building number 3 and to a large, empty room, where six of our *plantado* brothers from another gallery waited. While we had spoken to them often over the years, we had not seen them for quite some time.

There were no sheets or blankets—only clean new bunks with fresh mattresses and equally new pillows. While the accommodations were hardly the Waldorf Astoria, to me, they ran a close second. I had just chosen a bunk and laid down when another set of high-ranking officers arrived and outlined the situation for us again.

"The hour is late. You men should get as much sleep as possible as tomorrow will be a tiring day for you. In the meantime, we will be getting your passports and exit visas in order."

After the military men exited and I heard the lock on the door click shut, I talked with my brothers from gallery B for a few minutes, then settled down to sleep. It had been an exhausting day. I closed my eyes for a moment as I struggled to create order out of the chaotic jumble of emotions, memories, and hopes bombarding my brain. I couldn't sleep. So much had happened. Again, dozens of questions bounced around in my mind—questions for the immediate future, the distant future, and the past. My life was changing faster than I ever imagined possible. The United States—was it as great as Paulina claimed? How would I adjust to freedom after living almost half of my life behind bars?

At four-thirty the next morning, a guard unlocked the door and announced, "Dress quickly for breakfast."

I scrambled to my feet and gathered up what personal belongings I'd carried from my cell the day before. The twenty-five other *plantados* did the same thing.

Noticing what we were doing, the officer politely suggested, "Just leave all your possessions here until after you've eaten breakfast. You'll have time then to pack everything you wish to take with you."

We formed a line and marched out of building number 3 into the early morning sunlight. We heard the door close and the guard snap the padlock shut. Without looking at the guard's face, we knew we'd been suckered once again. How foolish, I groaned. I believed him when he said we'd be allowed to return for our things. Hadn't I learned anything in twenty-two years?

We turned to glance back toward the pitiful little possessions we had treasured, that had given us courage over the years, now snatched from us forever, only to have one of the guards shout, "Get moving! Snap to it."

Instead of heading toward the dining area, the prison guards marched on each side of us from building number 3 across the prison compound to headquarters. While we waited at headquarters, we shared our prison experiences with one another— the hunger strike at La Cabaña, the beating and killing during black September at Pinar del Río, the genocide at Boniato Prison, the Isle of Pines—Cuba's equivalent to Siberia, and our testimony of faith under fire. We had gone through so much together, and now we faced a new destiny, alone. A new team of officers arrived. The lieutenant in charge ordered us to strip out of our homemade undershorts. They were careful that we left the prison and Cuba with no prison memorabilia that might be used as evidence against them.

"As you leave this room, continue marching past the guards," the officer in charge ordered. "Do not stop walking at any time. At the far end of the line, a military bus will be waiting, and an officer will check your identity."

The first guard handed me a pair of undershorts; the second guard handed me an undershirt; the next, socks; the fourth, a shirt. Size didn't matter; big or small, you took the garment and kept walking. If the garment was too big, that was your problem. You could change with another prisoner after you boarded the bus. The fifth guard shoved a pair of pants into my hands; the sixth a belt. The seventh guard dumped a pair of shoes atop my mountain of clothing and waved me on.

A lieutenant and four petty officers waited at the bus.

"Name?" he shouted.

"Humberto Noble Alexander."

"Number?"

"3-1-4-5-0," I replied.

"Date of birth?"

"February 12, 1934."

"Place of birth?"

"San Germán, Oriente."

The identity check sounded strangely familiar, like the one I went through the night of my arrest.

"Mother's name?"

"Beryl."

"Father's"

"Christopher."

He completed his list of questions, then ordered me to board the waiting bus. The vehicle had been specially prepared to prevent the passengers from seeing out of the windows and any curious passersby from looking in.

Once on board, another officer took a second roll call. Then a third questioned each of us individually, going through the long list of questions the officer outside the bus had just asked. After the third questioning, the G-2 men boarded the bus and made their way to the reserved section at the back. Though I didn't look, I knew from experience that they held their gun hands poised and ready should trouble erupt.

The bus grunted and sputtered to life. A sigh of relief swept through the bus as it cleared the last guardhouse and turned onto the busy street. Out of the corner of my eye, I glanced toward the steely-faced G-2 men behind me. A motorcycle policeman preceded the bus, and two patrol cars followed.

After what seemed like the longest ride I'd ever taken, the bus slowed down. We inched our way through Havana's heavy midday traffic to G-2 Headquarters. Guards hustled us off the bus and into a large reception room, where a number of relatives waited. For most of us, no one was waiting, since the families of prisoners from the other end of the island would not have had time to learn of our release and make the 1,000-mile trip to the capital city. We consoled ourselves, knowing that our reunion would wait until we could greet one another in another land—a free land.

After a short time, the officer in charge ordered the family members to leave and instructed us to reboard the bus, where we again went through the roll call and interrogation process. The bus inched out into the busy traffic toward José Marti Airport.

Our procession snaked through the crooked, winding back streets of the city in order to avoid stirring up the interest of the local population. Once the bus eased past the airport gates and onto the concrete runway, the driver killed the engine. Under the noonday sun, the temperature in the bus climbed swiftly. I glanced at my seatmate as I wiped my shirt sleeve across my face and neck. Tiny black dots danced before my eyes. The excitement of the last few hours and the intense heat were threatening to do me in. I took a slow, deep breath and prayed, "Oh, Father, don't let something happen to me now—not this close to freedom."

I glanced out of the corner of my eye at the G-2 men in the back and smiled. They were wiping their brows and necks with government-regulation handkerchiefs. "Good," I thought. "At least they're just as uncomfortable as we are." As one hour melted into the next, my mouth dried out from thirst. I kept licking my lips, but to no avail. "One last test. Always one last test," I thought.

The difference between this time and times in the past when we'd been forced to wait in the hot sun was that the guards allowed us to talk with one another. However, with the G-2 men so close by, no one wanted to risk saying anything that might jeopardize his release. We had lots to say, but not until we reached Washington, D.C.

After filling out a couple of documents for the Cuban government, we lapsed into an uncomfortable silence. We waited for four hours for Jackson's plane to land. During the hours while the Cuban government processed our release, he had flown to Nicaragua on a second mission for the U.S. government.

At seven that evening, two jets—one American, one Cuban—touched down. I could feel the excitement in the bus escalate as the two jets taxied over to the terminal. When they'd come to a stop, the motorcycle policeman revved up his engine and signaled for our bus to follow him onto the field, where we waited for another hour while the ground crew serviced and refueled the two planes. Our anxiety level soared when a high-ranking Cuban officer and one of Jesse Jackson's associates climbed aboard the bus.

The American introduced himself and delivered greetings from Jesse Jackson. "Rev. Jackson will meet with you all when we reach Washington," he explained; then he relaxed and smiled. "Rev. Jackson wishes each of you a smooth flight, gentlemen."

In contrast, the sober-faced Cuban official explained the flight procedures in abrupt, clipped tones as if he uttered each word under protest. "All Americans will board the American jet, except for the following." He read off the names of four Americans. "And all Cuban nationals will board the Cuban airline, except for the following." He read off the names of four Cubans. He went on to explain that the eight individuals mentioned would switch planes. The four Cubans would fly in the American jet and the four Americans would fly home in the Cuban airliner. "You will now exit the bus in an orderly fashion and board your respective planes."

I stood to my feet and stretched. It felt good to stand again after sitting in one position for so many hours. I stepped down from the bus and felt the cool evening trade winds refresh my wilted energy. I walked across the concrete and climbed the long staircase leading to freedom. Stepping inside the plane, I found an empty seat. The usual murmur of passengers searching for and adjusting their seat belts could be heard throughout the cabin. By closing one's eyes, one could almost think this was just an everyday flight on an everyday plane.

I buckled my seat belt and glanced out the window. Tears swam in my eyes as the plane's four jet engines roared to life. It was happening; it was truly happening. For the first time in twenty-two years, no uniformed guard or officer hovered, shouted, prodded, cursed, or swore at me!

Havana and Home

A hush fell over the passenger cabin as the plane's four jet engines roared to life, then inched forward and out onto the runway. After taxiing to the end of the runway, it turned and paused. A horrid thought taunted my mind during the few seconds we awaited clearance for takeoff. What if, at the last minute, the Cuban officials were to order the pilots to kill the engines, and a sneering Cuban lieutenant should step from behind the cockpit door, into the cabin, and announce that it had all been a joke—a cruel, sadistic joke.

But no, after a moment or two, the plane leaped forward, down the runway. The passengers cheered as the plane's landing gear left the pavement and the big bird arched skyward. As the jet leveled off, silence returned as we craned our necks to catch one last glimpse of our homeland. I looked down on the red-tiled roofs intermingled with the grayish tan rooftops made from the fronds of La Palma, the royal palm. Then I spotted a royal palm itself, standing straight and tall above the buildings.

Indigenous to Cuba, the royal palm's gray-green trunk grows very straight and smooth instead of curving gracefully like its relative, the coconut palm. And out of the top, above the deep green fronds, one fingerlike stalk points, like a lightning rod, into the heavens. La Palma never wavers, never bends, even during the worst tropical storm or destructive hurricane force that may beat upon it.

Emotions imprisoned within my heart for so long broke free at the sight of this stately palm. I wept openly at this symbol of Christianity under attack. I recalled the times when I had teetered on the verge of collapse and my God had infused me with a surge of strength that helped me stand tall. Without Christ, I would have, like the coconut palm, bent and swayed to the pressures, but through His strength, I was able to stand straight and tall—a royal palm. I also remembered the faces of my brothers who, like the royal palm, refused to bend, only to die in their faith.

I didn't have to worry that my mates would see me crying, for they, too, wept openly as our plane circled into the sky and headed north to our new home, the United States of America. The sun neared the horizon as I watched my beautiful island home fringed with its delicate white beaches and vivid blue waters disappear into the shadows of night. Within seconds, we flew above the deep blue ocean waters, and Cuba disappeared from view.

At the moment my plane lifted off from Havana, Tom White telephoned my mother and my sister from Washington, D.C. "Good news, Mrs. Alexander. Noble's name is on the release list. I think it's a go this time."

Congress had summoned Tom to Washington to testify regarding the disgraceful human rights violations being committed in Castro's prisons. By the time he called my mother again to tell her that I had indeed been released, she had already seen me on "Good Morning America."

During the flight to the United States, we prisoners discussed the future. "What about Rev. Jackson?" someone asked. "Obviously Castro snookered him."

"Tell the truth. We have to speak out," said Esturmio Mesa, a political prisoner. "We have to let people know that there is nothing good about a man's trying to represent Castro as a great humanitarian leader; he is just a beast."

"If only the world had resisted Castro's takeover in the first place," I lamented.

"Well," one of the other prisoners admitted, "that's in the past. What we have to do is prepare for the future. We need to make free people everywhere aware of the price tag attached to their liberty, and that it's worth maintaining no matter the cost."

"All the liberty we lost," I argued. "It will be difficult for Americans to understand."

"But we must make them," Mesa added.

"And us," I interjected, "what about us? We can't live out the rest of our lives harboring hate."

Mesa shook his finger. "True, but we can't just go our separate ways and forget our brothers still chained in Castro's inferno."

We agreed that our freedom brought with it an obligation toward those we had left behind. Our cries of injustice were the only voices the world could hear. We had lived closer than any natural-born brothers ever could. We'd suffered, we'd starved, we'd prayed together twenty-four hours a day for years. Steel bonds of Christian love and understanding held us together. No filial brother or sister could understand the experiences we survived. No mother or father could relate to the nightmares we would relive. Once we left the confines of the plane, our fates would be forever altered. Before we got off the plane in Washington, D.C., we cried, embraced one another, and vowed never to lose contact with each other.

My legs felt like jelly as I walked through the long tunnel into the airport. I thought I had managed to compose myself adequately until I saw my friend and brother, Tom White, waiting for me at the end of the tunnel. We bounded toward one another in an embrace—weeping and laughing, pounding one another over and over again on the back. Cameras flashed all around me as others waited to welcome me to freedom—Guillermo Esteves, Armando Valladares, Diego Abeche, Carlos Calson, and so many more. Television and radio reporters jabbed microphones into my dazed face, badgering me with questions. I fought an unreasonable urge to run back to the protection of the plane. My friends and United States officials rushed me through the mob at the airport to a waiting limousine, which took us to the Cuban-American Foundation and Human Rights Association in Washington. Once outside, I inhaled deeply the perfumed air of freedom, smog and all.

One of the first things the officials suggested I do was to call my mother in Massachusetts. From then on, during the next two days of interviews by more than twenty-one television, radio, and newspaper journalists, my mother called every twenty minutes or so just to hear my voice. She still couldn't believe that after waiting and praying so long, her prayers had finally been answered.

For the first time in years, I ate uncontaminated food. I looked at the buffet table full of foods of every kind and remembered the hated maggot-filled macaroni we'd endured, the tainted Russian canned meat, eight-to-ten-year-old frozen fish that gave me such a bad case of food poisoning that it left scars on my arms. "Never again," I vowed, filling my plate with cheeses, entrees, and other delicious foods—and there was no fish, macaroni, or canned meat.

A psychologist checked each of the prisoners to determine whether any of us might develop problems from culture shock. Friends took me on a tour of Washington, D.C., to help me adjust to the fast pace of life in the U.S. They drove me through rush-hour traffic, took me to a restaurant for dinner, a department store, and finally, to a subway. I experienced no noticeable trauma.

After our Washington stay, I flew to Logan Airport in Boston, where my relatives gathered to greet me. My seventy-three-year-old mother engulfed me in her arms and buried her tear-stained face in my shoulder. How many times had I dreamed of my mother's arms holding me, comforting me, easing my pain! And here she was—my dream come true.

"God bless America," she exclaimed again and again.

"It's like a dream. I can't believe it is you—my son, my son." We had twenty-nine years to catch up on, so much to share. The noise all of the family members made equaled the clamor of the reporters when I'd landed in Washington, D.C. The constant stream of conversation continued as we drove to my mother's home in Salem. Every few seconds, my mother reached out and patted my hand, almost as if she needed to reassure herself that my presence was more than just a dream. "I can die happy now," she said.

Our automobile turned onto a quiet, tree-lined street and stopped in front of my mother's home. "This," she said shyly, "this is my home, son, and yours too, as long as you need it." By the porch, she'd planted a tree covered with a bevy of balloons, along with Cuban and American flags. "I call it my freedom tree," she explained through her tears. "I planted it, looking to the future when you would come home to me."

Between news interviews and TV appearances, I kissed, I hugged, I overdosed on family love for days, until I was totally drained and exhausted. My mother, with the help of Paulina, my sister, cooked up a storm, serving all my favorite meals during the weeks that followed. Yet no matter how much I loved and appreciated their efforts, I could not make myself eat any macaroni products or fish.

The doctors at the New England Memorial Hospital, after giving me a complete physical checkup, couldn't understand how I'd kept in such good health during my incarceration.

After a short time to rest and adjust to the idea of being free at last, the Northeastern Conference of Seventh-day Adventists asked me to pastor the Maranatha church in Hartford. Excited to get on with my life, I kissed my mother goodbye and moved south to Connecticut into a little apartment of my own.

On my first Sabbath as pastor of the Maranatha church, butterflies flitted about in my stomach—not from fear but from eager anticipation. In His time, God had fulfilled the dream I had imagined so often during my years in prison. I engraved each detail of the service in my mind that morning. I never wanted to forget the thrill I felt. After the choir sang special music, I stepped up to the podium.

"My sermon today, brothers and sisters, is entitled, 'The Origin of Sin'—the last sermon I had preached in Cuba as a free man."

While the sermon contained the same basic story of Satan's fall from grace, a new depth had been added to the message. I shared illustrations of sin, experienced firsthand. I told of a brother who, about to renounce his faith, looked heavenward, viewed Christ hanging on the cross for him, and stayed loyal. I recalled Olegario Charlot, who died pleading for his Bible; of my friend Seruto, shot for his faith; of Roberto Chaves, pleading for religious freedom even as he died; of Chino Atan; of the "brother of the faith," Gerardo Alvarez, who sacrificed his life caring for others—all faithful unto death, awaiting their crowns of life and a far better existence beyond the crystal sea.

Epilogue

Beginnings and endings inherently possess a poignancy that stirs the soul. With each, you lose something, you gain something. I changed during my incarceration. I am no longer the impetuous young ministerial intern that G-2 agents arrested in February 1962. I have lost my youth. I am now middle-aged, my hair streaked with gray. Yet I have a confidence in my Lord that one day I will possess eternal youth. Beyond the physical changes, I lost my freedom of choice, yet I gained incredible insights as a Christian. I settled into my faith. I acquired a peace, an acceptance, and a certainty in God's trustworthiness and His constant love for me. I saw men die; I saw men born again. I watched men deny their Saviour for a few crumbs of spoiled bread, while others refused life itself to remain true to their Lord.

Even today, the memory of my brothers in Christ lingers on the fringes of every celebration, of every holiday, of every simple pleasure I experience. As I bite into a brightly decorated Christmas cookie or taste my mother's candied sweet potatoes at Thanksgiving time, I pray for my brothers and sisters languishing in Cuba's filthy prison cells. Have they remained strong in their beliefs? Is the church behind Castro's bars growing and prospering still?

On the Fourth of July, when barbecues and firecrackers sprout up across America, I ask myself, how did I escape death to enjoy the freedoms of this country? I had vowed to die free, but so had so many others. At church potlucks, I picture the promised ones gathering about God's silver table in the new earth. I see myself seated near precious friends who died for their faith. Over and over I ask myself, Why did I survive and they die? I don't know. I don't have the answers. But I do know that one day Jesus, my Saviour and my Friend, will sit me down beside the sea of glass and reveal the depth of His plan for my life and for the lives of my brothers.

Today, my heart aches with the bittersweet memory of my ex-wife, Yraida, and my son. In 1989 I received word from her. She said she'd been rebaptized and begged me to forgive her. I wrote back, assuring her that I forgave her the very day she divorced me in 1965. As sweet as the news of her baptism and repentance was to my senses, a bitter aftertaste remains. My son Humberto is a mechanical engineer and a product of the Communist revolution. From a human standpoint, there is little hope of his ever knowing and accepting Jesus as his personal Saviour.

In spite of the painful reflections and memories, I have no time for bitterness. My life is filled with too much happiness, too many loving, caring people to allow myself to be devoured by the cancer of hate. I rejoice. I sing. I laugh. I celebrate, because I know that my God reigns supreme over all the forces of evil and destruction Satan has ever devised. And best of all—my God reigns supreme in me!